The Manse Calvo

a novel

Brian Budzynski

For Abby and Dorothea

Resignation, not mystic, not detached, but resignation open-eyes, conscious, and informed by love, is the only one of our feelings for which it is impossible to become a sham.　　　—Joseph Conrad prologue: <u>The House on Lemarchant Street</u>

THE COLLISION OF THE VESSELS *Imo* and *Mont-Blanc* on December 6, 1917, in the strait of Halifax Harbour known as The Narrows, which resulted in the explosion of the *Mont-Blanc*'s cargo of fuel drums and munitions materials and laid waste to nearly half the city of Halifax, did not so much as shake a tile from the roof of the Calvo house on Lemarchant Street.

But never mind that; its purpose was transformed. Its fate determined.

In the column of what it imprinted inexorably on the city that day and many to follow, The Explosion, such as it has come to be known, gave birth to the Manse Calvo — for that morning Aaron and Tilde Calvo perished in the testing suite of the Bedford Brewery on Agricola Street, while Annelie Calvo, just eight months old, survived.

Aaron Calvo came into his money the old-fashioned way; he inherited it. When Aaron announced his intention to marry Tilde Simms, his sweetheart since time out of mind, in the spring of 1916, his father Morton Calvo, who held the lion's share of property deeds in the city and along its outskirts, yielded to Aaron a sizable chunk of his bequeathal. Morton was not, however, the sort to simply hand over money on faith, even to his own son. There were two caveats of the gift: that Aaron find and establish a respectable home and that he cut his own swathe in the world of business. Aaron felt these reasonable terms, and so with the unblinkered confidence common to young, ambitious men, he set out to satisfy them. Soon his household was settled and in order and Tilde so demonstratively pregnant that her movements were curtailed to short walks around the grounds. But while the house on Lemarchant Street had been relatively easy to obtain — the Calvo name opening a vast portfolio of available properties — Aaron struggled to satisfy his father's second condition.

His habit of strolling the streets of Halifax's business district, peering owl-eyed through windows in hope of inspiration, a means to conjure an idea by which he might divorce the name Calvo from the lengthy shadow cast by his father, was proving deficient.

He sank several hundred dollars into the restoration of the Orpheus Theatre on Barrington Road, but this was greeted as an act of civic duty, of philanthropy. Admirable but profitless. He chanced a thousand on a restaurant, located just up-wharf from the ferry depot that shuttled workers to and from Dartmouth across the bay. Unfortunately, what had shown real promise on paper failed within a month, when it was revealed that the proprietor was shining on not only Aaron but four other investors, and one night simply vanished into mainland Canada. (The land was eventually sold, at a loss, to the city to expand the ferry depot.) Then there was a small franchise of laundries that, while honestly operated, stagnated monetarily; Aaron had only the pleasure of knowing he kept their operators out of arrears.

Annelie came into their lives on a temperate, hazy afternoon in April 1917, by which time Aaron was convinced he simply did not have the

2

stuff of success and that continuing to push forth announced him too ignorant to have learned from, if not copied, his father's example.

But then, like an unexpected gift, came an overture from the Bedford Brewery.

The brewhouse dealt in lager and did a fair return. But its proprietors' ambitions were undercut by the market share owned by Alexander Keith's and its celebrated ales, the familiar stag head crest topping three pulls at any pub to Bedford's one. Thus was the purpose of Aaron's presence in the testing suite the morning of December 6 — to entertain sales and distribution of a new, so-called "export ale" as a potential investment.

He imagined the pride that would overtake his father on learning of such inroads made with an evergreen establishment, and so of course, in his frazzled desire to finally strike a singular mark, he would happily attend a tasting first thing in the morning on the 6th, if that was the best time for all involved. What's more, he would bring his wife and daughter, show them firsthand all those stunted early ventures had finally led him to the threshold of true success.

The *Mont-Blanc* exploded at 9:05 a.m.; the inner mechanism of the clock on the tower of City Hall, disrupted within that minute, offering testimony of the event. The innermost wall of the brewery's testing suite was not load-bearing and fell like a domino. It landed, at an acute angle, on the sudden rubble of the wall opposite, which had been blown in by the force and lightning shrapnel of the blast, killing Aaron, Tilde, and the officers of the brewery who attended them.

In a small triangle of space uninvaded by rocketing debris between the fallen wall and the suite's washed wood floor, supine in her bassinet in a fug of brick and stone dust, Annelie's delicacy was preserved only by a thin sheet of satin that functioned, ordinarily, as a shade from sun.

It was several hours before her cries caught the ear of a fisherman wandering dumbfounded through the fractured landscape.

His wind-ravaged mouth gaped in silent awe of the faint howl of desperation coming from — of all things amidst the piles of rubble and glass baked black — a bassinet. He swept the satin veil, caked in a duvet of filth, away to find a child's tiny, red, furious face. Struggling but alive.

He carried her in the shroud of his gamey wool greatcoat to a YWCA Emergency Hospital. Though he refused to give his name before hastening away from the cacophony of cries spilling from so many rooms packed with frightened children — the sheer number of suddenly orphaned, later tallied, was astounding — he was captured nonetheless by a stroke of well-timed luck in the aperture of a reporter's camera. A news clipping of this photograph from the *Halifax Herald* would be placed, years later, behind a thin pane of framed glass in the Manse Calvo's manager's office, its odd caption — "Unknown Loller Claims Rescue from Brewery Blast" — at various times serving as a point of strange humor for the house's denizens, *loller* meaning *good for nothing*.

Annelie remained in the care of the sisters of St. Mary's Basilica for nearly ten hours before her father's brother, Myron, claimed her. He took the child back to Lemarchant Street. The great, brick hulk of a house sat empty but for a single servant, Loretta Wyndl, who took immediate control of the child, while Myron went out to face what lay at the site of the brewery.

A storm tore into Halifax and Dartmouth in the days following. Hail, sleet, blinding winds. Deep cold fusing feet of snow into a slick, icy shell over the city.

The lights of the Calvo residence remained dim, the shutters closed, as a practicality. Hundreds had begun to wander down along the unaffected neighborhoods to the south, seeking anyone to take them in, some not looking to ask permission. It was all Myron could do to deal with the total dependence of a child, to say nothing of what addled his mind — it ran madly, unreasonably deep into the future — as to how on earth he would ever explain to his niece what she had come through, what fate demanded she eventually reconcile herself to, and the impeding event she innocently, unknowingly, withstood. Strangers lurking about was out of the question.

There were stores of food in the pantry and enough firewood to get them through a month. There was no need to acknowledge the malevolent world outside.

Morton Calvo and his wife, Careene, also died that gray morning. They were found in their bed beneath a collapsed roof, their supine position suggesting they had slept through the moment of their death. Their loss provided a tragic maelstrom of financial benefit to Myron and (in her father's stead) Annelie alike.

Afraid that if he did not apply himself to some purpose, he might wind up a secondary victim to the tragedy, Myron indulged a daydream he had carried since adolescence like an undeveloped photograph and wasted no time putting it into action.

It is unlikely Morton Calvo ever intended the accumulated wealth of his life to find its legacy in a rooming house — but that is precisely how his eldest son applied it.

The house was, after all, quite substantial. It lent itself to more than just private residence.

Built in 1871, according to a small bronze plaque fitted into the yellow and brown-green brick façade, the house had served as an in-residence all-boys prep school until 1904, but had sat empty thereafter until its purchase by the late Aaron and Tilde. Its four stories contained twelve bedrooms, all en suite; four smaller servant's quarters; two ground floor parlors, one of which featured inlaid shelving along two of its walls and recessed lighting tucked into molded sconces along its upper trimlines and so served as a library; kitchen and livery suitable for a full staff; a dining room large enough to comfortably seat thirty, which fleshed out the rearmost portion of the ground floor in a long, clean run of glass panels; and an entryway that could withstand a fleet of horses. Falling in a gentle slope from the rear of the house was a small wood etched with a paved stone pathway that meandered along in a kind of figure-eight.

There were two eyesores: an unmanicured back lawn and an incomplete rear façade, which was meant to bear small balconies off the two fourth-floor rooms, which were the largest in the house, akin to apartments.

From the first time Aaron invited him around to show the place off, Myron, who lived in a comparatively modest two-story Georgian on Owen Street, had found it gargantuan, unnecessarily so for a single family. Myron had always suspected his brother's desperation to appease their father's impossible standards of success; the house had fully confirmed those suspicions.

It was this gargantuanness that would also inspire Myron to bestow the grandiloquent name *Manse Calvo* when the hotel finally opened its doors on March 21, 1920.

In the intervening years between the Halifax Explosion and the Manse Calvo's first registered guests, Myron expended fully two-thirds of his and Annelie's cumulative inheritance into readying the property for the public. First and foremost, the issue of the house's incomplete back area was rectified. The fourth-story balconies — cement platforms coupled to steel railings molded to suggest the elegant arching sway of swans — were riveted into place, and the lawn was sculpted into a fair mimicry of the landscaping of the Public Gardens on Spring Garden Road. A packed sand bocce pitch was dug and framed in rich cherrywood. The house's brick walls were washed and the mortar patched. The east wing of the house had its heating ducts replaced and the west wing its plumbing refitted. Flush commodes replaced gravity-drawn fixtures. A large, elliptical register, crafted in oak, was commissioned for the house's foyer to serve as a front desk. The weather-beaten front porch of the house was disassembled and rebuilt, at considerable expense, of redwood. Ms. Wyndl was named house manager and authorized to hire a small passel of cleaning staff, as well as a desk clerk and a live-in houseman to assume the task of general maintenance. Pamphlets were printed by the thousand. Myron arranged for all docking passenger ships, as well as the Halifax-Dartmouth ferries, to place them conspicuously in customers' ticket envelopes, on tabletops where commuting workers might gather, and in the glass boxes that displayed the ships' timetables.

During this time, Annelie lived in Myron's house on Owen Street, under the care of a revolving cast of temporary caregivers. Such attrition in nannies resulted from Myron's philosophy that any woman under his personal employ was duty-bound to keep the same interminable hours as he. After all, he was paying them a satisfactory rate. His promotional campaign proving successful, Myron's hours were many. It was rare that anyone lasted more than a few months before giving notice. Thus, Myron was perpetually eyeing any new face brought on the hotel's staff by Ms. Wyndl for potential ancillary child care, and Annelie learned early not to develop any deep attachments.

The constant aggravation of having to replace his niece's caregivers with such regularity grew tiresome for Myron, especially as the girl grew out of infancy and into adolescence, when the purpose of a nanny became as much a question of intellectual and emotional development and discipline as of care.

When Annelie informed Myron in the fall of 1923, in the precocious manner her age couched such declarations, that she would like to live at the Manse Calvo, Myron was only too happy to agree — on the condition that Ms. Wyndl likewise consented. After all, she would take charge of the girl. Outside of school, Annelie already spent a good deal of time at the Manse, often in the manager's office drawing on butcher's paper or in one of the two main parlors — named, respectively, the Aaron and Tilde — quietly people-watching or playing with the painted wood farm playset Myron had commissioned a local whittler to create for her fifth birthday. She would often grow despondent when it came time to gather her things and return to Owen Street. And what's more, by what Myron assumed was a transference of affection resulting from the gaping hole of feminine influence in her life, Annelie openly favored Loretta Wyndl and had begun to ape many of her mannerisms, figures of speech, and expressions of emotion.

Ms. Wyndl, who was entirely conscious of the girl's emulation and did nothing to dissuade it, was only too happy to have Annelie under her supervision and care. The only other live-in staff was the houseman, his room located at the Manse's west-most end. The other three servant's flats were in the east-most end. The idea was to move Annelie into the room directly across the hall from Ms. Wyndl's. Annelie, however, had a different idea. She demanded the lone flat on four. Coincidentally the largest of the servant rooms, nearly the size of a full registered suite.

Myron immediately refused. The girl must be within earshot of Ms. Wyndl, notably at night.

"You never know who people really are," he reasoned. "Anyone could be in these rooms."

Ms. Wyndl agreed. And so Annelie's things were settled into the room across the hall from her own.

Almost immediately, Annelie began to slip from that room after Ms. Wyndl's final check of her before turning in evenings, and go up to sleep in the welcoming queen-sized bed on four.

Ms. Wyndl withstood less than a week of the morning aggravation of retrieving the girl and issuing the same useless reprimand. She was too practical for such an untenable, unenforceable stricture. She ordered the houseman to bolster the door on four with a deadbolt and to give her the only key. As all servant's quarters were equipped with private toilet and washtub, same as the registered rooms, Annelie would have no need, provided a glass of cool water be left at her bedside, to be outside her room until morning.

Years, in this manner, accumulated.

Annelie shrugged off adolescence and Ms. Wyndl, forgoing the rigor of her nightly oversight, placed her on staff assisting with reception, reservations, and patron requests. Annelie did not need the money — and, with no spendthrift tendencies, had little use for it — but Ms. Wyndl felt it was the principle of the thing. You work, you earn, and fair was fair.

The relationship between the two was less a developed equanimity than an exercise in filial affection, at least for Annelie, who reasoned that observation was the easiest and best means of acquiring the disposition required of her. She became Ms. Wyndl's shadow.

Ms. Wyndl appreciated the diligence, but knew that introducing the supervisory dynamic meant rearranging the priorities by which her heart addressed pretty much everything about the girl. The difficult but necessary process of slewing away her quasi-maternal cast revealed a more temperate, less indulgent personage that threw Annelie for a loop.

One frigid February morning in Annelie's fourteenth year, a flu struck the kitchen staff. It fell to Annelie and Ms. Wyndl to prepare the breakfast service.

Annelie, well-rested coming off a school holiday, moved from counter to counter in the galley with an energy bordering on a show of impatience with Ms. Wyndl's even-footedness.

"Calmly, Annelie. Service is not expected, nor do the dining room doors open, for another hour."

"People never pay attention to the hours, Lottie. You know that. Better that we're prepared than scrambling to make up wasted time."

This last was a phrase Ms. Wyndl used herself often when speaking to subordinates. Of course the girl would have committed it to memory. In fact, it slid from her tongue with the same smooth cadence of practiced surety that it did from Ms. Wyndl's. *Lottie*, however, was a recent development.

Annelie had entered her teenage years with all requisite confidence. It would not be long before smugness took hold of her, and the struggle between the dissolving innocence of youth and the reticence to accept higher authority would begin. In short, Annelie was on the road to not respecting her elders. And though the playfulness of the nickname landed softly, the assumption of equality that underlay it, Ms. Wyndl knew, had to be corrected.

"It's best, I think, when we are working that you call me Ms. Wyndl." She laid a gentle hand on the low swell of the girl's back. "Should a guest or another member of staff overhear that kind of … familiarity between us, they may get the idea it is allowed."

"I don't see the big deal. I'm not like the others. They know that. This is my house."

"But my business to operate."

Annelie turned, her face smeared with disconcerting aloofness. She set the potato she had been slicing to fry down on the cutting board.

"I think of it as our business. Uncle Myron's and yours and mine."

"Your uncle oversees things, certainly. That is clear. But — look at me, dear. I am house manager. I am also the warden of your care. That will become different than it has been. Now that you are getting older, certain things between us will have to change, notably when we are both on the clock."

"Warden, huh? You make it sound like I'm indentured." Annelie's playful tone began to sour. "That's a way of looking at it. Since this is my house, that would make me Cinderella."

"Don't be dramatic, Annelie."

"I supposed this is a hell of a great prison then."

"Annelie. Language."

Annelie's hand, suddenly forgetful of the knife it held, slipped, and the blade passed across the knuckles of the opposing hand, yielding a thin but instantly seeping slash in the skin.

"Ah, fucking knife," she hissed, drawing in breath through her teeth. Spots of red flew over the food in front of her, dotted the cutting board beneath. The knife, released, pinged on the floor.

Annelie reached for a dishtowel and held it in a crumpled ball over her fingers. *"Fucking great,"* she shouted.

Ms. Wyndl, averse to the girl's dramatics — the cut did not look very deep — despite the honest shock behind them, wheeled on her.

"Civility is not merely the presentiment of decency, Miss Calvo. The curse word is an instrument of ugliness. It is language that diminishes the soul. It will not be heard from the mouth of anyone under my employ."

Annelie froze. Then she flung the bloodied dishtowel onto the counter and stalked out of the kitchen.

Later, once breakfast was complete and the coffee and tea service set out on the dining room sideboard, Ms. Wyndl located Annelie in the manager's office. She sat in a slouch behind the desk. An open first aid box lay on the desk blotter. On her right hand was a haphazard arrangement of gauze and white surgical tape.

Ms. Wyndl pulled a guest chair from around the front of the desk and sat down. She took up Annelie's damaged hand. She removed the wrapping and gently cleaned the cuts with an antiseptic swab. The knife had caught three fingers but only one incision looked like it would take more than a few days to heal. Using fresh gauze, she wrapped each finger individually and secured them with torn-off squares of tape.

"The tape doesn't need to go all the way around. The better for the skin to breathe," she said, sweeping the discarded bandaging into the wastebasket.

Ms. Wyndl kept Annelie's hand folded between hers. She felt she owed the girl a small surrender. Annelie was, after all, at the age when one's emotional barometer buries the needle at extremes with little or no middle register.

"I do love 'Lottie'. The endearment reminds me of my mother. It's from her I got my personality. Its good and its bad." Annelie's fingers curled slightly, and Ms. Wyndl felt a clammy pressure on the heel of her hand. "I only want you to grow into an intelligent, confident woman. That is about the best I can do for you, if you come right down to it. But those traits are impossible when arrogance is mixed in."

"You called me Miss Calvo. You've never called me that before."

"That was a reaction, Annelie. Just a reaction."

"I felt like you didn't know me when you said that."

Seeing that Annelie was a hair's breadth from melodrama, but also that there was no point in rising to the bait, Ms. Wyndl kept calm.

"You can call me Lottie when we are alone and not working. When we go out for walks or to the cinema or the Gardens. And I will call you Annelie, as always, and that will be that."

Annelie smiled, and after a few minutes' chat about some things that would need doing that day, Ms. Wyndl returned to the dining room. Annelie remained and began to open and sort the mail.

The day continued unabated, but an inexorable change had occurred. It was something she felt but could not speak to. Pride, like a sliver of light under a closed door, had become entangled with a kind of instability of the sort one felt standing on the deck of a ferry — legs taut, spine poised for persistent correction. It was not unwelcome, this off-balancedness. It seemed like a necessary step toward an equity she had not, up to then, known was missing.

The coming years withstood a few further conflicts, all readily mendable, and Annelie matured voraciously. Ms. Wyndl's manner did not waiver, and the girl was a quick study. Ms. Wyndl felt the girl's mission — what else could she call such blindered determination — mattered more to her than success in her studies, or the possibility of continuing on to college. In fact, she observed the disparate, but ongoing conflict on the topic between Annelie and Myron so often, she felt that the mere idea of higher education grew more and more distasteful to Annelie with each argument.

Myron began after the mid-1920s to take a looser and lessened role at the Manse Calvo. Hotel stationery still billed him as Proprietor, but he took on the almost mythic presence of Jay Gatsby. Purveyor and host of one of Halifax's finest and most tasteful establishments, but himself enigmatically absent, possibly in the periphery, but who could say. He preferred, instead of being the face of the Manse, to simply enjoy the stipend his venture provided. One would have more luck finding him holding court at the rail of Henry House's basement bar or the back garden of the Collier Club than at the sideboard of the Manse's smoking lounge. Via the hotel's success, Myron had achieved a position his brother never had in the subset of society that valued one's business acumen. He was conscious of this fact, though he felt a measure of residual guilt that it was his brother's property and father's accumulated means that had made it possible.

Despite stepping back from hotel operations, Myron remained very much in the daily life of his niece. It was his duty — and his pleasure — to keep himself apprised of her development and aims. But he was not without his opinions as to what was right for the girl and her prospects for the future. A common opening salvo to what Myron called "the college issue" was to lament his own lack of a higher degree.

"Damn it, kid, if I *had* gone even to just Dalhousie, never mind the big places like Toronto or down in the States, imagine where I might be. The hotel's great, no question. But I'd have five, ten of the damn things by now. Hell, I could be on the board of regents somewhere. And it's not just that, it's the respect that comes with that certificate. Folks look at you differently."

Aside from the patent untruth that he had ever given one good damn about higher learning, what Myron overlooked in such disquisitions was that he focused too strongly on things of little importance to Annelie. She had no bearing for big business. Entertaining, even briefly, the idea of shuttling herself between multiple enterprises called up the faint echo of a looming headache. Had Myron paid closer attention to Annelie's coming of age, he might have begun his argument by saying that a college education was crucial to a well-formed mind and that Annelie would find herself engaged with things and with people she might otherwise never be, except to serve them at the hotel. Higher education would preclude her from spending her life subserviently. But to Myron the reaping of reward and the degree itself, the stamped slip of paper, seemed his best and most consistent shot at getting through to her. What he never seemed to understand, though Annelie felt it should be the very first thing he *would* understand, was that the future already in wait for her was precisely the future she wanted. The Manse Calvo. Her room there, neither too small to bear, nor so large that it required the massing of unnecessary objects in order to fill it. The familiarity of the house and grounds. The Manse Calvo did not need her to go off someplace else to earn her way back to it; it was hers. It was her family's. It was itself family, as though kindly haunted by the past.

So, whenever Myron started going on about *was she ever going to be ready for college*, Annelie's battlements were already fortified.

"I wonder sometimes," she would say, "whether when you look at me what you see is a girl of ten with no path in life, or the woman I am now. You see," and here Annelie would lean forward, tip herself almost conspiratorially toward her uncle, because doing so wiped out any impulse in Myron to scoff at her use, at eighteen, then nineteen, then twenty, of *woman*, "I have a position already as co-owner of a large rooming house. You would think that I'd already achieved the sort of position in life schooling is supposed to prepare you for. And let's not forget that admission slips make no promises. Who's to say I would get anything out of more schooling."

Myron would shake his head. The similarities were uncanny. To Loretta, of course, but to Tilde, as well. Annelie possessed the reserved assurance Tilde had wielded like a well-concealed weapon. Aaron had been rather handsome, seen as "a catch" to those young women in the "social know," but Tilde won his heart, in Myron's opinion, with her subtly exuded confidence. For Aaron had been, above all, an aspirant, and Tilde represented to him both the measure of how he wished to be regarded and the person he himself wanted to be — sure-minded, yet wearing it lightly. Myron could never explain this to Annelie, however. The portrait painted would be nothing but complimentary, of course, but he feared rupturing whatever image of Tilde he felt the girl must have developed on her own in secret, and which would have become over the years as real as her mother was ever going to get.

"Annelie, you're in no position to," Myron would begin, but the retort died there. He knew she had his number. And though it distressed him in the moment, later his mind morphed the fact into a demonstration of affection — *ha ha that girl's always had me over a barrel*.

On one occasion, however, this was not the case. After Annelie played her usual defense, Myron said, quickly, as though the words might bite him, "Annelie, you're in no position to scoff at the idea there are things outside your life that would be good for you. For starters, you need to be better with people if you expect to be in charge of this place one day. Ms. Wyndl's a fine role model but she can be soft as sandpaper sometimes."

"Isn't that why you placed her in charge? I don't see how anyone would respect, say, a sponge." Annelie's admirable self-possession was underlain with an exactitude, a look of innocence veiling the piercing equipment beneath, and once more it put Myron back on his heels. In her mind, the conversation had come to a close directly upon its start. The plain cast of her face as she volleyed her seemingly innocent remarks would again render Myron mute, leaving him to hope that next time he might find the right rejoinder.

It was therefore something of a shock to Myron and Ms. Wyndl alike when Annelie announced, in the spring of 1939, that she had accepted admission to Prince of Wales College on Prince Edward Island.

Ms. Wyndl had always suspected an underlying impregnable aspect to Annelie. This announcement firmed up that supposition. She did not even think it odd or inflexible when Annelie offered no reason or explanation for her sudden turnabout. The girl was twenty-two years old. If she didn't know what she was doing, Ms. Wyndl could hardly offer better alternatives. As she told Myron, when he blanched at his niece's seemingly rash forfeiture of will, "For every person there comes a point, I suppose, when the accounting of life ends and a yearning for its testament begins."

Annelie left Halifax on May 18, bound for Charlottetown. A wire assuring her safe arrival reached the Manse Calvo two days later. She would not return to Halifax for nearly three years and then only by an unfortunate circumstance that left her, to her mind — so she would confess to me — no other choice.

i. <u>Transatlanticism</u>

MY NAME IS WALEK SZEYK. My place of employment and of residence is the Manse Calvo, where since Fools' Day 1941 I have been what is known, in local parlance, as a useful man. What exactly that means will come along in due course.

It is presently June 1958. I sit in the breakfast nook of a rental house on Prince Edward Island, in the rare interlude of darkened quiet just before dawn.

From the vantage of time removed I find that the past has, of late, assumed a terrific immediacy, notably those years of the war which for so many folks I imagine continue to resonate in a manner perhaps even their own childhoods do not. I suspect it is indicative of the point my life has reached — demonstrable middle age is just around the corner. Or perhaps it has always been there, looming like a great shadow, and only now do I risk a backward glance to see what is there.

Is it enough, I wonder, that what reason propels the telling of a story is simply that the story exists to be told and that it can find value or perhaps meretricious life in the telling, and that the manner of the telling is all? Ms. Loretta Wyndl, by whose favor I first received my odd moniker, once remarked to me, "We are in continual conversation with our past." I feel that only now am I opening up to the largeness of that statement, to the idea that what stands of me is the culmination of passions and peculiarities embraced

— and not merely my own. Thus, the impulse to make this record.

As you might readily suppose from my name alone, I am not natively Haligonian, let alone Nova Scotian. My people are what is known as "come from away."

My father was born and lived out his youth in the village of Maljenka in the Baltic region of Poland, not far from the port city of Gdansk. He inherited some land and a small house fronting it after my grandparents, Adam and Jadwiga, were shuffled off by influenza in 1910. He was no farmer, my father. He leased the fields to a local farming outfit, which provided him a monthly stipend that facilitated his studies in literature. His intention was to teach.

My mother grew up in Wejherowo, some 50 kilometers to the north. Her family came to Maljenka in order to be closer to an aunt of my grandmother's, who resided in a retirement flat on the outskirts of Gdansk.

They came together in the midst of a blizzard in 1914. A terror, evidently. Toss a quilt over the eyes and leap from a cliff, my mother once told me, and you'd know its enormity.

Having boarded the windows of the house, my father went out to the barn to secure the horses. The winds were such that the barn door had been taken off, the bolt driven from the wood. The animals stamped madly, throwing up a veil of dirt. My father managed to get them tethered to a foundation post and distracted to calm by a halved apple, when a cracking sound reverberated through the air. He turned at the sudden violence of the sound.

A figure stood before him, a mass of steam curling off brazenly black hair. He soon realized facing him was a woman. She strode toward him, fists balled, lips in a crimp.

"Where's your storm cellar?" She took hold of his forearm, just above the wrist, where the skin was exposed by the sleeve of his coat. For a moment, he could not find a word. In all the world, there was only, it seemed, the pressure of her hand on his arm.

"The storm cellar, where is it?" Grip tightening, voice urgent.

"I haven't got one. There's just the dry store." He kicked at the raw wood hatch at their feet. "But it's not much deeper than a wheelbarrow. And it's full up."

Without a word, the stranger released her grip on his arm, hoisted the lid, and began chucking blocks of frozen meat and cloth-packed vegetables over the lip and onto the sand-thickened dirt. When she had entirely emptied the space, she stepped down, pulling my father in after her by the tail of his coat. They lay on their sides and she drew the hatch shut.

Above them the horses chortled in fear. My father wanted to raise his head, coo them down, but was packed in too tight for movement. They were nearly face to face, my father and this apparition, his knees tucked up so that she could form around him, her legs drawn straight, boots pressed firm to the shallow earth wall. Her body like a viola. The lid began to rattle at its hinges as the horses' stamping again grew manic. My father threaded the rope pull through the loops of his trousers and tied himself on like the spindle of a kite. In so doing, he brushed against her once, twice, thrice — the fourth an awkward elbow to her stomach, which she reciprocated directly.

Seconds later her hand once again found his arm and came to rest there.

They rode out the worst of it like that, curled together, one within the safety of the other, both hemmed in to the confinement of the dirt walls.

"Marianna," she at some point whispered.

"Karol."

Later, their muscles cold and stiff and movement tenuous, they hobbled out of the store and surveyed the damage. Some planks had broken out of the barn walls, but the roof looked good and the animals were calm, drinking water and huffing breathy plumes into the air. My father tied quilts to their backs and was able to get a fire up in the stove, which he dragged to within a few feet of the stall gates.

They made their way uneasily — the cold deepening in the fading dusk light, ice forming before their very eyes — to the house, to blankets, the kettle, coffee, warm soup.

In the course of conversation came her full name — Marianna Biga. Her family had bought a cottage opposite the main road, a tick from the schoolhouse.

Family? he inquired.

Yes, her parents. No mention of a husband or children. Automatic as a blink, he smiled.

"How did you find me? I'm pretty far from the schoolhouse."

"I took my parents to the sundry. The people there put them under the counter. There was no room at the schoolhouse. My parents are older and I do not know our house well enough to trust its strength. I was going back, but the wind was coming in too hard. I saw the lamplight in your barn."

"You went back out?" My father was incredulous.

"Yes, I did. It is still my home. I wanted someone there." Her eyes thinned. "Wipe the smile away."

He kept it, but it hollowed him somewhat.

He draped a blanket over her back and handed her an enamel mug nearly spilling over with steaming black coffee, admiring how the expression of her face rode the loft of her emotion: a divot in her otherwise cream-smooth forehead and crow's feet at each eye that gave the aspect of a feather lightly breezed. The simple courtesy of a coffee — and suddenly an insolent mouth became one he suddenly imagined placing against his own.

The fire began to take as the blown-in snow went to vapor. They shared the quiet.

An hour later, they went side by side across snow drifts hip-high. My father's hand sometimes supported her shoulder, sometimes the small of her back, sometimes touched nothing of her but was held in ready.

They found my maternal grandparents, Thaddeus and Amelia, standing in the yard of what used to be their house. The house's clapboard walls had splintered and fallen. Rough gray insulation was strewn across the snow-shielded grass like shaved wool. Just the frame of a house remained, but the sight of it gave my father hope of salvage.

He offered his own home to them until theirs could be rebuilt. Moreover, he volunteered his own hands to the task. Hands that knew nothing of farming or manual labor.

He slept seven weeks, nearly fifty nights, bone-stifled on his own couch, often easing down in the dead of night and submitting himself to the wood floor. Thaddeus and Amelia were given his parents' bed, and Marianna his. She claimed to change the sheeting herself every few days but never once did, preferring the truth of his smell. And the creation of new, the alchemy of her body's nativity and his.

This was her first intimacy with him — not in the dry store, which had been his first intimacy with her, but there in his bed, my father a room away but a breath from her still.

The Bigas were easy people, and my father was grateful for their company. They took a drink with supper, another by the fire, yet another down the hall to quicken sleep. Though my father had lived comfortably alone going on four years, he found himself easing back on his own idea of what a house was meant for. His sheets soothed their bodies at night, his plates held their food, his floors creaked beneath their weight.

While Thaddeus helped my father rebuild what needed of the barn — refit the wall slats, rehinge the door, a matter of only a couple days' work — Amelia and Marianna kept mainly to the house, throughout which one could discern what lingered of my paternal grandmother. The lower surfaces were topped with intricately woven doilies themed on spring flowers, their edges yellow and crisp, centers soft as they had been in my grandmother's fingers during conception. My mother thought it unlikely that my father had chosen the babe's yellow and eggshell blue papering the sitting room walls, but credited him the blood orange in both bedrooms. She found the entire house to be an amalgamation of small nostalgic beauties and the resignation that accompanies an absence of solicitude. The rooms' corners, where gravity and daily activity cast their detritus, were grimy. Wool was needed to clean them. The skirting was washed, dried, sanded, repainted. She otherwise laid a gentle hand — yet the sitting room now revealed hidden comforts: the lush side of a pillow; the softness of a well-swept rug (appreciated by my father at three in the morning on the quick descent from couch to floor); how the walls and trim were separated but one degree of yellow and yet daylight through the gauze of now-washed curtains gave the room a fine quaintness.

My mother knew the house had not been lived in like a home in some time. A home absorbed small abuses, depreciated steadily in one kind of value while growing intangibly in another. She did not wish to maintain a curatorial feeling. Expunging it was not the matter of a clean slate but one dirtied by herself and my father equally. She wanted to see the effect of her touch. And she knew what she was doing.

The two of them went around one another like nervous animals. Looks, smiles. Each aware of the very fiber of accidental touch, the agitation of vellus hair. Fabric gently abrading. When the weather changed and the Bigas' cottage began to go up, my father found his arms curiously lax. He fidgeted nails, couldn't keep a straight beam. His thoughts roamed away across town to where Marianna sat in his kitchen with her mother, concocting what manner of meal would await him and Thaddeus at day's end. He wanted this family to have their home back but did not want to surrender *her*. Yet he lacked the wherewithal to be explicit.

She had to do it for him.

One evening, dinner done, they shared the washing up. She to wash, he to dry. A convenient slip of her hand, a plate shattered on the floor. Crouching down to retrieve the shards, she leaned in. As they kissed, strands of hair fell loose over her forehead and slipped into their mouths, thinning from the wetness until they were no longer felt.

My mother asked, apropos of nothing, "Have you considered changing things about? The tables and chairs, the figures of your mother's above the fireplace. The smelly rugs. That sofa. You."

"Me?"

"Yes. You. A change to the house would be like a change to you. Because, you see, I must take you both together."

"You can do anything you like."

"I'm going to hold you to that."

Nothing more needed said. A few weeks later she moved her mother and father to their resurrected house and then walked back across town to her own.

In 1916, my father took a post at a technical college in Gdansk as a junior instructor. He was given a fine salary for someone just starting out, and living in the village as opposed to renting a flat in town helped skinny things down financially. For a time, he and my mother, then married just over a year, lived in quiet satisfaction. My mother kept house and volunteered at the district's lending library. There was a war, the one to "end all wars," but it was elsewhere in Europe and had the effect on Maljenka of fiction, in the sense that it did not affect anything one did not allow it to. When it ended, my parents, like all in their community, believed the world was headed for an earned and hopefully prolonged period of peace.

This belief did not enjoy a slow fade.

When what is now known as the Polish-Soviet War began to escalate in spring 1920 from isolated skirmishes to full-blown conflict, colleges and universities throughout Poland began to repurpose their collective role in society — a society that welcomed the coming conflict if it meant keeping Russian ideology in Russia where it belonged, never mind that it nipped at the heels of the recently concluded World War. My father taught communications and literature, two fields suddenly considered superfluous against industry and science, which could actually do something to strengthen Polish society.

At the midpoint of the spring 1920 term, in unfortunate harmony with the news that my mother was expecting, my father was forced from his post. The college would now function as a kind of vocational trade institution, its new objective to grow a fresh generation of engineers, architects, and applied scientists for the free Polish state.

"Do these great minds of the future not need to communicate intelligently?" my father reasoned in the wood-walled claustrophobia of the provost's office. "To understand the breadth of humanity captured in great works of literature? To learn how creativity yields innovative thinking, how the well-rounded person is all of a part?"

That is what primary and preparatory schools are for, he was told.

This held as much water with my father as the palm of his hand, but there was no arguing against it. He cleared his office, returned home, and began the arduous, tedious process of typing letters of inquiry to any college or university he could think of.

One such letter went to Dalhousie University in Halifax, Nova Scotia. One of the last letters he wrote, it came of a brief fit of desperation, wherein he feared that no institution in Poland, in Eastern Europe for that matter, would have him. He liked pronouncing the name. *Dahl-ooo-zie.* Liked what it did to his lips, pushing them forward as for a kiss. According to the directory of international universities he had lifted from the Tech's library before quitting campus, the school had a department of communications — what was the harm? But he had no real interest in the place and never intended to uproot himself and my mother. Not for Canada, certainly not for a sort of waylaid island, floating out there in the water like a shard.

Then came the proffer.

Ignorant of the value of the Canadian dollar, my father could only compare the number on the page with what he had been earning in zloty — which was no accountable comparison at all. What truly caught his eye was the stipulation, undersigned by a dean, of a five-year contract and mention of a university-sponsored mortgage, "a considered means of reinforcing Dalhousie's resistance to turnover and a qualifiable gesture of faith in the long-term tenability of its faculty."

A packet of photographs accompanied the letter. The images displayed the sort of idyllic marriage of urban and rural usually found in such materials: The houses wax and neat, the lawns trimmed and green, the sidewalks seemingly safer for being decorated with children's chalk, a cloistered world friendly to dog-walkers and garden enthusiasts. A strain of romanticism ran like a sea current below my father's surface countenance, and these photographs churned it to a froth. While my mother remained circumspect, my father fell almost stupidly, as though he had been handed a corsage. But it was the narrow type of infatuation, often mistaken for love, commonly felt for the unattainable. Pure only so long as the vision one has remains uncorrupted by actual experience of it. With no tempering element, it can only grow richer. What's more, his intellectual vanity was prickled. *Teachers never stop learning* boasted one particular information card. And did he ever swallow that line.

"What a sight your father made," my mother recalled to me many years later. "He was stock-still in our sitting room, standing right in front of his favorite armchair, so taken by those pictures it never occurred to him to sit down. But when the clock on the mantel hit the hour, his wheels seemed to turn so fast, I would not have been surprised if steam had poured out his ears! He had to draft his letter of reply three times, convinced his 'tone' was all wrong."

My mother's reaction to the situation was an act of simple devotion. Without a word, she lowered the hinged staircase that led to the house's attic and went in search of their suitcases. The arbitration of the Szeyks' transatlanticism was literally, comically, that simple.

Within the week, the house was sold, along with its larger contents, to the same outfit that had been managing the acreage, and man led wife and vestigial child into the unknown.

They were at sea nine days. Gaining berth was the relatively simple matter of two hundred zloty. This got them a small crewman's quarters on the *Hullabaloo*, a decrepit steamer aimed at delivering what they knew only to be "goods" to ports in Newfoundland, Halifax, Cape Breton, and finally the northeastern United States. My father played gin with the captain and saw to my sea-sickened mother, who kept to the darkness and relative quietude of their quarters, sustained on deliveries of warm and cold teas and breads plain or lightly layered with honey. Though the vessel never experienced a truly extreme condition in the days they were on board, the water was a constant chop and the wind was ever there, rippling the flags and singing over the tow lines. My mother said little to me about those days at sea, but I picture her in discomfited repose, hands resting gentle as starfish over her belly, silently suffering her sea cradle so that I might not suffer in mine.

In quiet moments topside, seated along the railing, my father would turn a certain phrase over in his mind, a phrase my mother favored, as her mother had before her. *The wind has a fine voice and a sly purpose.* It referred to the passing of knowledge, or more directly the methodology of gossip. The way a piece of information concludes its short life in the shell of its initial forging but with all its components switched out one by one as it filters person to person, household to household, before dying away, a fresh rumor then blooming out of its ashes like a phoenix. He hoped that this new city, this new university, would be decently divorced from the political implications that had scuttled what he would eventually refer to as his "old life." Every workplace has its own inherent bureaucracy, he knew, but let it be common squabbles and pedagogic tiffs and interdepartmental intrigue. Let the behemoth of government keep out of it.

On the final morning of their journey, the *Hullabaloo* hovering just outside McNab's Island in Halifax Harbour, there was little noise but what

31

the water made against the hull. The air had grown calm. The wind seemed reticent to invade the bank of fog that hovered over the harbour. A breeze brought traces of gasoline, rot, the stew that was being cooked in the wheelhouse over a portable gas ring. The captain handed my father a brochure which had been stuffed into the paperwork a runner boat brought out to them upon entering the mouth of the harbour. THE MANSE CALVO. The pictures really made it look like quite a place, *the* place.

He saw fortuity in the fact that Dalhousie University was just two blocks from the establishment.

The very next afternoon, suit newly pressed, my father met Dr. Otto Hapstrath at his office in Burbidge Hall. Upon introduction, the dean, pumping my father's hand as though priming a machine, smiled expansively and said, "Well, well, your English is excellent, let me say. But how does it stand up to your Polish?"

Dr. Hapstrath's appearance betrayed the day-to-day life of sedentary academia. Moon-shaped face, jowly, flushing easily to a mottled red. Robust about the middle, but more from doughiness than puissance, like an athlete gone to seed. His eyes were pale and slightly rheumy, his voice a popish baritone. My father, sitting opposite him across a dark wood desk disheveled with papers, imagined him to be, in his private life, the jolly, constantly winded uncle of a gaggle of nieces and nephews, the rarely seen family member who materializes at holiday dinners with his pockets full of candies and stays just long enough to drink a bit too much.

"So," Hapstrath said, "Poland. Quite a long way to travel. And, well, you've only just gotten here. I was deeply intrigued by your letter of reply. Deeply. I just had to meet you, sir. The letter said that your wife, well, she's expecting, yes?"

"That is right, sometime around the New Year."

"Family. So important. Never married, myself. Or you could say, well, I married my work. Of course, nearly every member of faculty can say the same to one degree or another. But many are married proper. Families as big as a hutch of rabbits, a few of them. But it was never for me, I suppose. Still, I always like to see a young family just starting out. Gives one a sense of permanence. I suppose there's nothing more permanent than welcoming a new life into your own."

At first put off by expectation, my father warmed quickly to Hapstrath's delicate, if obstreperous nature. He was absent the vague air of superiority that taints what my father referred to as "nosebleed academics" as a stain ruins cloth. Perhaps the affectation that holds up younger men of learning, he considered, falls to the wayside as one grows accustomed to one's position, not unlike an actor who in his winter no longer needs the audience to gauge the quality of his effort; the effort simply becomes him. As he would later explain to my mother, "It was that bit about welcoming a new life into your own. So many men like him, university types, view children as a burden, a necessary concession to the woman." (To which I can see her scoff — "*The woman*" — and sink her fingernails into the meat above his kidneys.)

A quick swell of pride opened within him at the mention of fatherhood, and he now found inexplicable tears coursing over his eyelashes. He made no effort to hide this from Hapstrath or to imbue its presence with false weight by breaking down in the shoulders or using a sleeve to smear it across his face. It was merely eight days' travel catching him up, roping him like a lame steer.

Hapstrath stared back, not unmoved or impatient, but with the reserve of one who has encountered such an emotional display from many a student.

"It has been a long few days," my father said, releasing a long, deflating breath. "I am sorry."

"Oh, no need for sorry," Hapstrath insisted, pulling his hands up from the desk and fanning them out before him, as to keep further apologies at bay. "Journey like you had, well, anyone'd probably do worse. And, well, travelling with a pregnant lady is one kind of risk. Doing so with the knowledge that you'll not be returning the way you came is quite another."

They shared a smile. Then Hapstrath went on, a bit uneasily.

"That letter you received from this institution is a bit sticky. You see, I did not send it. My predecessor did. And, well, the reason I am in this chair now and he is not is that he tended to, well, indulge his whims regarding financial matters within the department. That letter was, well, a sort of parting shot to us upon being asked to resign. But before you get downhearted, let me say I have every intention of honoring what the letter stipulates. I just don't know *how* I'm going to do it. The term is due to start in nine weeks. The summer session, which is a bit new for us, has turned out to be surprisingly popular, and most of the folks hired on to handle those courses have made it clear they would like to stay on. Adjunctively, you see. There are only so many course sections to go around. We may be decently financed, but there are still limits on the types of courses we can offer. Both in size and number, you understand." He paused to check his pocket watch. "I have a departmental meeting which now that I see the time is due to start in a few minutes. I see no reason why the teaching roster for this year won't come up. Someone always brings it up, even in the middle of the year when the thing's already put to bed. I will present your situation."

"Perhaps they might like to meet me? I can answer questions —"

"No," Hapstrath said. His brusque tone seemed to surprise him. He stumbled back into his chair, his arms rising for balance. "What I mean is, look. This is going to, well, *get tongues wagging*, if you get the meaning, and not necessarily with the most pleasant breeze behind them. I've got to feel out the air. What a trial it's going be. My predecessor was not what you'd call beloved." He patted himself down vigorously, finally producing a gold pen from the interior pocket of his suit jacket. "What plans have you and your wife made by way of lodging?"

My father gave him the number at the Manse Calvo, to which Hapstrath made a passing remark that he was familiar with its owner. Then, in a stunned mope, he let Hapstrath walk him to the stairs that led out of Burbidge Hall.

As it turned out, one of the English department's grammarians doubled as a French tutor and therefore attended the Languages department's meetings as well. This person had come into the faculty lounge that afternoon "all shivery with gossip," as Hapstrath put it in his call later that evening to the Manse Calvo. ("That fateful call," my mother would recollect. "Not a second too soon. Your father's ruse was see-through. A poor performance of 'we've crossed the ocean and all's well.' That's what I get for marrying an honest man.")

A vein of conservatism had begun, postwar, to stain some corners of the university. And in some corners of those corners, it had become perverted into a rash nationalism. One latent response regarded the further instruction of German. The Languages faculty, with the exception of two abstentions — the German instructors themselves — felt it was no longer appropriate to offer the language in light of how it, to their collective mind, smacked of "international ingression and hostility."

"That's how it was put!" Hapstrath's voice barreled over the line at such volume that my father had to hold the receiver several inches from his ear. "Amazing, the intolerance! After all, now is precisely the time to protect the German language, to offer it sanctuary within academic halls from the besmirching it gets, generally, outside them. They put it, well, they *agreed* to put it to a vote, but before they could draw ballots, the German teachers, well, they left the room! Rightly so, I say. What else could they have done? Just stood by and watched it happen? Oh, they voted anyway, of course. And ballots! I would have demanded an open vote, yes or no direct from the lips. Hands in the air, at least. Well, anyhow, once Ms. Penning — that's the lady's name, by the bye — once she finished her summation of the situation, before I even knew what I was doing, I pulled out your letter. Mind you, this meeting was in *my* department, and, well, has nothing *whatever* to do with the doings of the Languages folks, but, well, it was suggested — suggested! I was *told* by

Ms. Penning that should I approach the dean of Languages, well, my appeal *might* fall on sympathetic ears."

"You are saying," my father began. Summoning all professional reserve to maintain a semblance of calm, his mind raced into the future: to the preparation of his blue flannel suit, which he felt was more collegial-looking than the brown wool he'd chosen to meet Hapstrath; to what like as not would be a series of short, urgent meetings full of palm-pressing and measuring up; to the urgency of slapping together a lesson plan; to the eventual process of finding a suitable and respectable place to live.

"I'm saying that a gap exists. It's all but done now, German. Something, well, *another type* of language, by which I mean the same general geographic area, is what is felt to be needed. And, well, you'll forgive my saying, yours has been a language of late repressed. Looks like they fancy themselves the champions of a wanting people! Phobes to philes in the space of a heartbeat. I must say, politics in the classroom is like trying to race a horse on foot. There's simply no winning, and you know that going in. I suppose coming from your end of the world, you know that all too well."

My father kept mum, lest he quash the opportunity before it could bloom. After a long pause he asked, "Have you spoken with the dean?"

"Straight after our meeting let out. Partially to let him know how little I appreciated our workshare commandeering my meeting." He paused, then said as if to himself, "None of *our* business was even mentioned."

My father was by this point ringing the receiver's cord around his hands as though taping them in preparation for a fight. His hairline broke out in sweat, his eyes bulged like a cat's at some far-off clatter — so he stared back at himself from the mirror hanging over the courtesy phone table in the Tilde Salon.

"As predicted," Hapstrath continued, but suddenly stopped. A rustling came over the line, followed by a brief, sharp slap, as of a book striking a hard surface. "Oh, for God's sake!" And the line went dead.

My father stared dazedly at the receiver for a few moments before returning it to its cradle and making his way back up to the room. In his confusion, it didn't occur to him to ask the front desk clerk to redirect the call.

He tried on a pleased expression. My mother saw straight through it. She demanded every detail.

"He may have dropped the receiver," she suggested after my father had given a satisfactory recital. "Or been interrupted by a student. The call came from his office? Go back downstairs in case he calls again. That boy on the desk seems unreliable."

He did as he was told, taking a chair along the windows that looked out on the hotel's east lawn, amused at how easily he accepted his wife's directive. She who had consigned herself to his quiet world. He hadn't even taken the time to use the toilet or take a book with him to keep company. He laughed aloud, until he noticed the attention he began to draw.

After an hour that saw as many shifts in posture as minutes, he began to doze. He was about to send for a nightcap to secure sleep when a call for him was announced.

Hapstrath apologized for the abrupt disconnection but offered no explanation for it; he began to speak as if their earlier conversation had merely been held in pause and was now fit to resume.

"The dean was sympathetic. That's not even the correct word. He was damn eager. Please forgive me, Mr. Szeyk, but I cannot believe such irrationality as I have encountered today. It's quite simple, really. It appears there will be a position for you after all."

Though Hapstrath's distaste at the whole thing was undisguisable, his ire seemed to be solely for the doings of the department. My father hoped that once he settled into the position and demonstrated his worth, Hapstrath would accept him as a colleague.

"And after all," he later declared to my mother between urgent sips of brandy, "no one forced him to pull my letter out during that meeting. He could have kept his mouth shut. He *was* gracious enough to accept my thanks. I am wary of the sort of people who toss out two of their own on a baseless prejudice. But straits are straits, and I want the job."

To which my mother added, not unkindly, "Of course you want it. It's what we're here for."

My parents' stay at the Manse Calvo was otherwise unremarkable. Once the position was official, my father wasted no time setting the terms of the agreement into motion, starting with the particulars of the university-sponsored mortgage. Campus residence was put into play, but my mother, after touring the faculty flats and seeing in them the same sad absence of quality and light that had underscored the tenement in which she had passed much of her own childhood, quashed the idea.

"Storage," she opined.

She was adamant their child be raised in a neighborhood. She desired a yard, a fence surrounding that yard, and a sense of placement that a glorified dormitory could not provide.

"How bad could it be?" my father reasoned. "Plenty of instructors like it well enough. Families are raised there, you know."

"Families are fermented there, as in a laboratory. I would rather our money be wasted on this hotel."

That closed the book on campus housing.

For the next three weeks, they were shuffled fruitlessly by a realtor from one disappointing property to the next. Finally, they decided to give one temperate afternoon to a postprandial walk through the neighborhoods northwest of the downtown business district, sans realtor. The homes in this particular area were some of the oldest in Halifax, and some of the best maintained. Plants and bushes and trees were well-manicured and arranged with precision, invoking airs of loveliness and affluence. The streets were of laid brick. Poking from the crevices were fallen leaves and small branches and clusters of dead-mown grass, disarray that grounded the seeming perfection of the neighborhood in something resembling accessibility, the feeling that *you* could belong there, too.

It wasn't exactly love at first sight, the house on Pepperell Street. The landscaping of the lawn was simple compared to most others on the block, but its line was clean and straight. The grass ran uninterrupted on a slight sloping decline to the sidewalk, suggesting from that vantage a modest manor. A run of hedges skirted the sidewalk. Tight bunchings of daisies hugged the front door. The drive was of packed white stone, at the end of which stood a small garage.

The house itself seemed compact on the ground, but the roof peaked remarkably high in the sky. It was styled with an obvious Queen Anne affection: eggshell blue with bone trim about the windows and along the outer porch railings at both ground and second story. Its asymmetrical façade featured a narrowly angled but grandly pitched and almost unnoticeably cantilevered front gable, giving the impression that the structure leaned slightly to one side, as one might offer an ear to conversation. The third-story attic windows were of stained glass. The roof tiles were slate, deeply black.

All was not pristine, however. The porch showed years of neglect. Paint came off in ribbons, boards were warped and coming up at the ends, revealing white-topped nail heads like dandelions. Around the back of the house, they found a disintegrating gazebo courting the middle of a scrubby lawn packed in at all sides by a smattering of dead or dying foliage. Arteries of living vine ran up the house's back wall.

The house invoked a mixture of unease and potential. It possessed just the right combination of stateliness and shabbiness to make its acquisition feasible.

There was no answer when they rang the front door bell, so my mother simply pocketed the notice of sale. She would have my father place a call that evening once what was generally understood to be the dinner hour had passed.

Their lunch that afternoon at Abigail's Coffee Shoppe & Book Stop on Spring Garden Road, the beginning of a sustained patronage, was awhirl in lofty planning. Schemes for repainting every room they imagined the house to hold. The buffing and waxing of hardwood floors. Purging cabinet dust and polishing cobwebbed light fixtures. The first night when the smell of fresh cooked food would drive out any remnant of the previous owner and leaven the very air with their possession.

So inspired were they by the possibility presented by the house, they even talked names, which they had previously agreed should wait until the birth itself. Amelia, being my mother's mother's name, was the obvious choice for a girl and thus closed to discussion. But there was no supposition were it a boy. Neither was particularly fond of their fathers' names. One Adam, one Thaddeus, and enough of both.

Wit, sounding as *veet*, my father suggested, which my mother vetoed, reasoning that the child would forever be known as Feet.

"But it means *life*, Marianna," he pleaded.

"By the time he's ten, it will feel like it means death, Karol." She preferred Pawl, meaning *little*, which was vetoed, for the sake of getting even, by a blustering, "Little? No, he will not be!"

The rejected ran on: Adrian, Aleksandr, Anatol, Augustyn, Casimir, Damian, Dominik, Eryk, Felicjan, Feodor, Fryderyk, Gerard, Grzegorz, Henryk, Jakub, Jan, Jerzy, Josep, Justyn, Konrad, Leon, Liuz, Ludoslaw, Michal, Patryk, Rafal, Stanislav, Stasio, Szymon, Tomasz, Wicent, Wiktor, Zarek. Some were ousted arbitrarily, some because they knew the Anglicized substitution — Greg for Grzegorz — would be what was used in classrooms and thereafter socially, and they wanted their son, should it be a son, to bear a name that spoke directly, unequivocally, to his heritage.

They settled on a derivation of Walerian, meaning *strong* or *brave*.

On July 1, 1920, the house on Pepperell Street was theirs. The summer was given to restoration.

On September 1, my father proctored his first lecture at Dalhousie. And four months and one day later — me.

ii. <u>Briefly, Adolescence</u>

MY BIRTH TOOK PLACE just after the stroke of
twelve midnight on January 2, 1921, in the very
room that would become my nursery, supplanted
in later years by a larger room up the hall. I would
remain an only child. I even now sometimes
wonder whether if I'd had a sibling, I might be
greatly different than I turned out. Less inwardly
directed, more generous with my affections, that
sort of thing. I drift there from time to time, but do
not much dwell. It's not exactly an original
thought. Every only child in the history of the
world, I imagine, has wondered the exact same
thing. I was not coddled, neglected, pampered, or
silenced. I was allowed, for the most part, to form
my own definitions and given leave to pursue
them. I was always aware that my flaws were my
own; I bore singular responsibility for them. This
burnished side of the coin traded fairly, I believe,
with the foundation of independent thought and
quiet confidence that underscored my parents'
mode of parenting. Conflicts within the family
amounted largely to common penny-ante
misbehaviors on my part that were, over time,
conditioned away and are not worth rehashing.
Disciplinary measures were restricted to the simple
utterance of my name as though it were being
severely squeezed — *Walek* — which invariably
did the trick of straightening me out. I was not put
through the anguish of infidelity or emotional
neglect or psychological violence. Theirs was a
workable marriage, and it bore the earnest, even

44

mundane, flavor of two souls giving one another a good life. In Maljenka, they had been practicing Catholics, though not terribly stringent in their piety, to say neither believed missing mass or doing without pre-prandial prayers were hell-worthy trespasses. Yet, lax in ritual though they were, my parents believed raising me in the church would yield moral benefits that would see me through to the age when I could decide for myself what I chose to believe. My Sunday mornings where therefore devoted to early morning mass followed by an hour's classroom study held in an annex to the main stable of the church, in preparation to receive the Holy Communion (age 7) and Confirmation of Faith (age 14). By high school, however, I substituted a few bedside prayers for actual attendance at mass, a choice that caused only a brief hiccup of protest before my parents succumbed to the pleasure of the extra hour of sleep. The God of my choosing was not so petty that He might damn one boy for not sitting in a certain building at a certain time of day on a certain day of the week and repeating the same phrases and songs and giving over the same number of coins to the same plate. The God of my choosing saw more into a person and relied less on rote ritual. I was protected as any parent protects their child from what their own philosophy deems untoward or frivolous influence, until such time as my parents realized their combined role in my life had shifted, irreversibly, from exemplar to counsel. Along the same line of self-inquiry as to what might have become of me were I not an only child, I occasionally wonder what my moral compass would respect had I not been molded in Christian doctrine. I knew plenty of kids who belonged to other denominations, other faiths, and they all seemed like pretty good eggs. Misbehavior, sure, but never out-and-out venality. Lunch money got pinched every now and again, but you were never laid up with broken bones. Kisses were stolen from the opposite sex on playgrounds and under the shade of backyard tree limbs, but that's where it ended. The thrill of the encounter was its own end. By the time I escaped puberty, I figured that unless I was wholly isolated from some secret, pervasive adolescent nature — and I did not think I was — whatever guilt I might carry for quitting organized religion was assuaged by a pretty decent moral fiber that had developed filially, rather than from respecting the metaphysical writings of old. In short, I had gotten everything out of religion that was useful to me. As for friendships, a reservation of manner kept me apart from those with whom I might otherwise have connected. This is not to say I lacked friends, of a sort. Boys drifted in and out of one's social scope, was all. One year you'd get in good with a score of fellas and be embraced by the allure of their collective companionship, like a flock of birds that knows precisely when to pitch into the wind. Then, summer. Quiet, asocial, your nose in a rotating series of library books. You return the following fall to find that the circle has changed; it has become smaller and the square footage saved in the bargain belonged to you. You seek another circle; sometimes you find one, sometimes not. Suspicions greet you. If you weren't good enough for circle X, then circle Y would have no reasonable expectation of moving up the ladder by making room for X's castoff dregs. Any standing member of circle Y kept quite understandably poised to make the jump unhesitatingly upward. There's always next year, you'd tell yourself as you moved along. Social matters settled for me at the beginning of my junior term of high school. Seen as studious and friendly, I was generally well-liked, but it was the sort of well-liked easily categorized and filed away, like paperwork. I had no declared enemies, nor any close confidant. I floated easily on pleasant smiles, invitations to the occasional get-together, and a vague admiration due not to any specific achievement — my academic distinctions were so muted as to be uninkworthy — but to the cross-stitching of heritage and an unorthodox name with a quiet *less said, more assumed* nature that disarmed fellow classmates into thinking I was mentally advanced or artistically natured, when I was neither. I kept my own counsel, as the saying goes. Rarely without a book tucked underarm, be it textbook or casual reading. To this I turned at spare moments or in times of stress, times when most people might turn to a friend. I turned inward and found it quite satisfying. I failed my parents in only one respect: Polish. I refused to speak it, read it, or write a single phrase. Though my parents both spoke it to one another in my presence, I was content to live by my adopted language. Children of immigrants are meant to be the bridge by which heritage crosses, though it diminishes along the way, and it is more acceptable that the children of those children become the philistines. I, however, was content to keep *what was* from tainting *what is*. Only later, after they were lost to me, would I recognize my regret, for I believe one's parents breathe beyond the scope of a single life, in the body of their beloved.

iii. The Occurrence at Abigail's

MY FATHER RETAINED HIS POSITION in the Languages department at Dalhousie University until March 19, 1939. His tenure ended along with my mother's years in the Circulation Department of the Halifax Public Library system's Sackville Street branch with horrible poetry at the same café where they had nearly twenty years prior planned their future and chosen their only son's name.

Ms. Abigail Evry by this time knew their preferences. Two coffees, one black, one dosed with cream and cane sugar, two glazed coffee rolls, warmed. They would exchange pleasantries with Ms. Evry as she handed over the day's newspaper to my father and the latest Hollywood exposé to my mother, who often justified her embarrassment with, "I love a new gossip rag."

They favored two dark wood chairs near the shop's front window. There the sun was kept at bay by a broad eave of dense blue canvas. Thus shaded, they could toggle their attention from reading material to what passed along Spring Garden Road and back again.

In the official statement — I was shown the police typesheet, as well as the slightly more sensationalized version in the next day's *Halifax Herald* — the driver of Municipal Number 17 admitted to mistakenly depressing the gas pedal rather than the brake as he steered the bus toward the signposted stop in front of Abigail's. A common mistake, an officer later explained to me, made circumstantially by perhaps every driver at one time or another in their life, though usually in their own driveway or in a parking lot.

Ms. Evry was quoted on page five of the *Herald*: "It was quiet, just a regular Sunday. Then it was like a chandelier dropped. It was so fast. I don't know that they saw it coming. Professor Szeyk was holding up the newspaper. Pointing something out, I guess. They were looking at it together."

The bus reached a speed of thirty-five by point of impact with the window, continually accelerating once entering the space of the shop. Apropos of nothing, the typesheet noted that the hazard lights had been properly switched on to signal a full stop. The driver, according to on-site authorities, was not injured.

In the published photo of the scene, a quarter-page black and white image, most of the History/Geography shelving is demolished, along with the wide oak table that displayed new acquisitions. Ms. Evry, who wears a simple dress of light color, holds a book in her hand, its title facing the camera but grainy, unreadable. Dark gray is splattered across her chest. Flecks of deep black like acne mar her otherwise elegant, stricken face. Clearly blood. Clearly coughed up. From this I deduced, though never demanded to know, that she was with at least one of them in their final seconds. (I have never since set foot in Ms. Evry's shop, nor asked for a private meeting with her, a kindness she has returned.)

The *Herald* article closed by stating the shop would hopefully re-open by the end of the month, provided repairs could be met efficiently. The city would foot the bill (as it later would all funeral and burial costs). The driver was suspended and eventually dismissed, but charges were nullified due to possible mechanical error. The entire write-up, including photo caption, came to just under five hundred words. I counted.

A common aftereffect of loss is a need to retain the order of things. For the possessions of those who've gone to keep the precise positions they held upon their last handling, their last interaction with the dead.

In an effort to abstain from the temptation to root through the material stuff of my parents' lives, to fall prey to a possible propensity for reading too much into common things — *My mother must have sensed something horrible was coming from the way she threw her nightgown over the chair that morning* and so forth — I bivouacked in the sitting room beneath a makeshift bed-tent over the sofa. Despite having full run of the house, this seemed the sanest way. I knew that were I to feign organization, to shift things about, they would just immediately be shifted back again. I would not be able to bear the differences.

On an end table in the sitting room was a photograph, silver-framed, taken shortly after the first Dalhousie graduation ceremony at which my father gave the invocation. I stand in front of them in the black and white image with my hands grasping, respectively, the long drape of my father's graduation robe and the delicate pencil-stitch of my mother's skirt. My line of sight is protected from the sun by a shadow cast by my mother's broad-brimmed hat. My eyes have the stunned appearance of a meerkat's. Above me, my mother beams, while the sunlight causes my father to squint. His eyes look almost closed. I recall nothing of the day; I was only four years old. But I do know it marked a kind of bested hurdle for my parents. My father being asked to keynote the graduation ceremony, an honor usually assumed by the provost or one of the deans, reconfirmed the fortuity of their new life in the West. I did not take this picture down; I let it be. People of a certain religious disposition believe that the dead watch over the living, a belief propagated via the medium of specific objects. I was not of that disposition. I did not believe that my parents were literally aware of me through some interdimensional photographic rift. I simply took a measure of comfort in being able to lay eyes on them whenever I wished. The photograph reinforced a state of what I thought of as sustainable melancholy by which I held them in memory. Its presence made me feel less alone.

The funeral services, by the way, were dignified, if unremarkable. I shook many hands, suffered many iterations of the idea that they were *in a better place*, and bore two groveling representatives of the bus company — there, I supposed, to assure I did not develop a suddenly litigious disposition. A striking moment came when the twin daughters of a faculty colleague of my father's declared in astonishment that the matching coffins looked like "hugely big bullets." Far from upset by this outburst, I appreciated it as a moment of levity. It propelled me through the morass of hours, the rictus of a sad smile aching on my face. I would, after each aggrieved interaction with some new stranger from my parents' lives, recall the exclamation quietly to myself. My only regret of that afternoon is that I did not, though perhaps should have, intervened on the girls' behalf before they were roughed out of the room by their angry, embarrassed father.

In May, my high school diploma was bestowed in absentia. I received the certificate by post. I was offered the choice of whether to attend the graduation ceremony, but anticipating some awkward testimonial, I declined.

As the summer weeks crept by, damp and sweltering, I availed myself of the myriad volumes that lined the sitting room bookshelves. With the exception of a series of pocket-sized Oxford Classics my father had subscribed to briefly in the 1930s, every single book in our home came to us via my mother's habitual skimming of what was donated to the Sackville Street Library. The library catalogued the occasional donation, if it plugged a gap in its collection and if the book's condition justified it. But everything else, to say ninety-nine percent of all donated books, was carted out to the library's foyer and marked for sale, a nickel a piece. Since it was just a nickel, as opposed to the dollar-plus cost of a new book, my mother felt it reasonable to staunch her critical faculty and to err toward open-mindedness. (I can see her now, sneaking her fingers into the cardboard boxes, filing her nails over the spines, breathing the pleasantly musty scent of aging paper.) One would not peruse our collection and find any strategic interest, any rhyme or reason. Beside compendia of Sinclair Lewis, Mark Twain, Herman Melville, Joseph Conrad, and Henry James were volumes on chemical formulation techniques, advice manuals for career planning and social decorum, cookbooks, oversized collections of photographic essays, American Westerns, gardening guides, and cheap lurid serializations of every variety. Most of these books were never read, not cover to cover. But it was not uncommon for my father and I to find my mother occupying the sofa, calm as an oyster, casually turning the pages of some random volume spread across her lap, her face cast with a clear openness to intrigue.

On lonely, owl-eyed nights that summer when my vision lolled and my eyes leaked passive, exhausted tears, I would take down a volume from that odd assortment, wondering if by some osmosis I might chance upon an interest in something unknown. Usually, I just fell asleep with the book weighing pleasantly on my chest.

I retained little of what I read that summer. My mind seemed waylaid in the same hypnotic state that drivers encounter when, sleepy behind the wheel, they realize they have no recollection of how they got home, a state I once heard referred to as "automatic pilot." There were, however, small pockets of cogence during those quiet weeks — four of them, in fact. The four times I read my 1902 Heinemann edition of H.G. Wells' *The Island of Dr. Moreau*.

The book had been an unexpected gift, just something from the donation box my mother thought I would like, and its sudden appearance in my life at age ten was all the dearer for coming on neither birthday nor holiday. A person imprints emotionally on certain objects, items that swell the heart. The book's well-handled, almost sticky leather cover, when in my hands, gave the sensation of my mother's presence so acutely, like a brilliant rush of chill air on a hot day, that I often had to sit down on the floor, book to my chest, for several minutes before continuing to read. The *book* was *sacred*, you see, even if the story remained entertainment.

"There must be things in your life which are sacred," my father once said. This was only a year before the occurrence at Abigail's, by which time he had begun lecturing in world literature to cover a vacancy left by an emeritus retiree. My mother and I attended the opening lecture of each term, as a kind of tradition. He made these remarks during one such lecture. "You *must* put such weight and meaning into certain things. You cannot only put this weight into people. Our natures are entirely too transitory to be trusted entirely with the interplay of another's soul. Investing in a book or article of jewelry or photograph, anything you wish, is investing in the individuality of the soul. It renews the slender piece of you that only you will ever truly know."

As each reading was a new avenue of ingress, a subtle shift in the light of meaning, my retreading the same literary ground that summer was both a means of incubating the memory of my mother and a renewal of my father's belief in the sacred. Thus did *The Island of Dr. Moreau* bear the touch of both mother and father as it related to my soul.

I only once set foot outside that whole summer. (Blessed be the grocer who makes house calls.) The exact date, I forget. June, perhaps. The boneyard where my parents lay is sandwiched between Robie and Summer Streets and skirts the gradual incline of Citadel Hill. It was a brisk twenty-minutes' walk from our little parcel of Pepperell Street. I stood before the new cut stone, my family's name — SZEYK — stark as propaganda. The dirt over the grave, even with the delicate sprouting of new green grass already present, looked fresh, for it had rained that morning.

There was a horrible beauty to my visit. The sun sat behind a long run of clouds, but you could tell that soon the clouds would dissipate and the heat would arrive, making the dew on the grass shimmer briefly before boiling away. It was a moment of undue clarity for me. I was only there because they were dead, and yet I wished that we had all been there together expressly to see the promise of that sky.

I opened the front door one late August afternoon to the sight of Dr. Otto Hapstrath batting rain from a gray trilby against the porch railing. I had not seen the professor in the flesh in a long while. He had retired emeritus at the close of the spring 1935 term — the last time we spoke was, in fact, the retirement dinner my parents held in his honor — and had since been living quietly in a house on Owen Street, where he worked on a short history of George Ramsay, 9th Earl of Dalhousie and founder of the university, commissioned by the administrative board. He had begged off the funeral. Condolences came in the form of flowers. I was not offended by this. Had the funeral been for, say, Ms. Evry, like her though I did, I would have given it a miss, too.

Age had less thickened him beyond his usual girth than drawn his accumulated bulk downward, as though his skin could no longer withstand gravity. What hair he had left was true white and he now sported a thin, well-manicured beard over lip and chin. He shook off his coat as a dog shakes off a bath. I hung it on a hangar on the outside knob of the closet door in order to let it dry.

Since I could not easily explain my living condition — the lean-to erected around the sitting room sofa, the general detritus scattered across the floor — I turned Hapstrath casually by the shoulder toward the kitchen, promising coffee.

After a brief inquiry, I was told the biography went "swimmingly." Hapstrath then discoursed on Ramsey's supposed affection for that particular word.

"From what I've been able to gather, and, well, it's been no small amount, it was his sort of *go to* expression. He used it quite extensively. Apparently, he found it the correct marriage of playful and prohibitive. It usually drew a smile and just as usually precluded further probing. Heck of a smart thing, you ask me. There is even a record, the handwritten journal of the grandson of one of Ramsay's fellow Lords who testifies to Ramsay saying 'Swimmingly!' when asked how his 'schooling property' was coming along. Don't you like that, his schooling property! Were I lexicographer, I bet I could make something of that usage. Anyhow, I let the expression out now and then just to, well, test it in the social waters, if you'll pardon the pun. I've even tried it out on the people down at the college. Some of them look at me like I've gone half dotty, which, between you and me, tickles me no end."

"Are you on campus often? It must be a hassle to step out of retirement."

"These administrative folks seem to want my opinion about all the big-ticket decisions now, the ones that used to be, to borrow military language, above my pay grade. Committee meetings and so forth. I never quite know what to tell them. I contribute very little. They just seem to like having a full room for these types of things. They're very good at making you feel needed, though. Any decision is less informed without rolling me into it, apparently."

"You can't, I don't know, abstain?"

"No, no. Have to earn the honorarium. The burden of financed retirement. And I do miss the air on campus. Always seems charged with something that is missing in the rest of town. Rest of anywhere, maybe. Like you can, well, *weigh* the potential surrounding you." He downed his coffee at a gulp and wiped his mouth. "Speaking of which, have you ever heard the name Marian Rose Collier?"

One of the matters *requiring* Dr. Hapstrath's opinion was the awarding of the Marian Rose Collier Fellowship, named for a past graduate turned moneyed philanthropist. The fellowship was awarded annually to an incoming student and was renewable in subsequent years should the student meet certain academic criteria. Hapstrath had suggested me, though I had not even applied for admission to the college.

"Your case of need perhaps speaks for itself," he explained.

While my potential nomination was ultimately quashed and that year's fellowship granted to someone else, mention of the Szeyk name drew a certain interest. In light of my father's tenure at the university and the generally positive opinion had of him as an instructor and colleague, the door to what Hapstrath called "filial exemption" — gratis admission entitled by having a parent on faculty — was thrown wide. I need only walk through it.

"I would not go so far as to say this is a complete rarity. Any faculty brat can take advantage of this admission policy. But for you, Walek, things are different, and I do not mean because we've lost your father. I do not mean because you are not the child of a *present* instructor." He drew his words out carefully, as he might were he speaking to an agitated student in need of reassurance or clarification. "This arrangement, and this is what I mean by different, is *unconditional*."

Meaning that short of outright flunking my courses or setting fire to one of the buildings, I would be safely carried to a diploma on the current of the college's largesse.

Then Hapstrath looked at me from the very tops of his eyes, as over invisible spectacles, and said, "Not only would it make your father and mother proud to know you went on to college, and to the college they chanced so much to find a place with, but honestly Walek, if they saw what you've let happen here, well, it would have hurt them something fierce."

Several thick seconds passed. I said nothing.

"Would you like to tell me about the sitting room? You didn't turn me about quick enough in the hallway that I missed it."

I did not attempt to control the sobs that followed. I have no negative bearing against demonstrations of grief and do not look down on those who perform them, but I had not cried like that since childhood, when you don't know how to stop and instead must take your cue to calm from others. I disliked the feeling entirely. These were not tears of loss or pity, but of shame. The expression Dr. Hapstrath wore was unbearable. I felt I was shrinking down inside my clothes, losing years, reverting to a younger self. I turned away, drove my face into the collar of the three-day-old shirt I wore. Hapstrath sat passively and said nothing. (I later appreciated this. It was like being alone without having to leave the room.)

"College will be good for you," Hapstrath eventually said, in the same gently measured tone. "Not like school as you've known it. You'll be more in control of things. You wouldn't even have to live on campus, although it is a bit, well, nerve-wracking to imagine you living here like some fugitive."

"I can't change things around," I said. "I can't change things." I had not before said the words aloud, acknowledged the truth of them with voice. It sounded both confessional and somewhat ridiculous.

"Too much stuff up there," Hapstrath said, turning his eyes up as though he could see the rooms above through the kitchen ceiling.

"Something like that."

"Would it help if I walked up there with you?"

"I don't think it would."

To my shock Hapstrath's patience dissolved.

"Walek, snap out of it. Please. I truly am sorry I was not here for you. God, that I let months go by without showing my face!" The thin skin under his eyes went red, as though stung. "No one can convince you. I know that. But you have to see your way to, well, moving on. Moving forward. At least if you're in school, forgive the expression, you will be out of your own head."

I saw his point, of course. Before the accident at Abigail's, matriculation would have been the natural order. *Of course* I would go to college. *Of course* that college would be Dalhousie. I was embarrassed to have so aggrieved Dr. Hapstrath, even as I recognized the truth in his not having "shown his face." But the man was under no obligation to me. And his point was clear.

iv. The Looming Hook

I STAYED JUST SHY OF FOUR SEMESTERS at Dalhousie, but you couldn't call it matriculation. No dormitory for me. Summers and winter breaks aside, my evenings alone on Pepperell Street were regimented affairs. Hours were earmarked to respective subjects, and sleep came satisfyingly of mental exhaustion. For a time, I sank very agreeably back into studenthood. Off-campus residency made me something off a drifter, blowing into the halls to attend classes, then dissolving into the ether until the following week. I conducted life, I believed, according to my own star. Few obligations. Frugal living, both out of necessity so the savings left to me could stretch, and as a matter of choice. I collected no new possessions, acquired no standing debts. I took on neither friend nor acquaintance.

As for romantic pursuits, my inconstant presence on campus rendered such things moot. Ditto sexual exploits — though, as I have committed here to as much transparency as memory will allow, a single evening midway through the fall term of 1940 stands forth as the sad, full measure: the opening of that year's student art gallery, a historically well-attended affair.

Events that mixed students and faculty on a relatively even keel were rare. (And there was a cash bar.) I was ignorant of art, or at least willfully ignorant of what passed for student art. My reason for being there was Theodora Roth. After a passing flirtation in two classes prior to one we shared that fall, I decided to buck up my courage and make a pass.

The gallery was packed when I arrived. Chatter bounced off the high white walls like the scrum of buzzing bees. I stood on the landing at the top of the stairs and cased the room for Theodora. In a far corner of the gallery, a pack of narrow-shouldered boys, who were up to then silently focused on something or someone beyond my line of sight, dispersed and suddenly she was there, like a bolt of lightning. She was, to that point, the most beautiful, exciting-looking thing I had ever laid eyes on. How she looked that evening redoubled the fizzy, lustful urgency of my wanting. Her hair seemed to capture the light. Neck like sculpted cream. Calves dimpled by the lift of her shoes. Thighs strong yet malleable (or so I imagined) beneath the easy silk of a limpid yellow dress.

I crossed the room — so stridently I'm sure I was nearly jogging — and came to an almost skidding halt beside her. At the squeal of my shoes against the floor, she turned. Slow, as though she had been expecting me at that precise moment. Her expression was inscrutable. Not enjoyment, but not boredom either. Then a glimmer seemed to catch her eyes and a slow, smoldering smile — one I am certain was mastered over untold hours of practice in the mirror — spread across her face.

Theodora stepped forward, to within inches of me. "You're like a movie, do you know that?"

I smiled and pushed my chest out, lassoed entirely by the light of her.

"You haven't even said hello yet, the show I bought a ticket for hasn't even begun, but here's the coming attractions." She nodded toward my waistline then tilted her head slightly to the side, the motion familiar to me from observing her in class. She tilted her head in just this way when she felt she was doing someone a favor.

I looked down. Froze. In my rush to get ready earlier that night, I had missed two shirt buttons, and the resulting gap exposed a swathe of hairy belly, which owing to my inherited Eastern European complexion was pale as the underside of a herring.

She drew her hands up to her chest, laced her fingers together. As my eyes traced their way upward, they took in a constellation of freckles on the inner exposed side of her décolleté, a sort of pink parallelogram. My eyes lingered half a second, momentarily affixed, before finishing their journey up to her amused face. A hiccup briefly troubled my breath. I began to sweat at the armpits and the tuck at each leg where thigh becomes buttock.

"The only question is," Theodora said, now confidently in charge of me, "what kind of movie are you? Have I gone for a romance, or a comedy?"

"Looks like a documentary," someone nearby (one of the narrow-shouldered pack?) scoffed. "A boring one." To which another voice added, "One of those school reels about the dangers of VD."

Theodora turned on them. "Run fetch me a drink, huh? Oh, wait, you're both only, what, seventeen? They won't give you one." I took the opportunity of her distraction to repair the gouge in my façade.

She slid her arm through mine, gripped my jacket sleeve — "Bye, boys." — and led me away.

At the bar Theodora handled herself well amid the constant coming and going and shouting of drink orders, even as like a black hole she pulled in the attention of every orbiting male. She was easy to laugh and kept her hand on my arm the whole time. I ordered us Haig & Haig whiskey, because it was the first label I noticed when the barkeep approached. I was inexperienced with liquor; it leaned on me. It leaned on Theodora, too, but less heavily, it seemed. She was clearly a with-soda-or-juice type, and the neat amber made her eyes go wet. We lasted two rounds before agreeing it was time to find someplace quieter.

Which was why, less than an hour later, like a cheating husband, I sneaked through the halls of the women's residence with a small cylinder of scotch weighing down the left interior pocket of my sport jacket.

I figured the key to successful entry to the residence was knowing precisely which room I wanted and bee-lining for it. Catch the eye of a hall matron or student who felt it was her duty to police the virtue of her sisters (this type was often a gifted lurker) and I was done for.

Stepping into the empty stairwell, I pulled in the odor of cigarettes and the odd allure of talcum powder. The scotch I'd bought at Theodora's request sloshed against me. I kept an arm slung tightly to my chest to keep the bottle from dragging the jacket's collar down across the back of my neck. I thought only of getting there, *getting there.* The moment her door eased open. The perfume she surely circulated into the air. The promise of her bed sheets. Theodora told me her room was on the fourth floor, first room off the stairwell. I hoped she had the good sense to leave her door unlocked so I could slip right through without knocking.

The scrape of my shoe on the first step past the third-floor landing ignited a renewed anxiety, and my mind flooded with details of physical interaction (of which I knew experientially nothing). It did not even feel lewd to think *I am going to have this girl tonight. In a few more minutes, I will have balled someone.* The particular word, *balled*, too silly to be lurid when spoken aloud, seemed the only word available. My notions of Theodora were, in the way a boy gets notions about the particularity of girls to which he has no reference, romantic. But I had no sense of love, and no ambition to get it. My motives were utterly base.

The girl whose bare foot I smashed with the heel of my oxford midway between the third and fourth floors was familiar to me, but in the moment I didn't know it. She shared my Modern Theories of Curriculum class. She, in fact, sat directly in front of me. Her wide, round shoulders had absorbed weekly doses of blind-eyed daydreaming. Yet even when her howl of shock and fresh pain filled the stairwell, I did not realize who she was. I looked her dead in the face and could think only of how close I was, a mere seven steps.

"I am very sorry to have done that, but please, if you could just —" I was poised to sweep past her.

"Margot."

"Okay, Margot, why don't you —"

"Margot *Lincoln*. From *Theories*."

"Yes, sorry. Margot. I am very sorry about your foot."

"Ever had your bare foot trampled like this?"

In the low light she held up a pale foot as evidence.

"It was because of your bare feet. Because you were so quiet. I didn't hear you coming."

"You didn't see me?"

"Uh, no."

In that lone stairwell, I could hardly have missed her. I was, of course, already deeper into the night.

"You *still* don't know who I am. You're already up there, where you were sneaking off to."

I kept quiet then. It was the way she said *sneaking off to*.

"Your plans have changed. You're going to have to help me back to my room."

"Look, Margot, I have said that I'm sorry."

"Maybe you would like me to scream again. Or limp to the floor matron's room. I could introduce you."

"No. Please. I'll help you." What spirit had bolstered me to this point deflated like a torn kite. "Wait, don't you have a roommate?"

"She is presently on the fifth floor of the men's residence wrapped around Mark Boyer."

"Never heard of him," I said absently.

"She's not in our room is my point. So, come on."

Margot Lincoln's room seemed to mock the atmosphere in which I (yet) hoped to pass the night. The walls were stark white, unadorned with photographs or poster pictures or even scissored news clippings. The air smelled vaguely of paint. Along the wall opposite the door, the radiator sizzled. It was markedly warmer in the room than it had been in the hall. The closet's accordion shade was pulled shut. The bed sheets were taut and tucked down. On the desk were stacks of books, leaved with makeshift bookmarks of torn notebook paper. If an emergency arose right that second, the room could look uninhabited in less than a minute.

Margot, having apparently forgotten her injury, trod easily across the room to her bed, where she sat with a dainty flourish of her skirt.

"At least there are no peepholes in the doors. So she couldn't have seen you come in," she said. "I assume a certain someone is your *why* for slipping around here. Betcha I can guess."

She raised her right hand in the air and pitched her fingers into the semblance of a duck and made the duck quack at the door. The door opposite Theodora Roth's.

"You're about the sixth guy she's had up there this term, you know. And its only October. That ought to give you the shivers. Or is that the appeal? Ugh, don't say it. Maybe you were lucky I left my slippers in the common room. This little mishap did you a favor, is my opinion."

I sat down on the bed beside her.

"You're not, um, you're not going to rat me out, are you?"

My voice eked out, as though I had just run a mile. The fullness of the evening began to accumulate. The bottle of whiskey sat heavily in my jacket pocket, dragging one side of me involuntarily into Margot's immediate air.

From the other side of Margot's door came the sound of hinges working. A ring tapping sharply on a plane of wood. The hinges working again and the soft thump of a closing door.

"I think we can arrange for you to get away with this one," Margot said. Her voice became

66

something different than it had been. It lost the veneer she had been laying over her words.

My attention was with the phantom sounds from outside the door and so this dissimilitude washed past. Only when the weight of her hand registered through the trouser cloth at my thigh did I return to the moment, thinking it was the whiskey bottle that had settled against my leg, the pressure being so high on the leg, so much a part of unquestionably intimate space.

Startled by how close her face had now come, I kept still and for the first time really looked at her. Lank hair, eyeglasses like opaque upturned turtle shells, a rather mannish jawline. But her eyes were like pieces of raw crystal behind the horrid glasses and her mouth was full as an unbloomed bulb, an oasis in the bland landscape of her uneven complexion. She even had what is on children called a button nose, a feature that seemed to exacerbate the smooth fairness of her cheek before it segued into splotchy red at her chin and neckline.

Several seconds went by. Quiet seconds in which a threshold was breached, the space between our faces slimmer and slimmer. A kiss now inevitable.

Margot's mouth was cool and soft, offering an almost meek resistance, easily overrun, and her breath tasted surprisingly of gin, though she did not, to look at her, seem the type. The light dampness of her lower lip invited me to push harder, to test the boundary before our teeth mitigated the assault. My hands, perspired and lightly sticky, slid up the hem at either side of her skirt, expanding like starfish to encompass the width of her legs, the curve of her hips, their path determined to culminate at her breasts. They broached the waistline of the skirt, meandered briefly on the fabric of her blouse.

Then once again, from the hall, the hinges whined. The ring tap tap tapping. And I slipped out of the moment.

Margot's hands rose up to my ears, rubbed aggressively over the oystered skin and slipped like dull knives into my hair.

Again, the muffled thump of the closing door.

I tried to reengage, pulling as best our shared posture allowed her body toward mine. But in the motion, the capped top of the bottle in my jacket twisted into the tender meat at my armpit. Releasing a gasp, I pulled immediately away. In the light whoosh of air produced by our separation, I inhaled off her neckline the odor of laundry soap thick enough to lay on the tongue.

"Look, Margot," I began.

"Be nice or I'll make you go down and get my slippers."

She pulled me back to her. Hands vicing onto my scalp. The kiss had heated her mouth and now her lips felt gummy, viscous, their previous coolness boiled away, her saliva tough. I was hit by a sudden, vague flutter of nausea, as when a yawn is interrupted.

It might have seemed funny, were I watching from a slight remove where the evening had already come to a successful close and this little episode had merely provided a mild jocularity to the proceedings — how I wrenched her hands away, stood up, stumbling backward over my own feet and jamming the bone just above my backside into the edge of her desk. But again: the goddamn hinges. The tock of the ring.

I turned to the sound.

Margot stood and smoothed her skirt. Strings of hair hung over her forehead like kelp.

"The floor matron does rounds at half past eleven. You better beat it, because when I hear her coming, I'm opening that door."

"I really am sorry," I said. In awkward stasis between flight and reconciliation. "About your foot."

Margot's eyes grew round as saucers, then folded quickly into slits of insulted fury. I closed my eyes, knowing I should have just shut my mouth and left.

"Get. Out."

The hallway was bare. In my rush around the corner and down the stairs, I did not see Theodora Roth's blue eyes peering from the receding space of her closing door, but I knew they were there. The hinges told me.

To this incident there is little to addend. My return to Pepperell Street that night paced out at approximately a third of the scotch. All I took to bed that night (what pathetic substitution!) was the fug of liquor. I had never felt as grateful for the solitude of the house as I did then. Falling like a plank of wood onto the duvet, I tried and failed to strip from my mind the subtle taunt of that other door opening, closing. The click click click of Theodora's nails on the doorframe and how they were attached to the fingers that should have been running through my hair. (Margot had gripped my head as though testing a melon for ripeness. The base of my skull ached.) Nor could I excuse the acute refrain of Theodora's smile behind my eyes as I closed them, and how in the struggle to maintain some sliver of sobriety before plummeting finally into sleep, it all fell to pieces.

Over the following weeks, Theodora staged a brief but effective campaign to make me as unviable a sexual candidate as one girl could. I was branded a rake and liar and — worst — *boy*. I felt I possibly deserved her ire, though I knew she didn't really care. A bruised ego was all, but that's a dangerous injury because there is no sure prescription for it; one just flails about until the inflammation cools, damned be the damage to anyone else.

As for Margot, while I could not shake off the idiocy of those minutes in her room, she would eventually accept my apology. But then she'd have to, wouldn't she? She would sit directly in front of me for nine weeks yet before the semester ran out.

The spring term passed with quotidian dullness. Summer brought stretches of sticky heat unusual for Halifax; I kept the windows of the house open even during bouts of rain. The scathing nature of those months had no greater effect on any part of me than my appetite. I lost my desire for anything other than tinned soup and cold coffee (which I acquired quite a taste for), and consequently lost 26 pounds. I did have the presence of mind to schedule a check-in with my doctor, who remarked, smugly I felt, that I had "finally achieved a healthy weight."

As I began my second fall term I was as-yet undeclared in my study track. One's second year is typically when concentration narrows, and you are taxied onto the runway toward graduation, but I began to dissolve away from things. The muted but tensile enjoyment of academic reward began to wither in the stark light of subjects of utterly no use to me — laboratory science, mathematics, sociology. While I never felt I owed it to myself to get settled on a major, I did feel I owed at least some measure of concerted effort to Dr. Hapstrath, whom I still saw for the occasional lunch or coffee when he visited campus for administrative reasons. But in quiet moments of inward honesty, often during the dim nights when trying to will myself to sleep seemed to only enliven my mind, the answer to the simple question, *what did I want*, was *nothing*. I felt no pressing need to function in the adult world. With what remained of the money left to me, though not a grand sum, I could easily drift through another year, maybe two, in perfect isolation, and I was in very real danger of veering into this tempting pattern. I was not terribly enthused with any vocation; rather, I wanted to read books, take long empty-headed walks, and lead an obsequious life free of the need to answer to any significantly higher authority. In other words, an abstention from maturity, a life that had not existed for anyone in civilized history save for those few vaunted individuals born into the absolute cherry of a caste society. A life that, for someone like me, clearly was not going to work.

I felt I should bounce this strengthening ambivalence toward my studies off Dr. Hapstrath. I hoped he would be able to put me to rights. But I never had the chance.

Otto Hapstrath died of a stroke on January 3, 1941, one day after my twentieth birthday. This was not, I suppose, an entirely unexpected event. Dr. Hapstrath had always exuded an unhealthy air. It was usually easy to overlook in light of his native enthusiasm and warm manner of dialogue, but it did not go unregistered. I would later learn from an overheard bit of chatter at his memorial that the stroke had occurred at a New Year's Eve

71

gathering at Dean Talorford's home. He was hospitalized, unconsciousness, for the three intervening days before finally succumbing.

In the immediate aftermath I felt greatly affected, though I see in hindsight that I did not honestly feel my world to have been tossed asunder by his passing. He was a terribly kind man, but his impact on my life had practical implications, not visceral or emotional ones. Only once was I ever granted a glimpse into his heart. Interestingly, it had taken place almost precisely one year prior to the date of his passing.

I had been invited to celebrate my nineteenth birthday at Dr. Hapstrath's house on Owen Street. The professor had also invited, unbeknownst to me, a small gallery of guests. I arrived, bone-chilled by the early January wind, to a half dozen faces bearing amused, already liquored smiles. I myself got absently drunk from nerves, and Hapstrath insisted I stay in his guest room. I did not argue. Nor was I aware of sleep; it was one of those nights when the body is so wracked, so entirely pent-up, that submission to the pillow is instant and you awake unnaturally chilled within your clothes, as though you had only just closed your eyes.

In the morning when I emerged from the guest room, face aflame and each footfall a delicate matter of keeping my vision steady, Dr. Hapstrath was seated at his kitchen table, the day's *Herald* open before him like a sunshade. At first blush, I assumed we were suffering the same predicament. The professor's slouch was so pronounced he could easily have taken to the floor with little or no impact on his posture. But when I skirted the dining area and entered the kitchen, following my nose to the coffee pot, the newspaper fell to the table, revealing him to be smartly dressed and clear-eyed and peering out at me over the top of frameless reading glasses.

"I made enough breakfast for us both, but then I wasn't sure when you would be coming around, so I put your plate in the bread box." Hapstrath sat forward, rested his elbows on the table. "I'm not used to doing for, well, for anyone else, so I wasn't sure how much is enough, or even how to make sure it would keep until you woke. I suppose the bread box is not the best place. I just didn't want it to all go cold in the icebox."

After clouding a coffee with milk, I opened the bread box to find a plate almost spilling over with eggs, toasted bread, and a small hillock of bacon. Pathetically grateful, I eased the plate from the narrow aperture. It was warm in my hand as I walked it to the table, where I took the chair opposite Hapstrath.

"Thank you," I said. "This all looks wonderful."

I felt some kind of apology was in order for appearing in such a state, but couldn't muster more than a meek "I'm sorry."

Hapstrath folded his newspaper squarely and laid it down beside his empty plate. He picked up the steaming mug at the plate's opposite side and held it in both hands.

"You weren't the only one," he said, his tone accepting and dismissive at once.

I ate ravenously until the plate held only a small pool of crumby butter. My head began to clear, the tightness at the temples dulling to a vague pressure as from a hat that's a bit too small.

"I had a very fine time," I said.

"So, you remember it then."

Hapstrath struggled through wheezing laughter at his own remark that ended in a harrumphing cough.

"I didn't expect you to have a gathering," I admitted. "It was very nice."

"Yes, well, it was the perfect excuse, your birthday. Only the day before I was in bed with a nagging sniffle, but yesterday my head cleared up, well, just in time. I'd spent New Year's Eve in the dark with a wet washcloth over my eyes. I consider last night a conciliation prize."

"Some of the other guests seemed surprised to find out it was my birthday."

"Oh, I didn't tell them. It was a surprise for everyone that way."

Dr. Hapstrath's home was simply but tastefully decorated. The walls were empty of hangings and papered with rich green and blue vertical striping that exuded an appropriately collegiate tone. Bookcases at each end of the sitting room broke up the potential eye-strain of the wallpaper with their color spectrum of book spines. The lower surfaces were free of knick-knacks, save discreet ashtrays on the coffee and end tables. This absence of décor drew your attention to a single framed picture that sat on the mantel above the sitting room fireplace. It was a large black metal frame, perhaps too big for the depth of the shelf (it would have been more appropriate to have hung it by a hook), containing a casual snapshot of Hapstrath standing beside a woman about his age and height and a teenaged boy much taller than either of them, taller by two heads.

He caught me staring at the photograph.

"My sister, Agnes, and her son, Luck."

"Luck?"

"Indeed. Agnes, well, the pregnancy was difficult for her. She'd always been a brave person. Hers was a quiet type of strength. She was not unlike your mother in that respect. Her personality erred on a, well, a sort of humor in things. For instance, she assigned the Hapstrath name to Luck's birth certificate. She saw the writing on the wall, as the expression goes, with regard to some false promises made to her by the boy's father — an inconstant reprobate, if you ask me. She figured if responsibility for the boy was going to be hers alone then, well, he was going to be *hers*, period."

"Why the name Luck?"

"Not so common, is it? Agnes was a bit older than I. She was thirty-seven when she became pregnant, and for a spell it looked as though she might not be able to carry it to term. So, when the boy arrived, ten fingers and ten toes and howling like a banshee, she knew he was a gift. He was her great good luck. Unusual name, but a very fine one."

"Are they still here in Halifax?"

"Agnes passed in '33. Heart attack. Not the type of thing you see coming. But then death never is, as you well know. Luck was just twenty. It hit him quite hard. He came to stay with me for a little while, but I could tell from the start that it wouldn't last. Luck inherited a good measure of his father's willfulness. After a few weeks, he decided to take his chances in New Brunswick. I doubt he knew what he wanted, only that he wanted something *else*. Who was I to argue?"

"Is he still there?"

"Oh yes. Dug right in. Factory work. A foreman now, according to his last letter. Running a staff of seven." He paused then and looked down into his cup. "An impressive young man. So much like his mother."

I had never known Dr. Hapstrath to be one for sentimentality. What emotional weight rested in his words, in his general view of things, was usually couched in the sort of genial tone one takes with a crowd of strangers to keep everything light and friendly. (However, this was not strictly the case, as evidenced by his visit to Pepperell Street those months before when he yanked me out of my self-imposed oubliette.) I felt he was now but a thread from lowering his usual battlement. I was duly taken aback by what he had told me, but as I was still recovering from the aftereffects of the previous night, I selfishly coaxed the conversation into shallower waters.

"What about the book you wrote? The one about the guy who founded Dalhousie?"

"That book queered me on *ever* writing another one. I got it finished, of course, no problem there, and I thought it was a very fine job. The board practically sang over it when I turned it in. But when the chorus died down — and it died swiftly — the book received a small printing and then was archived. Two years' work collecting dust on a shelf few people visit in the basement of the college library. I'm glad to have done it, no question. But now I can say I've tried my hand at it and, well, that's good enough for a life. Publish or perish does not apply to retirees."

The conversation dwindled down after that — Luck Hapstrath was not discussed again — and soon it became time for me to head home.

After a return walk that felt much less cold than the same route the night before, as I stepped up to my front door, I found myself thinking of Luck Hapstrath. Though I would never know this person or ever even meet him, I felt there was something to say for what a rash decision could do for a middling or directionless existence. This was no epiphany, but I did feel Luck had conjured the stuff of adventure. No threatening villains, no mortal peril, but a risk nonetheless. Chance brokered by the need of the heart. Small 'r' romantic, but romantic all the same.

Though the intensity of my grief at Dr. Hapstrath's death was short-lived and thereafter took the form of simple regret that what thanks I made for all he had done for me, for the Szeyks, had been piteously meek, in the days after his burial I underwent a brief bout of terrific enthusiasm, a bolt of confidence that I might persist through school after all, if only in his honor. But this was merely a product of how I processed my regret. I awoke one dim, blanched morning a few weeks later to find that this fervor had dissolved like salt in warm water.

Thereafter, school became a slog. I dumped my entire course schedule into Tuesdays and Thursdays, hoping that three unconstrained days might help wriggle me out of my preterm funk. A resounding miscalculation. As winter intensified through February before yielding to a sopping early March and the spring term was in full swing, I stopped going to campus altogether.

I suppose it is not terribly unusual. College doesn't agree with everyone, or them with it. But of course, that's not good enough, is it? I was a college proctor's son. I was a library manager's son, also. The accumulation of knowledge was a constant in my life for as long I could remember. Institutional education paid for my cushy little life (and I count Dr. Hapstrath's gift of filial exemption in that column, as well). I inherited many traits from my parents, perhaps the foremost being resignation to the notion that people's indecipherable motivations are, at base, romantic. A deliberate life cannot exist on an island — and I was surely on a goddamn island. But I had put myself there. No one did that for me. Not even the driver of Municipal Number 17.

I think that when you come down to it, I saw the end game and turned up my nose. And since reading books was the one thing that seemed to matter to me then, the only result I saw of continuing to halfheartedly pursue a degree was to become exactly what my father had been — except that I would have made, at best, a shadowy reflection of a superior model. A mere likeness of the genuine article.

Had my father not been a teacher, nor my mother spent her life in a library, I doubt this would ever have bothered me. Had they held blue collar positions, or been involved in clean-handed levels of commerce, I might have conditioned myself to seek a target career and to strike. Instead, I let myself grow lazy on the idea that what whirled about in my mind would eventually catch me up to a calling as yet unrevealed to me.

By the long weekend's break that signaled the midterm of the spring semester, I was decided. So, I went in search of the paperwork I had signed two years earlier, to find out exactly who I would need to speak with and what steps would need taking in order to dissolve the arrangement of my attendance.

My mother's secretary sat in the rear part of the downstairs foyer, which fed by a narrow hall into the kitchen. It was where she had managed all our monthly bills and yearly taxes; my father had no head for numbers. I had not picked through the drawers and cubbies since they died, though looking back I see that I should have, that it should have been one of the first things I did, in order to apprise myself of the practicalities of my situation. One thing I did use the secretary for was as a place to stack mail, which I only sifted through about once a week, the take being so lean. Mostly advertisements and offers from local businesses.

I was unable to find what I was looking for in any of the drawers, so I picked through what was on the desktop, including the unopened mail, figuring the papers might be mixed in with other unrelated but identical white envelopes. I was right. The envelope I wanted was tucked beneath a small sheaf of old tax papers that bore my parents' signatures. But before I located it, I first found an unopened letter from the Canadian Royal Mutual Trust and Loan, which I recognized as the lender to which I signed the monthly mortgage check. It was the bank, I assumed, that functioned as intermediary with the university on my parents' original 1920 loan.

I had a sketchy memory of a conversation my parents had in which mention was made of how close they were to closing off the mortgage. It seemed that our house would belong to us free and clear very soon thereafter. What I had not heard was the context of this conversation, which now that I read the summons, I realized was them trying to justify to themselves refinancing the house. Closing off one mortgage to open another.

As for the substance of the summons, it stated simply that an officer of the bank requested a meeting to discuss the potential default of the loan issued to Karol and Marianna Szeyk on June 12, 1937, and now entrusted to the present resident of the house, which was me. This meeting was desired at the present resident's first opportunity.

I dealt with Dalhousie first. Seemed easiest.

I expected more resistance from Dean Talorford, to whom the registrar's office directed me for signature and stamp, but found him oddly genial and receptive.

"I respect your decision," Talorford said. "I disagree with it, of course, but then what might I say to my twenty-year-old self had I been through what you have these last years."

I could sense him trying to inject a thread of concern into his words, but the man had not really known my father so far as I knew, having come out of the arts department before being appointed to the English deanship. And this was only the second conversation I had ever had with him, the first being a brief, customary handshake affair that sealed my initial entry into the school.

His desk held a shine in the lamplight. His blotter, pristine as a putting green, seemed an extension of his own physical grooming. His fingernails, which he tapped with reserved cadence on the blotter, showed half-moons pale as ivory. The hair on the back of his hand, as black as the brilliantined hair on his head, looked like it had been carefully brushed. He could not have looked less like his predecessor, Dr. Hapstrath.

As he went on at some length about the "stolen freedoms of youth," I pictured a wheel turning in his mind that tallied the amount the university would save from having one less faculty brat riding its tailcoats. I returned his genial tone with a genial smile, and after securing his signature deposited the refutation papers with the registrar.

All told, it took about as much time as it takes to shower.

As I stepped out into the afternoon air, somehow, even then, with my decision filed and final, it all felt like a rouse, a gesture. I believed I could turn on my heel, retrace my steps, and take it all back. It would have been all the same to Dean Talorford, I imagined. He might have even allowed it — out of amusement, if nothing else. A giddiness rose up in me. The air smelled unusually fresh, perhaps because the sea wind was languid that day. I had no great impulse to return home, where the summons awaited and where I would likely fidget myself into a sleepless night in anticipation of the next morning's appointment.

I walked down toward the quad. The sun would be down in an hour and the small quadrangle would light up softly yellow. The dining hall would flood and the residences' front steps become occupied by those waiting for friends or looking to have a quick smoke, until blackout regulations drove everyone inside to their books, their beds, their liquor, their seemly and unseemly ambitions. As I went along, I seemed to part the air in a way I can only describe as parting it willfully with my entire body. I could not finger exactly why I felt this openness; I didn't know what kind of openness it was. I didn't know it was that of a shell responding to the calming lassitude of a temperate current, ignorant of the looming hook.

I reported to the bank the next morning, March 25, after which things tumbled very, very quickly. But at the risk of stringing out with false intrigue a fairly straight-forward series of events, let me burn through the particulars.

I was assigned to a loan officer. He vetted the documents I had found earlier that morning in one of the secretary's cubbies against the bank's files, confirming that the house had been refinanced in June 1937, the debt remaining to Dalhousie paid in full, and that the bank presently owned the loan, which was set to run through July 1957, at the monthly rate disclosed in the agreement. Furthermore, my account, which I had been blindly using to pay mortgage, utilities, and domestic costs such as food and upkeep, but which I had not actually sat down to reconcile on paper since the previous summer (I am my father's equal as regards finances), sat at an amount equal to two months' payments with little else to spare.

I took this news with the plainness it was offered. The officer then put me through a series of questions to ascertain my present ability to meet the terms of the loan.

Was I a student?

Employed?

Receiving income from any alternate or undeclared source?

Was I a member of any branch of His Majesty's Royal Service?

Had I considered applying for status as a bedding establishment, as a means to draw income?

I answered each question in turn — heedlessly, for I seemed not to be in my body. The previous day's exit from university seemed at once prescient and terribly foolish. Would being a student have offered me some protections? Or would I have had to jettison it anyway, in order to make myself available for … what? Some sort of job. What job?

I found myself beginning to perspire. I was given a glass of water. It was at this point that the bank officer changed his tone and spoke with hushed urgency to me.

"Mr. Szeyk, I'm afraid I see little avenue here. Unfortunately, your parents' untimely passing does not dissolve the contract, not when the terms of their codicils expressly passed the property in question over to you. You have maintained the property as a residence, having never abandoned it or assigned rights of the property over to another person."

He sat back In his chair, the leather softly exhaling against his weight. His eyes in the light now touching his face from the window seemed pellucid, and a small patch of bristly hair on his cheek stood out, obviously missed during his morning shave.

"These are unusual times, what with the war and all. Living space is at a premium. That is why I asked about the option of applying to have the house zoned in as a business. But I can see that is not something you are fit to — not interested, rather, in doing."

He was correct, but I said nothing. I only nodded my head vacantly.

"Your situation is as simple as this. You have some money remaining. Either you secure a paying job before it runs out and nothing need change. Or you consider the likelihood that you will default on this loan and that the bank will assume the property, leaving you in a difficult situation. If you are unable to find a source of income before your savings is exhausted, there is little I can do. An alternative would be to forfeit the agreement here and now, surrender the property and its assets, and we'll see what can be done about the bank not pursuing satisfaction against the amount that sits in your account."

It felt like a kinder form of blackmail; I wasn't sure If he was expecting an answer or not.

"Housing, as I've said, is becoming a problem in Halifax," he went on. "There are many households — most, if you want my opinion of it — that are quietly taking in boarders. Whether soldiers or factory workers or anyone in between. I don't imagine these people draw enough money from what they are doing to keep the lights on from that alone. They must have jobs, too, you know? But, you see, the bank is presently pursuing the procurement of properties by which to act as landlord. A direct challenge to those doing it on the sly, you see."

I felt I needed to issue some counter, but could find none. I fell back on politeness. "Thank you for your suggestion. I'd like some time to consider it."

"Of course. It is a big decision. We are always here, Mr. Szeyk. Please come back when you are ready." We both stood, and as we shook hands, he leaned slightly toward me. "But don't take too long. Time flies when you're turning over a decision like this."

He smiled, revealing a row of jagged, unkempt teeth. A shark's mouth. I knew right then that one way or another, the bank would try to take everything I had, and this man would find some excuse for why.

So, after stepping out of his office cubicle, I went to a teller whose window was on the opposite side of the main vestibule and closed my account. I walked home with $576 sitting like a brick in my front trouser pocket.

~

It is clear what kind of person I was. My life hinged on nothing more than the days following one to the next. A person plans for his future as a means of focusing the present, making the steps in his life matter. I didn't seem able to do that. The terrible schism of cowardice is that it removes you from what idea you previously held of yourself. I could have resisted. I could have made appeals to alternate channels. I could have done what was needed to secure a job, any job, even three jobs, if I truly had wanted to tough out my life in that house.

Instead, I began to weed my possessions.

It was a process I strangely enjoyed. There is something lifting, I discovered (or perhaps willed myself to accept), about jettisoning the material stuff of your life. The judgment process requires perfect honesty about what matters and what, ultimately, does not.

The furniture was easy to cast away. The garrison stationed at the Citadel sent a panel truck and small detachment of men to retrieve it as a donation to the families of those with fathers and sons already overseas. They were a gruff bunch, speaking in monosyllabic directives. Their practiced efficiency stripped the house of its larger items in an hour. I was thanked. Each of the men shook my hand, from which I absorbed a brief rush of unearned patriotism.

The house, once emptied, was a virgin space, as though a family had not spent nearly two decades in it. Before turning in that night, I roamed the empty rooms in my bare feet to enjoy the gentle suck and lift of my damp soles on the wood. I drew my fingertips along the walls like a child who felt he was getting away with something, giving the moisture of my skin to the dry texture of the wallpaper. My parents' bedroom and the study were part of this evening tour. Bare, they were just rooms, identically white-walled with identically curtainless windows. They no longer contained the residue of tragedy.

Standing before my own bedroom window, I wondered what legend I might make if I were to stay on in that naked house, and amused myself with Dickensian manifestations of children tear-assing along the sidewalk, weary of movement at window corners, for the hiss and creak of the front door opening to reveal the solitary creature within.

Apart from the clutter in my bedroom and the plates and flatware and miscellany in the kitchen, my parents' personal belongings were mostly what was left. (I had liquidated their clothes closets at Christmastime for St. Matthew's Church.) There were books, so many books, and the more intimate items that seem to describe a person with an accuracy often those closest cannot quite summon. My father's hair brush, for instance, on which lay a shiny film of pomade. The oyster shell dish — a real oyster shell, polished — that held my mother's assortment of hair clips and barrettes, all useless to tame the frazzled onyx mass of her shoulder-length hair in summer. My father's shaving kit, a common leather sack holding a razor, a small paper envelope of replacement blades, and a jellied cake of shaving soap, all kept to professional standard. My mother's ironing board, folded and hung from a metal hook on the back of their bedroom door, bearing more than a dozen arrowpoint-shaped scores from her absentmindedly ignoring the hot iron while reading a book or watching the robin's nest that every spring appeared on a bough just outside their bedroom window. I remember how my mother once found, cast asunder in the tall needles of unmown grass, four hatchlings that had been rocketed from the nest during a rainstorm and had been abandoned by their mother. Using gardening gloves, she retrieved them one by one and set them back into the nest, which I had pulled down in one remarkable piece from the tossed bough. She covered the nest with a kitchen towel that had been warmed in the oven and together we walked the innocents to the library on Sackville Street. One of the women on the children's collection staff had turned her greenhouse into an aviary, and gladly took possession.

I wished to keep all these things, and many more I do not here inventory. But sentimentality takes you only so far, and my pathetic means of addressing these items was to treat them like all the rest of the stuff in the house. I was as discriminating with these things as with my own possessions.

In the recess of my bedroom closet was a matched set of luggage. Three pieces with snap-lock closures, upholstered in felt. The largest of the three would hold all the clothing I wished to retain, the smallest all my personal items, my sundries and such, my most precious books. The middling suitcase I gave to the past.

I kept: the framed photograph from my father's first graduation speech; my mother's oyster shell dish; a collection of handkerchiefs that bore my father's initials and had been a gift from me on my father's fortieth birthday; the shaving kit, minus the cake of soap; a framed antiquarian map of Halifax and environs, dated 1894, (elegant deep black fonts, quays and docks etched into an eye-blue harbour like the uneven bristles of a

brush) that stood atop my mother's dresser; my
father's wristwatch, a weather-worn 1935 Timex;
a few volumes cherry-picked from my father's
Oxford Classics collection, *David Copperfield*,
Roderick Hudson, *Youth*, *Lord Jim*; the sterling silver
compact and hair brush from my mother's vanity,
tarnished slightly at the scalloped edging but
otherwise very fine-looking, which I kept as a
hedge against the odds of my never having a
daughter to whom I could bestow such things; and
a petrified sliver of deeply black wood, hard as
slate and showing thin veins of scraped-off
barnacle. My father had pocketed this piece of
flotsam on the Halifax Harbour wharf after
descending the plank from the *Hullabaloo* the day
they first arrived in the city. It was a random and
uninteresting thing to keep, but its presence in my
hand both reinforced the authenticity of my
parents' long-ago risk and comforted me against
the imminent unknown.

From the garage — which I left as it was; we
had never had a car, and lawn implements were
too awkward to transport; they would benefit the
new owner — I took the wheelbarrow my father
used for gardening and spreading crushed rock
over our drive, and gave an entire day, from
midmorning to an hour past sunset, to hefting
loads down South Street to Fort Massey
Presbyterian Church and St. Matthew's Church,
respectively, both of which served as distribution
depots for the in-need. Fort Massey received the
entirety of the kitchen; St. Matthew's what things
were chaffed from my and my parents' bedrooms.
The rectors never questioned the sheer volume of
my donation, even though it must have seemed
unusual to them — not just the amounts I was
hauling but the means by which I was hauling

them. Theirs was a practiced discretion, and I wondered whether the charity of random citizens held a seat beside the quiet confidences of the confessional booth.

Not everything went to the churches, however. Eight trips were made to the Sackville Street Library — all of the books my mother had amassed disparately over the years returned once more to the nickel racks. I also made one last visit to campus. I could not return or resell my textbooks to the bookstore so early in the term, but I saw little reason that they should go to the racks along with everything else. I took them in a paper shopping sack to the women's residence and left them, along with a note that read, *No longer needed. Might get a few bucks out of them in May*, for Margot Lincoln. Who else could they go to? Who else did I know? (Theodora Roth did not enter into it.) I suppose I could have left them anonymously in the library or at the foot of any given door in the men's residence. I left them for Margot not to drop a small fraction of my discarded life on her, but rather as one final meek gesture of apology (or so it felt as I walked away from the residence hall). The books would be worth something at term's end, and what student couldn't use a little extra money?

On April 1, 1941, I signed away the house on Pepperell Street. I was shown to the same falsely sympathetic officer I had seen on my previous visit.

As I predicted, once my signature was had, he immediately turned his attention to my account. I was able to enjoy the look of mystification that coated his face when he was told by one of the tellers that the account had been closed days before. He dismissed the young woman with a wave of his hand.

"I suppose that's it then," he said.

I asked what would happen to the house now. I felt it was on the tip of his tongue to say that it did not concern me, that withholding this information would be his final card to play, trumping my account closure. But he briefly held a sigh and said that it would be held vacant until the arrangement of an auction, to coincide with that of several other similarly repossessed properties. He seemed to forget his earlier tale about the bank's entrée into housing management. Then he seemed to forget about me, too. His eyes rolled flat and he tucked his chin into his neck, suddenly absorbed by the ledger open on the desk before him.

It began to rain as I left the bank and headed up Coburg Street. (Precipitation is a perpetual threat in the Maritimes that carries no symbolic weight.) I turned up the collar on my jacket. I don't recall what it was I might have been thinking, or how it felt to walk so anonymously through my own hometown. Yet I was more anonymous than I had ever been before, unmoored to residence or purpose or clan. Since the rain was light, and the rooming house where I had secured a flat that morning before visiting the bank held all the appeal of an abattoir, I decided to chance a walk to Point Pleasant Park, hoping that the day could be nicely lost in casual motion before the drudge of finding work that would greet me in the morning.

I turned south onto Lemarchant Street. I had neither reason nor excuse to come down Lemarchant very much in my life, and so the Manse Calvo, far from ordinary to me, made a fine sight. The enormity of the hotel's façade, rising four stories toward the massing clouds and broad as a whale, made the maples that lined the parkway along its front lawn seem like saplings. The weather-washed yellow and faded brown-green brick of which the place was built looked like an old road that had been lifted in great sections and mortared upright into the foundation.

I stared admiringly at it as I paced along the sidewalk, and that's when I saw the notice posted in the inlaid glass window of the front door:

'USEFUL MAN' NEEDED
POSITION OF ASST. HOUSEMAN
EXPECTATION OF IMMINENT
ADVANCEMENT
INCL: QUARTERS, THREE SQ.S, FAIR SALARY.
ACTIVE MILITARY DISJOINED FROM APPLYING.
ALL OTHERS INQUIRE AT FRONT DESK.
SNGD: MS. LORETTA WYNDL, HOUSE MANAGER

v. <u>By the Favor of Ms. Wyndl</u>

"THE VALUE OF A HOUSEMAN, at its essence, is bent upon his knowing when to adhere to an established routine and when to roll with the punches. Ours is an unpredictable time, Mr. Szeyk, and a good portion of the Manse's revenue comes from the booking of events and receptions, few of which adhere to a framework. This provides interesting variety, but also requires staff to adapt to circumstance."

Ms. Wyndl's fists disappeared into the pleats of her skirt as she stood, squat and akimbo, on the grand staircase's second-floor landing. She made a remarkably proportioned form. The soft bloom of her sizable hips was matched by a pillowy, almost comically rotund bustline and an ovular volume of tufted silver hair that sat atop her head like spun sugar. Only a pair of mauve-colored house slippers, narrow of instep and with toe lines as stunted as ballet pointes, betrayed what might once have been a youthful litheness.

"Unfashionable though he may be in wartime, our finance minister, Mr. J.L. Ilsley, was perfectly correct when he stated that money and material things are nothing as compared with the freedom and dignity that idealism alone can bring as a benediction to the lives of common folks. A fine statement, I should say, and I am confident that I have not bungled it in recitation. However, it does not follow that what material things we have in this house are not to be cared for properly and maintained. Particularly in light of the flexibility we must display in our hospitality and service — and despite the unavoidable fact that mass production now makes nearly any item one might find use for available in frankly absurd quantity. The war has, in such regard, amplified the disposability of material things. The Manse Calvo, however, exists outside this contemporary turpitude. Point to any item, any fixture, any article of furniture, and you will find a story, a bit of history, and an elegance singular to anything else in Halifax."

I had been at the Manse Calvo for more than an hour at this point and had already received a lengthy and informative tour of the house and grounds, during which Ms. Wyndl provided a surprisingly frank history of its founding and inception. (These details included what I first learned about Annelie Calvo: the incident with the knife in the galley; the power struggle with her uncle Myron over continuing her studies; her sudden move to PEI. These aspects seemed somewhat out of place, though I suspected Ms. Wyndl could not help but betray her acute affection for Annelie, even to a perfect stranger.) I had been greeted with abrupt formality when I first stepped through the front door. Ms. Wyndl came swiftly from behind the main reception desk, her left hand extended, telegraphing as a man would the expectation of a handshake. She moved with an easy grace and determination, despite her relative bulk, and my immediate impression was of a person not to be trifled with.

"Let's move on, shall we?" She turned and led me up to the third-floor landing, where sat, in a small windowed alcove, a pair of wing chairs.

Easing down into one of the chairs with a slight flourish and quick tuck of her skirt, she said,

"I prefer to conduct the personal aspects of interviews here, Mr. Szeyk, if it's all the same to you." She tucked her short, square-nailed fingers into a threadless cat's cradle upon her lap, a gesture of calm assuredness. Her gaze was an odd mixture of cautious and piercing, and I found myself sitting up straight, as though it were role call at school, despite the chair's being pleasantly warm from the sunlight refracting through the overlooking window, welcoming me to sink sleepily into it. Instead, I squared my shoulders into the seatback. The better, I felt, to bolster myself physically against Ms. Wyndl's brusque manner of speech.

"I went through interminable frustrations when hiring our present overnight clerk not three months ago. Apparently, the twilight hours bring out every askew person in the whole of Nova Scotia. I would rather not suffer such an ordeal a second time. I would be hard-pressed to consider myself an intelligent woman if I did. What I *would* like to do is learn more about you. There is much to be said for the character of those with whom one works. After all, the best part, to say the largest part, of one's waking life is spent not in the company of loved ones, but coworkers. And this is what's called a live-in position. Therefore, what you have by way of character is relevant to your reasons for being here. You are from Halifax, is that correct?"

"Yes, all my life. We had a house on Pepperell Street."

"Is it not still on Pepperell Street?"

"I'm sorry?"

"We are in continual conversation with our past, Mr. Szeyk. I am asking what brought you here, to that chair you sit in, seeking a live-in situation, from a house that is at worst twenty minutes' walk from our front door."

What a question. Her tone suggested that I might have the job already in hand, a supposition supported by the open complaint about her previous hiring experience. But I felt that laying bare my failures and inadequacies might upset the whole deal before I knew for certain. What decided me was Ms. Wyndl herself. Her compactly plump carriage was at perfect attention, slumped not a centimeter into either of the chair's wings, but her hands, as she spoke, had become unclenched and now rested oddly at each hip, giving her the appearance of a doll that had been dropped by a distracted child. I read into her posture a mixture of pertness and calm susceptibility to persuasion — and to this I spoke. I made an effort to excise emotional considerations. I stuck to facts, in order to temper the outlandish lack of reasoning she would surely find on display.

While I spoke, Ms. Wyndl made neither sound nor movement. She maintained her silence even after I stopped speaking, to the point I began to worry I had said too much.

Finally, in a soft voice she said, "Orphans aren't just children, Mr. Szeyk. Even I know that and my parents both saw me enter my fourth decade with a full grasp of their faculties before the gradual decline. When you lose your family, you lose them for good, whether you are newborn or grown. I have had experience with this type of youthful loss. A vicarious sort of experience with Ms. Calvo, whom I mentioned at some length earlier."

From somewhere below, a clock marked the noon hour. I had been at the Manse since half-ten and yet I felt that everything to this point — my entry and approach to Ms. Wyndl at the reception desk; our tour of the grounds; her exacting remarks on the staircase landing; and now the seemingly direct, but in retrospect meandering chat in the company of the wing chairs — everything was a preface to what a proper interview ought to have been. But it never got so far as proper. As the last hollow chime faded on the air like the call of a foundering ship, and as if the very air in the third-floor foyer had changed, my interview, for all intent and purpose, came to a close.

"You are the first applicant to this position. I had the notice to which you responded drawn up and posted only yesterday. I have no desire to prolong the hiring process, for which reasons I have already explained. I will give you this job. You do want it, of course?"

"Yes, I do." (Though at the time the parallel did not occur to me, in composing this record I now hear the faint echo of my mother's voice – *Of course, you want it, it's what you're here for.*)

I was unclear what switch had turned in Ms. Wyndl's mind, for I had said nothing of note, aside from what weight my personal history carried, and she had pitched no pertinent questions. She now sat forward in her chair. Her neck betrayed a subdermal effort, a straining that provoked, in the sunlight, a twinkling of her eyes, which I now noticed were quite green.

"Mr. Joonblack, who has been the houseman here since our opening day in 1920 has seen fit to tender his resignation. His people originally landed in Digby and he means to return there to assume control of his family's plot now that his parents have passed. No tragedy there, just so you know. A matter of age is all. The natural sequence of things. Still, I felt I should be direct about it, seeing as you will be under Mr. Joonblack's wing, to so speak, until his tenure ends with this calendar year."

"That's a remarkable notice period," I said.

"When you have been part of a place for as long as Mr. Joonblack has, it behooves you to offer that place a remarkable courtesy before exiting it." Neatly refolding her hands in her lap, she went on. "At any rate, certain things will call attention to themselves here that likely did not affect you alone in your former house. I want to be perfectly transparent about that. Foremost of which is the issue of rationing. You may have encountered the general shortages when you purchased your groceries. They affect an establishment like ours something more significantly. Butter. Eggs. Most types of meat. Our cook is using what ingenuity she possesses in keeping our tenants from staging a mannered coup in the dining room. Alcohol in all its forms seems to be the only thing of which there is excess. We are not the least expensive place to get a room, and there are expectations that come with the ambiance of an establishment such as ours. The assistant houseman will be expected to procure certain items directly from the farming groups that stage markets in Truro, at the discretion of the kitchen staff. We have a car for such things."

She was poised to go on, but a bellow that seemed to ricochet off the very wallpaper redirected her attention.

"Doggins! Keep up now!"

My first sight of Troke Joonblack made for a singular impression. Five feet tall, but only just. Clad in a black sweater and faded green overalls soiled almost black at the knees and pocket slits. A tam-o'shanter less covered than restrained a ginger typhoon of wiry hair. His chin jutted out as if in challenge. His step was a slight drag and lilt that favored his right side.

As he clambered into the alcove, Ms. Wyndl rose from her seat.

"The folks from the auxiliary are here more than an hour before time. They want the room now, but I've been out dealing with that mess in the back garden." Troke Joonblack's voice had been leavened by his proximity to Ms. Wyndl but still danced to the lowest chord in the register and bore a touch of accent, which I could not then identify but later came to learn was Scots watered down by a generation Canadian. He carried the distinct aroma of chewing tobacco.

"Is that a problem, Troke? Surely the room is already set for them."

"Did you see the bocce pitch? Some guest's kids used it for a sandbox. And they tore up one of the flower beds. They left the poor uprooted things all over the pathway like some kind of message."

"Is the room not prepared, Mr. Joonblack?"

This sudden shift from the familiarity of his given name to the professional distance of *Mr. Joonblack* was accompanied by an inscrutable look. Though I did not know what the look contained, I surmised from it that the years had forged an affinity between them, perhaps a not entirely positive one.

Troke Joonblack said nothing.

In the thickening silence, I became aware of an echoic pitter-patter over the hall carpet. I looked down and saw its source in the long, dirty-white toenails of a small dog. A mottled yellow-white Jack Russell terrier, unbearded, with a stubby tail that reminded me of a smoked-down cigar and a pool of brown fur surrounding one eye. The eyes themselves were alert, as if seeking stimulation from all corners. The dog paced strongly up to me, satisfied himself that whatever scent was carried on one pant leg corresponded to that of the other, and then pattered over to its master and stood at attention.

Troke looked down briefly and whispered, "Keep still."

Ms. Wyndl, looking down at the dog with mild disgust, repeated her question to Troke. After a brief hesitation, he finally admitted that no, the room was not prepared for its intended occupants.

"How doubly fortunate then that Mr. Szeyk is here." Ms. Wyndl's eyes flashed. This time there was no uncertainty behind them. "Mr. Szeyk, this is Troke Joonblack. Troke, Mr. Walek Szeyk. Your new assistant houseman. And should he satisfy, your successor."

For the first time since barreling into the alcove, Troke directed his eyes at me. From the tilt of the tam-o'shanter on his head, I couldn't tell with what effect he was attempting to imbue his perspective. Frizzled locks of orange-red hair dangled in a disconnected curtain over the middle of his forehead, seeming to mingle intimately with the thrush of his eyebrows. Oddly, his face was clean-shaven, and I caught a whiff of shaving lotion off his collar.

As though acknowledgment of my name was a kind of signal, Troke's dog scampered forward like a befuzzed missile, and clamped onto the front of my trouser leg with his forepaws. He went up on his hind quarters before me, leveraging his sausage body against my shin, paws digging in just above the knee, his damp nose pressed into the fabric, searching out some suggestion of its contents. Awkwardly, I reached down and ran a hand over his coat, drawing away a shower of short, needle-like white hairs.

"You'd think with four floors of hallways and that huge back lawn to run around in, he'd look like I was starving him," Troke said. "Nope, not this one. I offer him one kipper, he barks for two. Then he noses the plate."

Troke's gravelly voice had a chuckle looming at its edge, like a tease. His dog, sensing its master's jocularity, began to bark a light, rapid cadence, as though he were trying to whistle.

Troke extended his hand to me. A paw, really. Nails chewed down to pulpy ellipses, fingers as thick and dry as corncobs, hair over the broad landscape of the top of the hand like a rash of crabgrass. His grip was powerful, an animalic grasp.

"Seems you'll start earning your way from the first." He released a thin reed of laughter, like the scratch of a pencil over paper.

"Where are the guild representatives now?" Ms. Wyndl's voice returned to its naturally prim haughtiness.

"The Aaron," Troke Joonblack said.

"Very well. I will go and speak with them. I will offer them a coffee and pastry service to amend for their having to wait."

"They're an hour early. There's nothing to 'amend'."

Ms. Wyndl's eyes traded time between Troke and me. I began to feel that I had stepped into some domestic farce and was expected to play the role of the ignorant interloper, the purpose of whom is known to all but the player himself.

"I know they are here early, but there is no reason why their suite should not have been readied last evening. They are today's only booking. Perhaps Mr. Szeyk's presence here is a minor felicity." She turned to me. "Mr. Szeyk, please accompany Troke to the second-floor conference suite and follow his instructions." Her voice now contained us both. "You have a half-hour to ready the room. With the usual amenities, don't forget. Mr. Szeyk, you may retrieve the guild members from the Aaron Salon once you are finished."

Troke looked like a lad who was being punished unfairly.

"Have you even looked at the north lawn? I've been out there all day."

Ms. Wyndl began down the staircase. "That occurred yesterday evening. You only realized the situation this morning. The suite should have already been done." Turning on the landing and looking up at us through the thin spires of the guard rail on which Troke's dog was now balancing its forepaws with a shivering energy, she added, "Stow that dog in your quarters. Its breath is like dirty mop water." There passed another cryptic beat, and when she next spoke, concern entered her voice so entirely I felt I hadn't the right to hear it. "You know how I feel about the tobacco. And you know why."

Once she was gone out of our sight, Troke turned to me and said, "Hell of a woman. She loves old Doggins, don't she? Hell, she's got to. Why else would she notice he's been into the mop bucket?"

Then he broke into a broad smile of surprisingly strong, square, off-white teeth. A stunning glimpse of a younger man breaking through an otherwise feral mess.

101

I followed Troke down to the ground floor and the task set to us. I was now employed.

vi. Useful Man

THE ROLE OF HOUSEMAN derives from the tradition of those grand English homes that required a large staff to run, wherein the position was junior to the house manager and the assignee largely tasked with menial and/or general maintenance. The alternate moniker *useful man* stood for the myriad ways such a person could be of service to the house.

Since the Manse Calvo made, by name, open aspiration to the status and regality of such traditions, naturally it would retain a houseman. In practice, the role ballooned over the years to encompass everything not assigned to the cooks, housemaids, or Ms. Wyndl.

So: there was no groundskeeper; there was the houseman. Carpenters were not employed, nor plumbers for basic repairs; there was the houseman. Banquets were overseen by the house manager, but the houseman put them together — raised the tables, draped and bracketed them, arranged the chairs, hung the tapestries and bunting, erected the wet bars and coffee stations, muscled the tureens of steaming soup and scalding coffee from the kitchen to the requisite room. He did not stack the cups or arrange the silverware or fold the napkins, but he did transport the wheel-carts of prepared food. He did not wash the interior windows, but he replaced those fractured. He took the hose and sponge to the exterior brickwork (and windows) and dried the patios afterward with a long-handled broom. He set stones in the pathways and did touch-up work on the front porch. He readied business meetings, luncheons, wedding receptions, screenings of short-reel cartoons for local schools. He did not sweep the floors, but he did sand and reseal scraped areas of the wood. He did not curate the library, but did arrange for its careworn volumes to be rebound or replaced. He changed light bulbs and stocked emergency kerosene torches. He was expected to be approachable by staff at all times. He was to not engage with guests unless given explicit permission.

I was amazed, after only a few weeks on the job, that Troke could have managed by himself for as long as he had, yet in coming to know him I understood why he fit as houseman. It was the disengagement from people that he seemed to appreciate the most. It was a service position, but not *patron* service. We served the Manse Calvo. Troke wasn't terribly good with strangers. Most were put off simply by his appearance. Those who looked past that would like as not be treated to a quick and final lesson in why Ms. Wyndl was their proper point of contact.

Example: A month into my employ a women's group booked the Aaron Salon for a meeting. I forget the organization's name, but I do remember that each of them was demonstrably overweight. The sort that wobbles rather than walks. They were very kind people, thanking us profusely for setting up the room for them, and commenting highly on the overall ambiance of the hotel. One of the women seemed keen to make Troke fully aware of her gratitude and went on and on about what a fine reputation the hotel had and how *clearly* it was deserved and how *clearly* the staff, most notably Troke, was the reason for this sterling regard. She had one hand braced on the sleeve of Troke's shirt as she expounded, as to take some mild physical possession of him, and in the other was balanced a plate weighted down by an assortment of hors d'oeuvres and a thick wedge of frosted white cake. (Their booking had stipulated, as most small groupings did, a small buffet.) Troke, standing patiently and seeming wholly devoted to the woman's remarks, glanced down at the plate in her hand, then slowly back up the landscape of her body, to her beaming eyes, and said, in a perfect facsimile of worrisome concern, "Oh, sweetie, *no*." He then gently relieved her of the plate and exited the room.

His dog, he insisted, was the best company for him. My asking after the dog's unusual name was, I recall, the spark for our first proper conversation.

We were sitting on one of the benches at the far west end of the Manse's yard, a quiet, well-shaded spot where Troke and I sometimes brought our lunch, when the subject arose.

Tradition had it that Troke would take a week's holiday twice a year to Digby. The waters off Digby Gut, which marries to the Bay of Fundy, are good scalloping. Troke's father, Conal, had brought the family over from Scotland to the Maritimes to trawl them.

The dog had appeared during one of his biennial visits home, he said, "like a tiny, shivering apparition on a blaze of an August day."

"I was taking breakfast on the back steps of the house. This was in '35. A bit of fried ham, two-day-old biscuit, coffee. Right in front of me, the low grass opened and this little haunch-starved thing ambles out. Filthy as a leper. I guessed him the shy side of three. He stopped a few feet from me and spread down on the scrub. We had a bit of a staring contest. Those eyes a'his, they were like fired chestnuts. I'd salted the ham too much and it was sucking in my cheeks, so I tossed the best of it to him. Boy, was he fast for such a scrawny thing. That meat disappeared mid-air! He followed me about the rest of the day, nosing at everything. Hay, birdshit, woodcuts, leather straps, this pile of busted oars out near the boat shed. It all deserved a good sniff, said him. Anyway, that night I set an old wool throw in a corner of the boat shed and led him there, told him to stay. Roughed a small pile of hay into a kind of shallow bowl, told him that's where you make. Then I locked him in and went back to the house. Next morning, I open my eyes and who's there but him watching me from the edge of the bed. Calm as a sentry. Smelling up the room. When I raised my head from the pillow, he pawed up and licked my face like I was made of hock. Now, I've no gift for cleverness and I never named anything before in my life, but when I finally got him to heel, I pressed up on my elbows and looked down at him and thought, *Dog's in*. Basically, that was it. I said that little phrase aloud and the letters slipped around on me a bit and it sounded good when I ran the words together. He's been Doggins ever since."

"You never found out where he came from?"

"I didn't see that it mattered. Whatever it was sent him my way, I'm the better for it."

"I never had a dog," I said. "We never had one, I mean. My mother was allergic."

"Ah, too bad. Finest company a man can have. Not as exciting as the company of a woman, but I've not met a woman yet who'll roll over for me just because I tell her to." Troke smacked his lap, raising a light cloud of dust that the afternoon

106

sun caught each particle of. "So never a dog, eh? Cat people?"

"No. I don't really like them."

"Why not?"

"Honestly, I don't know what you get out of them. They don't like to be held or chased around. They slink by the corners. I've seen them in alleyways. They have claws. And from what I know, they only pay attention to you when they're hungry."

"That about says it."

"My father had a dog once," I said, not ready to drop the thread of conversation. (I quite liked Troke's storytelling; it was my impression that had he lived a century earlier, he might have been some village's oral historian.) "But it died when he was a teenager."

"Mind if I ask how?"

"Accidentally shot by a hunter, I guess. My father was the one to find him and that's what he said."

"That's terrible."

"He said he named it after a stuffed toy lion he'd had as a boy. Adok. He told me the name meant, *Of the Adriatic, a soul in deep need of quiet*. It was a hound of some breed or other."

"Awful poetic for a boy to come up with. I suppose he didn't give much in the way of details, eh?"

"Not really, although I'll never forget he said that when he found Adok, its body was already covered in a layer of flies. He remembered the loud humming sound they made, so many of them packed together."

"That's stark biology for you. Did he ever find out who shot him?"

"No. After that, no more dogs. My grandfather and grandmother died of influenza a few years later, but my father never got another dog, even when he lived alone before my mother came along. I suppose that saved him having to get rid of it, her being allergic."

"Or getting rid of her!" He chucked me on the chest with the back of his hand to show me he was only joking. Troke was shorter than me even when seated, but the strength of the contact nearly made me keel.

"Well, it's a shame you've never had a dog. I suppose Doggins can be your honorary pup."

"That would be okay by me."

Such little bursts of commiseration were a good tonic to the taskmasterly disposition of Ms. Wyndl.

When Troke and I were not staging the salons for prearranged events, we worked off a long and very detailed list she drew up for us. As Troke was leaving by year's end, she intended to get as much out of him by way of general improvements to the house and property as she could. To illustrate what I mean by very detailed, one of the items was the stripping, sanding, and re-staining of the library shelves in the Aaron Salon, which had fallen victim to mold and bacteria incubated within the books themselves. A simple enough task, a day's work at best. But Ms. Wyndl wished the shelving to be stripped not by chemicals or scraping tools but sandpaper. And once the former veneer was gone, a second sanding should then be performed, against the grain of the raw wood beneath, and then a third with it. She also expected two coats of lacquer to be applied. Then every volume in the library was to be investigated, page by page. Any book bearing even the suggestion of mold or book lice or foxing was to be discarded, preferably in the salon's fireplace, and a list of the removed made so that we could then arrange with local booksellers to have them replaced. What ought to have taken a day ate up four.

Troke took Ms. Wyndl's instructions with a customary grain of salt. I, however, was concerned that the precedent being set could not be measured up to by myself alone, once Troke was gone to Digby for good.

One afternoon, in the midst of emptying, churning, and repacking the bocce pitch, I told her as much. This was about five weeks into my employment. It was the first time I questioned her about anything.

"What are you really concerned with, Mr. Szeyk?"

"Just what I said. That I won't be able to stand up to the expectations you set."

"What I think you really mean is that you do not understand why I cannot just get out of the way and let you and Mr. Joonblack do your jobs. Not an entirely unfair reservation. After all, I didn't hire you on the strength of an innate capability for failure. Nonetheless, were it not for the expectations I set, Mr. Szeyk, there would be little cause for my holding anyone to standards, would there? What argument do you imagine I might have were I to assign you a duty with no disclosure of the expected result and then express dissatisfaction with the outcome? 'Well, you never said you wanted things done a certain way,' would be your reply to me, and you would be right to give it. Better that I am clear from the first than I waste your time correcting a foreseeable error."

I never questioned her again. And she was never backwards about forwarding her assessment. All in all, I do not think I could have asked for a more valuable trial period than what I had under Ms. Wyndl's authority. She was a firm boss, but a fair one, rewarding the earnest and disavowing the lazy. If holding down a job is the least one can do toward demonstrable adulthood, then I gave the bare minimum. But into this narrow funnel I poured the best of myself. I was a volunteer to the regime of those who become what they do (as opposed to those who force what they do into the imperfect mold of who they believe themselves to be). I became, in a fairly economic span of time, a useful man.

Though I never bridged the chasm cut by our professional relationship, there was a subtle but clear warming in her approach with me. She began to use my given name, rather than the more formal "Mr. Szeyk." On occasion, her directives were issued almost as questions — even though there was ever any question about my obeying. When, for example, she needed me one evening to drop what I was doing and take a mop and pail to the main lobby in order to take care of a pile of sick left by a woman who must have had a disagreeable meal somewhere in town, she said, "Walek, could I ask you to leave the rest of what you're doing until the morning, and address a bit of an accident in the lobby?" Ordinarily, it would have been: "You can stop what you're doing, Mr. Szeyk, and proceed to the lobby. Bring a mop and pail and double-time it. What you need to do will be self-evident." I suppose such softening of her tone could well have been a betrayal of concern for the unfortunate sick woman, that she might be unduly embarrassed if the mess were not gotten rid of swiftly. Likely that was part of it. But it seemed something more. I could not call it warmth — though I realize I just referred to it as a "warming." Perhaps *defrosting* might be more to the point. More accurately, I was earning her respect and along with it her trust.

vii. Some Things I Learned About Ms. Wyndl

AS MS. WYNDL WAS ADAMANT that the
housemen refrain from direct interaction with
patrons, the brunt fell almost wholly on her. All
conflicts of an interpersonal nature were addressed
by her and her alone. Often these were minor
issues of guests needing help with the heating units
in their rooms, or in the summer months
requesting portable fans, an assortment of which
we kept on hand, as the house was not outfitted
with air conditioning units. There was also the
occasional complaint about the dining room
service or quality of the food or condition of the
salons or outer grounds, all of which Ms. Wyndl
handled personally and with what seemed little
consternation. Even when the complaint was
superfluous — for example (and I did actually
witness this) if a guest took issue with the fact that
leaves littered the walking path on the rear
grounds, despite the fact that it was autumn —
Ms. Wyndl would gracefully assure the guest that
they had been heard and that they had her
sympathy in the matter, even if there was little she
could do to immediately rectify the situation. (In
this particular case, I recall her "solution" being
that the coming evening was expected to be quite
windy and should take care of the leaf-cluttered
path naturally.) The guest was always greatly
relieved and would go on their way satisfied, even
in the absence of a definite course of action.

The one thing Ms. Wyndl avoided, however,
was instances of verbal conflict among guests of

the same party. Bickering couples. Children being disciplined. Lovers' spats. Unless an argument was disturbing to a general area, she was hands-off. Decorum usually kept such things from being an issue. But there was one exception.

I forget the exact date, but I do remember that just the day before I had been asked to begin the process of changing out the inner drapes in both salons from the dense cross-knits used in winter to the thinner, almost opaque cotton and silk put up in the warmer months. With evening blackout regulations in place, the exterior-facing drapery was simple black sackcloth, but Ms. Wyndl insisted that such drabness was in no way appropriate for guests enjoying the atmosphere of the salons, day or night. And, of course, she was right.

I was in the process of taking down the winter drapes in the Tilde Salon when the incident occurred. The ladder I was using rose to just shy of the curtain rods, and so I witnessed what happened from that perspective.

On that particular day, a man and his son were checking out of their room. Their suitcases had been set by one of the bellhops just a few feet from the smokers' cistern, an oblong copper thing that nonsmokers often mistook for a vase or trash receptacle, located just inside the front doors. It was common practice for departing guests to have their luggage so arranged, as a courtesy, in order that they could calmly settle their bill without their belongings clogging up the space around the front desk.

The man was aggravated; something about the charges disagreed with him. He was studying his receipt closely. The boy looked to be about ten. Short sandy hair, pug nose, dimples. He was dressed casually but smartly in trousers, a dark sweater over a white oxford, and tennis shoes scuffed up but not holey. He held one of the hotel's advertising brochures in his hands, and he was fanning it open like the wings of a bird, swooping his arm up and down and around and making *whoosh* sounds under his breath that echoed in the quiet lobby.

At first the father paid him little attention, then after making some internal decision (he nodded his head and let out a slight huff) he pocketed the receipt he had been studying and turned to where his son now stood beside their suitcases.

Exhaling sharply, he said, "Knock it off, Matthew. And what is that? You don't need that, we're leaving, not looking to stay. Toss it in the trash."

The boy did as he was told. He crumpled the brochure up and tossed it into the cistern, a perfect shot.

The ash accumulated in the metal grating housed just inside the cistern's scalloped aperture plumbed into the air like the discharge of a volcano. Layers like silt fell on the suitcases and coated the boy's sweater all down his left side, as well as much of his hair and face. He did not even have time to cringe back before the cloud washed over him, and he thus stood firm, a statue, in a rictus of shock.

Having witnessed what happened, I was likewise held in thrall, knowing that I was somewhat complicit, having forgotten to clear the grating that morning, being too caught up in the task of changing out the drapes.

The boy's shock lasted only a few seconds, however, before he began to laugh. Careless, amazed laughter, as though some trap he had set inadvertently backfired, much to his amusement. This, and not the silent eruption of ash, now drew his father's attention.

When he saw the effect of what had happened, the man stalked swiftly the ten paces between them and reached for the boy, his fingers crimped in a loose claw, as to grab him by the collar. But he held back when he saw that doing so would dirty his hand. Instead, he looked down at his son. Though it was certainly an effect of the light from a nearby lamp catching his face, the father's eyes looked flamed with anger.

"Is there nothing you don't mess up? Can you not do the simplest thing correctly?" His voice slithered out in a strangled rasp. "Look at yourself. Such stupidity."

As I said, the lobby was empty and so even though he had not been shouting, the man's voice, particularly those last words, rang through the air, followed by an even louder silence cut only by the subtle tick-tocking of the clock that stood outside the doors to the Aaron Salon.

The boy seemed to crumple down slightly. His shoulders withered within his clothes and his knees turned in, as though he suddenly had to urinate. His eyes darted around, nervous, to see if anyone might have heard what his father said. (He did not look up, though; he did not see me atop the ladder. I was pathetically grateful for this.)

The father held his eyes on the boy for another moment, then turned, almost directly on the heel, and stalked away. I watched him march past the front desk toward the short hall that led back to the kitchen and dining room, off which was the house's only public toilet. I heard the door to the washroom open and close.

I kept my eyes on the boy, now standing alone. He looked near to tears and seemed to be struggling with deciding if he should swipe himself clean or keep still so as to not create a larger mess. It took me a moment but I snapped out of it and began to descend the ladder.

It was then that a familiar cadence of heel-clicks echoed in.

Ms. Wyndl leaned down before the boy and spoke to him. I did not hear what she said, but when he looked up at her, his expression softened and his hands, which he had been ringing together (as one does when washing them), fell limp to his sides. She said something more, again I did not hear, and the boy nodded. She placed a hand on his shoulder, the one untouched by ash, and walked him out of my eyeline.

I stepped off the ladder and into the doorway of the Tilde in time to see them both disappear into the manager's office. There was a private water closet in there, as well as direct access, via a door, to the kitchen.

Several minutes later, the father returned, carrying a stack of damp towels in his hand. I was finishing with a mop-up of the lobby floor. I had wiped down the cistern and cleaned the grate with a brush. The father stopped short when he saw me.

"Have you seen a boy, about ten?" His tone was brusque.

"Our house manager, Ms. Wyndl, took him to her office. I think she was going to help him get cleaned up."

"Right. Far be it for him to stay put. Far be it for him to do anything I say." He squeezed his hand and water ran out of the sopping towels and puddled on the floor.

116

"I was in the salon, just there." I pointed to where the ladder stood.

"Excuse me?"

"You didn't ask him to stay put. You walked away."

I swung the mop out of the bucket and let it drop just inches from his feet, and slowly began taking up the pooled water.

He jumped back, an expression of outrage twisting his face. He raised his arm over his head and threw the bundle of towels to the floor.

"Where is this house manager's office?" he demanded. "I now have two issues to discuss with him."

"With her. Our house manager's name, as I already mentioned, is Ms. Wyndl. Her office is behind the front desk, but it is off-limits to guests."

"We'll see." He heel-turned crisply, as he had done before, and strode off.

Just as he approached the front desk, the office door opened and Ms. Wyndl emerged. She took immediate notice of the man.

"Oh, good, I believe you are young Matthew's father?"

She stepped primly up to the desk. It was her customary behavior to step out from behind the front register to address situations one might consider delicate. I saw clearly now that she instead kept the desk between them.

"Your son is putting himself to rights with the help of one of my kitchen employees. We were able to quite efficiently clean his clothing with the use of a portable steamer we keep for just such instances of sudden need. His salutary situation was also addressed."

"His what?"

"His hair and face."

The man's back was to me; his posture suggested what Ms. Wyndl said had further upset him. He made short, stuttering steps, turning left then right, then left again, as though he meant to begin pacing, as one does when anxious, but couldn't quite bring himself to it.

"Who is this employee you have my son being exposed to?"

"Her name is Fenella, and she has been with this establishment for some time. She is very professional and has managed to calm Matthew down. He was quite upset with the situation." Here I saw Ms. Wyndl's eyes lock the man in place. "The *entire* situation."

"Meaning what exactly?"

"Mr. Szeyk, have you finished?" she called out to me.

I nodded my head but said nothing. Her voice seemed to still hang in the air. I had never before seen or heard her in such a way. She had always, in my admittedly limited experience of her, been discreet almost to a fault.

"Then could I ask that you complete your work in the salon."

Again, I nodded. I hefted the mop into the bucket and walked them to the storage closet beneath the main staircase, passing the front desk in the process. Then I walked back across the lobby and turned into the Tilde Salon.

It took me just over a full minute. Ms. Wyndl and the man were silent the entire time.

As I went back about my task of changing out the drapes, I focused on the noise of the fabric and the metal-on-metal scrape of the rungs along the curtain rod. I heard nothing of how the situation at the front desk played out.

After a few minutes, the man and boy exited briskly through the front door. The boy had a green lollipop clutched in his hand and bore an odd look of caution and contentment — the former I presumed coming from his now being alone with his father, the latter from the treat he had no doubt gotten from Fenella.

I completed my work and folded up the winter drapes. I would have them sent to a local cleaner. I compacted the ladder — it folded into itself by a pair of locking hinges — and was about to carry it out to the garage, when Ms. Wyndl came into the salon. She was the very picture of composure, hands folded neatly at her waist, but I could sense some residual ire brewing beneath the surface calm. She looked over the condition of the windows.

"Were you sure to clean the glass thoroughly before putting the new ones up?"

"Yes."

"Very good. That's very good." She kept still a moment, then eased herself into a nearby chair. "I want to thank you for how you handled the situation with that man. Perfect discretion, and yet your walk to the storage closet and back sent a wonderfully clear message."

"I could see that he was making you upset. Or rather that he was looking to make you *get* upset. I heard what he said to his son."

"Oh, yes? I won't ask you to tell me what it was. I can only surmise."

"I think you handled the situation very well."

"It was the height of idiocy for that man to have left the boy standing there by himself. Which reminds me, my reason for coming in here. He left something of his own mess in the back hall washroom."

"I'll get to it straight away, as soon as I get the drapes ready to be sent out."

"Thank you. Luckily it looks as though today will be a quiet one, recent events notwithstanding. Otherwise, I would have you drop what you are doing and take care of it now."

"I can, if you'd like."

"No. As you suggested will do nicely."

Ms. Wyndl removed a small gold pocket watch from a fold of her dress and checked the time against the clock on the Tilde's wall. Satisfied that all was in line, she returned the watch to its home. She looked at me.

"The last person to change those curtains was Annelie," she said. "Though it is completely out of character for me, I never had Troke change them last year. I can't for the life of me know why. I suppose the expanded regulations that were handed down had something to do with it. As if the standard blackout times were not good enough." She exhaled. "Perhaps not. Perhaps I just wanted them kept the way they were. To have them there to remind me in some small way of Annelie."

"I didn't realize she did that sort of thing. The sort of work given to the houseman, I mean."

"It was one of Troke's weeks off. I remember quite clearly asking him to change them before he left, but he rather conveniently forgot. I'm not tall enough to manage it myself, even with the ladder. Annelie volunteered."

"That was very good of her."

"It was also her way of showing others that she was capable to doing things they perhaps felt she could not, or should not."

"She must have been very independently natured."

Ms. Wyndl suppressed a laugh. "That's a gentle euphemism, Walek."

I had never seen a photograph of Annelie Calvo, which at that moment struck me as odd. But there were, so far as I knew (and I had spent ample time in each public space in the hotel) no photos of her to be found. I'd never commented on this, there having never before been cause to do so, but now I was tempted. I supposed Ms. Wyndl kept one in her room, but it would have been indelicate to ask. In the end, I kept mum.

Ms. Wyndl sank back into the body of the chair. "Recollection is usually tinged with a soupçon of regret. But I find that is not true when I think about Annelie."

Not knowing how to respond, I stood and said it was time for me to go see to the mess in the public washroom. I took up the ladder and tucked it under my arm.

"I can phone the cleaners and have them dispatch someone to pick up the curtains," Ms. Wyndl said. She clearly did not wish to remove herself from the comfort of the chair.

"I appreciate that."

"Once you see what that man did to the washroom, you'll wish I'd offered to stow that ladder for you, as well."

Later that same summer, we put on a do for Canada Day. Troke and I put bunting out on the front porch. Guests were treated to a complimentary cocktail and appetizer hour on the rear patio. Lantern lights strung among the trees turned the wood into a playground where our younger guests played hide-and-go-seek.

We also hosted a private event that evening. A group of trainees from the Ocean Terminals

Facility on Halifax's south end arranged for a celebratory supper followed by a cocktail service in the Aaron Salon. The Terminals were the primary access point for immigration, and that particular business continued to boom despite the war, or because of it — refugees seeking asylum, ships having slipped through the net of U-boats, family waiting for them somewhere in Canada. There were twelve in the party, all about my age, men and women evenly, and they brought with them a youthful energy.

The evening began quietly with a supper of poached salmon, stewed tomatoes and green beans, several loaves of crusty bread, and a frosted cherry cream cake. Everyone drank water during the meal. Manners were on display, voices were kept conversational, though there was in clear evidence a bond amongst them, a camaraderie. Snippets of their conversation wafted into the kitchen with each swing of the door. I sat at the tile-top island having a shepherd's pie reheated from the previous evening's dinner service. It was curious to wonder what kind of person seeks work helping vet strangers' worthiness to enter one's own country. It seemed noble and also somehow troubling. The chance of having to turn someone away, the potential for emotional anguish looming always.

Once coffee was served, Ms. Wyndl came into the kitchen and asked me to double-check the setup in the Aaron Salon, and to help Troke stock the portable wet bar. (We kept house liquor under lock and key until the very minute it was needed, for reasons that should be obvious.)

Ms. Wyndl was dressed that day more casually than usual. A light, almost flouncy lemon-colored dress, accented by pale pink ribbon at the waist, neckline, and bottom hem. The thick-heeled shoes she usually wore had been traded for the same flats I recalled her wearing during my interview with her the day I inquired about the houseman position. Her hair, ordinarily spun up like a sculpted hive, fell in a loose bun over the back of her neck, controlled by a thin hairnet the same color as the trim on her dress. She looked ready for a picnic in the Public Gardens.

Her raiment reflected her mood. Her eyes were bright, every word and gesture accompanied by a smile.

"And be sure that Troke puts out enough glasses, will you? And remember, a nice range of spirits, too. We'll want as little intervention on these fine young people's celebration as possible."

Later, once our work was done, Troke and I looked on as Ms. Wyndl lead the group into the salon, gesturing like a docent, her speech sprinkled with light but precise remarks about the salon's features (as much to stoke the group's interest as to provide a gentle warning as to their conduct). She pointed out the location of the wet bar, in the corner of the room adjacent to the shuttered fireplace, and reiterated that assistance, if needed, could be had by ringing the front desk bell.

"Otherwise," she said, "I will leave you to it."

But they did not want to let her go. Each in the group offered profuse thanks for the quality of the dinner and the splendor of the Aaron Salon, and they insisted that she share a toast with them. To my and Troke's amusement, Ms. Wyndl acceded to a sherry. They toasted Canada and the women and men fighting overseas, and Canada again for being the sort of country that welcomed the displaced and dispossessed. I found it a genuinely moving moment. Even Troke had no snide remark to offer *sotto voce*, as I expected he might.

We stood by observing for another half-hour or so, and watched one glass of sherry become two become three, before Troke excused himself saying it was time to get Doggins out to do his business.

"I'll button up everything out back, then I'm heading up to bed," he said. "You can handle this once they've departed?"

"Of course."

He looked over at Ms. Wyndl, now seated primly in a wing chair and having an engaged conversation with one of the young women. Her eyes had gone a bit glassy; her cheeks had taken on a pink hue.

"This is quite fun to watch," I said.

"Yeah, well, I'd advise you to find something to do, even if it's just sitting in the Tilde and playing Klondike. She's certainly having a giddy one, but you never know. Slightly drunk doesn't mean inattentive, and she won't like you just standing around gawking."

Troke seemed consternated, though I could not have said why. I chalked it up to his usual manner with regard to the hotel's guests, and just the general weariness that comes at the end of the day. He trod off toward the rear entrance, calling out for his dog. I took his advice and slipped into the Tilde. I sat down on one of the sofas and tuned my ear to the goings-on across the lobby.

The next couple of hours passed in a steady current of laughter and occasional song, while I played patience with a deck of cards I took from the games cubby.

Just after midnight, a pair of taxis pulled up in front of the Manse Calvo, and our guests filed out.

Ms. Wyndl saw them to the front porch. I used the opportunity of her distraction to slip out of the Tilde and head to the kitchen, where I would need to retrieve a trash bin and the cage cart by which we transported our stores of liquor.

I was just ready to make my way back to the Aaron, when Ms. Wyndl swept into the kitchen, leaving the door to swing freely behind her, and sat hard, almost at a stumble, on one of the island stools.

"Well, that was quite an unusual time for me, I must say. I forget how energizing young people can be."

"I'll try not to take that personally," I said.

"Oh ... oh, of course! You know I did not mean ... honestly, Walek, sometimes your sensitivity level spikes like a church steeple."

"I was only making a joke. You looked like you were having a wonderful time. I watched for a little while, then I sat in the Tilde. I wanted to be out of sight, but within earshot in case I was needed."

"Troke?"

"Said he was turning in for the night. Asked me to take care of the clean-up. I was just on my way to the Aaron."

"I take it the kitchen staff has," her voice trailed off, the question hanging in the air.

"Yes, a couple of hours ago," I said.

"It will be an easy task, I can tell you now. Those young folks were quite responsible in their behavior, and I don't necessarily think it was occasioned by my presence. They were a respectful group. All the glasses are lined up neatly on the bar. Napkins and so forth rounded up and waiting in the bin."

"That's a relief. It shouldn't take long then."

She didn't seem to hear me. She looked off across the room, the kind of almost vacant stare where you suspect the person is looking not at anything in particular, but backwards into the past.

After several quiet seconds, Ms. Wyndl snapped back to realizing I was still there.

"Apologies." She smiled. "As you may well have gathered, I am not much for drink, and I may have exceeded my limits this evening."

"Would you like me to walk you upstairs?"

"No, thank you. I'm going to sit awhile, and perhaps make a coffee."

"Let me. Now that you mention it, I'd like one as well. Camp coffee is quickest, if that's alright."

"Perfect. And make it quite black, please."

I put the kettle on and took two mugs down from the cabinet.

When the kettle began to whistle, I took it off the heat and poured the scalding water over the grounds in each mug. I walked the hot mugs to the island and sat down across from Ms. Wyndl.

"It'll be a minute before we can drink it," I said.

"I don't remember the last time I had a cup of coffee after hours in here," Ms. Wyndl said. "I suppose it's been more than 10 years."

"That's quite a long time."

"Early to rest, early to rise, that's how I was raised." She took up her mug and gingerly sipped at the steaming liquid. "You know, I think I'll take some sugar. Would you mind?"

I took the sugar pot down from the cabinet and spooned a half-measure into her cup, leaving the spoon in for her to stir as she liked.

"I'll leave the pot here, in case you'd like some more." I took a sip from my own mug, content with the deep bitterness. "I'd like to get the salon over with. If I'm not back before you're ready to head up, just leave the pot and mug. I'll wash them so Fenella doesn't have to bother tomorrow." I looked at the clock above the door to the dining room. "Well, today, really. I can't believe it's already one."

Ms. Wyndl gave me a wave of her hand, freeing me to leave her. I took my coffee to the Aaron and bussed the remains of the celebration.

When I returned to the kitchen, I found Ms. Wyndl draped over the countertop, head atop folded arms, snoring lightly.

Unsure what to do, I watched her sleep. While it had only been a few months that I knew her, it was an incredible circumstance to stand there and witness her in that state. Her face was lost of all expression; her cheeks drew flat and her mouth seemed to slip down toward the countertop. Her eyes looked only barely closed, the skin around them smooth. Having never deliberately watched someone sleeping before, I paused at her eyes. I had always assumed that in sleep the eyes are crinkled, the brow subtly furrowed in dream concentration. Ms. Wyndl looked entirely peaceful.

I was hesitant to disturb her, but I knew I couldn't leave her there. It would cause her no end of embarrassment, even if she awoke before the kitchen staff arrived, to say nothing of the twittering it would cause if she didn't.

To delay the inevitable, I took our mugs to the sink and washed them. Then I emptied the kettle, rinsed it, and turned it over to dry on a towel I laid out on the counter next to the sink.

How to wake her? I wondered. Shaking her seemed incorrect, adolescence even, as did poking her on the arm. I decided I would just gently lay a hand on her shoulder and leave it there until my presence roused her.

I turned around and stopped. Troke stood in the doorway in a set of red flannel pajamas like some kind of Christmas elf.

He quickly held a finger to his lips to keep me saying anything. He looked down at Ms. Wyndl. The corner of his mouth flickered in a subdued smile.

"Go ahead on up, Walek. I'll take it from here."

I exhaled deeply, relieved. "If you say so. Sure you don't need me to at least hold doors open for you?"

"Nah, we'll manage." He crossed the room and gave me a chuck on the shoulder. "Thanks for staying with her, and for getting that room cleaned up."

I shrugged.

"Alright, off you go. Better that just one of us is here when she comes to."

Without another word, I left the kitchen and headed up to my room. I suppose I could have asked what brought him downstairs – was he hungry? Did Doggins wake him? Where even was Doggins? Was there something he forgot to do or to tell me to do? — but the adrenaline charge of the coffee burned out like a wick as soon as I made it to the second floor and all I wanted was my bed. It didn't even occur to me that Troke might have been waiting up the entire time.

Thanksgiving Day, the second Monday in October.

I sat across the desk from Ms. Wyndl in her office. It was late in the evening, around 10 o'clock, and the room was lit solely by a standing

128

lamp in the far right corner of the room and a small adjustable desk lamp that cast a shadow across the span of the desktop between us. Having now been on the job just over six months, I was about to receive my first official evaluation.

"I should have done this closer to Labour Day, both in fairness to you and in order to maintain a proper schedule with regard to this sort of thing, managerially. But circumstance precluded it. By which I mean, and admit, it simply slipped my mind. Still, here we are, so let's begin."

Certain holidays, I learned that first year, were unpopular for hotels. Thanksgiving was one of them. Unlike Christmastime, there was little in the way of return-to-home travel that would make a room of one's own an attractive option. It had been a quiet day and evening. There were only two rooms occupied, a middle-aged couple weathering the unfortunate circumstance of a burst water pipe in their home's kitchen, and a young woman whom I saw only briefly in passing and knew nothing about. Both occupants took supper in their respective rooms, and the kitchen staff had been dismissed by Ms. Wyndl around 7 o'clock. Troke and I had joined Ms. Wyndl in the kitchen for a hodge-podge meal of tinned beef, black pudding with steamed beets, and thick heels of rye bread. We opened a bottle of white wine and each had two glasses to celebrate the occasion. Afterwards, as Ms. Wyndl tended to the kitchen, Troke and I made our rounds, Doggins trotting loyally in our wake.

Troke volunteered to give Ms. Wyndl our final notice that all was well before heading up to bed. I was making my way up the main staircase toward my room, thinking I might be awake enough yet to start a new book before turning in, when Troke's voice caught me up short.

"She wants to see you, my young Walek." His voice bore an edge to it, tiredness combined, perhaps, with a desire for more wine.

"Is everything alright?" I asked.

"Fiddle-fit, if you ask me, but she says she wants to speak with you. She's waiting in the office."

"What sort of mood is she in?"

Troke laughed. "That's always the question, isn't it? If you're wondering whether I got the sense that she's upset with something you've done, or didn't do, I do not think that is it. She seems a bit tired, is all. Probably wants to remind you of something. Don't forget I'm off to the markets first thing, so you've got run of house in the morning. Not that it'll tax you much."

We exchanged goodnights, and I made my way down to the office, where Ms. Wyndl sat waiting.

It was a fresh experience for me, being formally evaluated. I suppose the closest I had ever come to such a thing was the degree to which I had been sized up by the bank associate I had dealt with at the Canadian Royal Mutual Trust and Loan. Not even in my courses at Dalhousie had I ever really felt I was being taken measure of.

I was, as I had been during my first interview with Ms. Wyndl, unsure what do to with myself.

Ms. Wyndl noticed straight away.

"You can relax, Walek," she said. "This is not what one would call formal. Clearly." She gestured out with her hand, a sweeping arc that pulled in the entire room, as to make plain that the confluence of dim light, the lateness of the hour, and general lack of pretense contrived to siphon out any inkling of ceremony.

"I've never been evaluated before," I admitted.

"I don't doubt that, given your age and station. There has likely never been cause. But I can assure you that neither is there cause for undue concern. In fact, the lion's share of what I have to say concerns the things you have been doing *right*. With a few recommendations for improvement, of course, as the goal of any person should be the application of one's self to continued improvement. Complacency gets one nowhere."

For the next half hour, Ms. Wyndl carefully limned my development. She was clear and concise, at times pointed.

"One area where I see a distinct opportunity for improvement is in your approach to the landscaping of the bocce pitch and patio area. It often leaves much to be desired in the way of precision. I am speaking of such details as the depth of the raking, the visual pattern of the pitch, as well as the amount of detritus that remains in the crevices of the patio paving blocks. My impression is that you rush through this aspect of your work, perhaps feeling it takes up more time than it should, keeping you from getting to other tasks as efficiently as you might like. My advice is to ignore this worry, and to give every moment of your effort the appropriate time and attention it requires."

I noted her use of *opportunity* instead of *need*, from which I was able to take some heart, her criticism accounting (quite correctly) for the mental approach to my work and offering a prescription for improvement, rather than just pointing out a deficiency and leaving me to sort it out on my own.

In all, it was an agreeable and, in some respects, revelatory evaluation.

When she was finished, Ms. Wyndl asked if I might make her a cup of tea. I excused myself, went to kitchen, and prepared a pot of water. I returned a few minutes later with a tray on which I had arranged the pot, a pair of enamel mugs, a pair of short glasses containing milk and sugar, and a plate of some of the gingerbread cookies the kitchen staff had left to cool overnight on the stovetop.

A metal bottle sat on the desk blotter, cap off, and I saw that it was aspirin. I set her tea down beside it.

"Just a nagging headache," she said, refusing my offer of the plate of cookies with a shake of her head. "They often come if I've forgotten to drink enough liquids. This tea should set me right. Thank you."

"I should thank you for what you said. It was all very helpful. I'm glad that I've not been a disappointment to you."

"You have not. I think Mr. Joonblack has also been pleased with how you've come along."

"I'm guessing you asked his opinion before speaking with me."

Ms. Wyndl smiled, blowing steam off the top of her cup. "Just before you came in, in fact. It was rather hurried. I should have gauged his mind in this regard beforehand, but as I said before, this all got away from me, sad to say. But he had only good things to say. It was a very direct, very brief, very *easy* discourse."

"I am glad to hear that." I sipped my tea. "I hope that you are feeling confident in this

132

arrangement, given how close it is coming to Troke's leaving."

Ms. Wyndl's expression darkened, though it could have just been a trick of shadowed light as she lowered her teacup from her lips. She kept quiet a moment. "I suppose I do not think directly to that fact, in all honesty. I should, of course. As house manager. And, as you say, the time is approaching." She looked at me. "Now that you have asked, I should answer. Yes. I am confident in the arrangement. I am also anxious about it, but that is nothing to do with you. It is only to do with my being set in my ways, one of which is having had a certain houseman in place for over two decades."

"It will be a big change."

"Not so much as all that. Less a change than a ... oh, I had the word right on my tongue. Now it's gone." She shook her head, her lips pursing in frustration.

I wasn't sure how to respond, and so asked: "Did you ever give Annelie Calvo a formal evaluation? While she was on staff, that is." I had no reason to ask this, other than to keep the conversation going. Annelie Calvo was still something of a mystery to me, but I cannot say that what I did not know about her compelled me to probe for more information.

Ms. Wyndl was quiet then for some time, long enough that I didn't expect her to answer and was about to excuse myself, thinking I might have asked an untoward question. But then she hunched her shoulders, snuggling back into the soft bearing of her chair, and smiled.

"I almost did, once." She closed her eyes.

"If you'd prefer to call it a night, I can sort this all out," I said, gesturing toward the tea tray.

It looked to me that her headache was getting the best of her, despite the aspirin and the general quiet of the house.

"No, no. I was just thinking. Ruminating, you might say. I remember being distinctly at odds with the degree to which formality applied when it came to Annelie. She was hardly an outside hire, yet standards dictate uniformity of procedure for anyone in the hotel's employ, myself included. Myron Calvo and I have a discussion each year on or around Dec. 6. It takes his mind off the anniversary of the Explosion, but it also serves to keep the hierarchy in place, which is something I appreciate."

"But you never went so far with Annelie?" I asked, redirecting her attention.

"In the end, no. I suppose I felt it would detonate the bridge between our shores, if I may use a wartime metaphor. And then of course she had gone soon after she graduated school, so the opportunity to frame such a thing in a different light simply never came about. Do you know I have received exactly one letter each month from her since her matriculation? Always the one, never more but never less."

"It's remarkable that none have been lost in transit. Boats and planes being targets."

"It certainly is. And I am enormously grateful. I do so look forward to my monthly update. Given the circumstance of the war, PEI seems as far away as London."

It would have been unquestionably out of place to ask about the subject matter of Annelie's letters to Ms. Wyndl, though I admit the temptation arose. My interest, previously neutral, had shifted into gear. The chance to learn something of this stranger's perspective of her own life — a stranger who may one day in the future have become my employer — intrigued me, in the same manner that a person might devote themselves to a collection of some writer's or artist's letters, the chance to peer into another's soul without a biographer's interloping opinion clouding the matter. I suppose what I really felt at that moment was a desire to *read* Annelie's letters, rather than have Ms. Wyndl remark on them.

This was, of course, out of the question, so I said nothing further. We both let the silence extend until the moment when conversation might be rescued had come and gone. Without another word, I collected the cups and saucers and spoons and took the lot to the kitchen. I rinsed everything but left it neatly in the sink for the morning kitchen crew to put away properly. Then I returned to the manager's office.

Ms. Wyndl had once again closed her eyes and looked on the verge of falling asleep in her chair. I gently laid my hand on her shoulder, and at my touch she rose and allowed me to walk her out of the office, across the lobby, and up the main staircase.

I left her at the landing, remembering that I meant to have another check of the fire door exit opposite the dining room. I watched her move steadily down the hall until she reached her door, then I went back downstairs, thinking about how Ms. Wyndl was correct that where Annelie Calvo was now seemed half a world away.

There were no other occasions of familiarity between us outside the ordinary day-to-day interactions of our professional association. Fleeting moments all — yet they resonated precisely because of their rarity. And yet, of all the things I came to learn from and about Ms. Wyndl, the most surprising came via the unfortunate deterioration of her vitality, hinted at, I only realized in retrospect, by her tired demeanor the evening of my review.

The first of what she characterized as "real" headaches came in early November. When one of the kitchen staff expressed concern over her pallor, she brushed it off, saying it was no different than "having had too much sugar or too little sleep." A nagging persistence easily explained by the rigors of her job: "Harder hitting, but still little more than an annoyance."

But these annoyances amplified with startling speed.

She soon began sleeping such stretches as a newborn; I even saw her like this once, when I happened to pass her room when the doctor was being shown in and the door was temporarily ajar — laid flat, arms up, fists at her ears in defiance of waking.

Troke's devotion should have made it all plain to me, but ignorant of romantic impulse I saw only human decency. He drew her shade, replenished her water glass, even slept some nights on the sofa in her room. When the mornings came and Troke's work was left undone, I hurriedly picked up the slack, while Fenella O'Dwyre assumed the responsibility of arranging bookings and reservations. Some afternoons Troke dragged her bed to an open window in her room, so she could feel the light, smell the dirt and rain, watch errant birds carry across the limited view, which she once remarked, wonderfully, were "oblivious to all but the soaring." I was usually asked to help, for as she withered, Troke's own robustness seemed to retire deep in his bones. Troke also placed wildflowers in thin glass vases at each corner of her room, so that no matter where she looked, her eyes fell on colors, on a small measure of beauty.

One evening toward the end — it must already have been December because the windows were shut against the howl of evening wind and the hallway had begun to grow musty as the heating units went into action — I stopped outside Ms. Wyndl's room before stepping into my own. Her door was halfway open. I heard a second female voice, which I recognized as Fenella's. I assumed the latch simply didn't catch when Fenella tried to close the door; likely she was carrying a meal tray or fresh linens and tried awkwardly to close it with the tap of a foot. I leaned against the jamb, careful not to make a sound. I had arrived at the end of a conversation. I heard the following, and it is the last thing I heard her say, though presumably they were not her final words on this earth: "I can feel his eyes even now roaming over me, going beneath these bedclothes. Like little stars peering from behind that awful rash of hair. That at my age I still inspire the occasional naked expression of desire is something I take a good measure of pride in. This is not shallow, Fenella. Not at all. Each of us, everyone, aches to be so desired."

The unmistakable clarity of *that awful rash of hair* hit me like a wave. I had myself never known what Troke and Ms. Wyndl were soon to lose. Her voice, stripped of all its bearing, its formal wit, called back to something she'd said during my interview as to my having earned my orphanhood. The same plain and simple grace. I felt a sudden urgency to cloak them both in what meager protection I might provide, which is to say I felt helpless.

A few days later, Troke was in her room, reading aloud from a book of myths he had borrowed from the hotel's library — I could hear his deep, distinct voice through my closed door — when she let go. I was just drifting off, but snapped awake when I heard the book slip to the floor, a slap to the hardwood followed by the ruffled unfurling of the scattered pages like a deck of cards being shuffled.

I cracked open my door, unsure whether it was right for me to cross the hall, just in time to catch Fenella slip lightly into the room, a plate of food her excuse for coming. I stepped into the hall and traced her step. She found them — well, I suppose we both did, as I could see clear into the room — at the last perhaps as they had once begun: Troke beside her in the bed, curving his awkwardly compact body around hers, their fingers threaded together like ribbons, their faces close enough to have traded breath.

The next morning, I was called to Ms. Wyndl's suite. She was tucked neatly in bed. The cover was smooth, the body diminished. Troke was there, as was Myron Calvo and a doctor called in from Victoria General.

There seemed a heaviness in the air as I sat down on the coffee table to take hold of myself. An odd thought crossed my mind, unbidden, that there had been so many casualties in my life in so short a period of time, and yet none of them was the result, even indirectly, of the war. I quickly admonished myself for thinking this — as though Ms. Wyndl's passing had anything at all to do with me.

I drew a breath and observed everyone gathered in the room. At a public service, the object of gathering — the dead — is made to look almost artificially restful. The heaviness that pervaded Ms. Wyndl's room seemed to settle on and rise away from my shoulders like a cape in the wind. That heaviness perhaps is what the air gains when a spirit unused to its new lack of matter begins to negotiate its way.

Seeing me there, Troke suddenly made as if to leave. His head turned, but his body remained rigid, as if instinct kept him footed. His face was blanched and his hands shivered lightly at his side. He bit into his lower lip. He seemed to wrestle with saying something, then succumbed.

"You know, boy, I'm a lucky man to have what time of hers I was given. And I hate knowing it." He looked straight at me, almost through me, eyes bloodshot yet sulfurous, like a field of maize afire. "I'm sure you have no idea what I'm talking about."

I flinched. The resoluteness of his words felt like a reprimand.

viii. <u>Awful Long Walk</u>

THE WAKE TOOK PLACE IN THE TILDE SALON. I
draped the walls in bolts of black cloth and erected
a setting for the coffin on a pair of dumb horses
provided by the mortuary that prepared Ms.
Wyndl's body. I also dusted the fixtures, set out a
coffee and sandwich service, and ran a mop over
the foyer's tile floor.

At the appointed hour, Myron and I stood at
the Tilde's entryway, greeting and guiding visitors.
Having arranged no burial since the awestruck
urgency of his brother's and sister-in-law's more
than two decades prior, Myron had done an
admirable job considering it was the last Sunday
before Christmas. In quick time, the salon was at
capacity.

In my limited interactions with Myron, I
found him to meet the image of a successful,
slightly aloof entrepreneur. He dressed simply, in
dark fabrics, but the details of his person were
precise and understated. His hair was cropped
short and cast only a slight gleam of pomade.
Other than a small pin in the shape of a mayflower
affixed to his lapel, he was free of ornament.

"I suppose Mr. Joonblack is otherwise
disposed," Myron remarked.

"I believe so," I said.

I had not seen Troke in the two days since
Ms. Wyndl's death. Not in the halls. Not his
quarters, though I did that morning use the master
key to let myself into his room (which I was
surprised to find as ascetic as Margot Lincoln's

dorm room, save a propaganda poster on the wall above the sofa depicting a German soldier in the midst of some apparent seizure brought on by Canadian mortars whining down from a black sky, the tagline reading FRITZ IS ON THE FRITZ). I even enquired at the basement long-bar of Henry House, a haunt on Barrington Road he preferred, but came up empty.

"Are you comfortable handling all of this yourself?" Myron asked me. His tone towed the delicate line between sympathy and concern.

"I'm not entirely alone. Fenella O'Dwyre is here, along with her staff. And you've been careful in the arrangements. I wouldn't be concerned about mishap."

"It's kind of you to say, but my concern is my concern." Then, realizing he had been rude: "But I appreciate your saying that."

Myron shot his cuffs and stretched a knot out of his neck. He observed the crowd.

"I should be able to find someone to stand for Mr. Joonblack regarding the coffin. There are a few guests here I am familiar with I could possibly ask to bear the pall in his place. At least that dog of his is not underfoot."

Myron let out a long, deep breath, clapped me awkwardly on the back, nodded gravely, and stepped across the foyer to a pack of ornately costumed women who welcomed him with sad expressions and mild cries of relief.

I wondered where Troke was right that minute. My mind could not account for all the possibilities, the unchecked places. I doubted he would do something like tuck himself into one of the custodial cupboards with a bottle. Though I knew that wherever he was Doggins was with him, I shuddered at the thought of him alone with his grief. Crowds can be lonelier than isolation, and I supposed the people who were filling up the salon were not exactly Troke's peers. But, I thought, at the least he would have me. I might have acquitted myself well, I felt, in holding him up. I might have been better than no one at all, having had some practice at getting through memorials.

Myron quickly moved on from the circle of ladies and was now amidst a pack of conversing men I did not recognize, other than the pastor from St. Stephen's. Standing somewhat apart from this group, yet appearing of a texture altogether divorced from those around her, was a young woman. A blue wool skirt towed a narrow line up the length of her legs, coming to a plateau just below her waistline. A schoolgirl's skirt. She had the kind of body that holds a bit of extra weight but wears it well. Her hair fell in brown curls over her back. I could not see her face — she was turned away from me — but the architecture of her ear and how it flowed by a delicate fold into the paleness of her cheek suggested a soft face. Her sweater was also wool, but gray, and its cable-knit pattern seemed to narrow the sculpting of her back downward before her lower extremities finished the hourglass. She had her arms folded over her chest, as one does to defend one's self against untoward or indignant conversation, though from the looks on Myron's and the other men's faces, whatever their topic, it was amicable.

I began to move into the salon in order to gain a look at the young woman's face, but before I could glimpse her profile, I was accosted by Tory Venish, the overnight clerk and now acting desk manager.

"There's a wrinkle needs your attention."

"What is it?"

"Well, I'd rather not say here."

This was typical of Tory Venish. My experience with him was as limited as that with Myron, but unlike Myron, Venish's manner never failed to annoy me. Mundane happenings were unnecessarily fueled into small fires. Direct questions went unanswered. Like as not this "wrinkle" was as simple as we were low on some brand of whiskey or gin, or a guest had a question that either could wait or be handled by Venish himself.

"Just tell me what it is," I said. "This is a memorial, you know."

"I think its best if you see for yourself." He leaned in conspiratorially. "It affects us all, maybe you and Mr. Joonblack most." He shook his head in mock frustration.

"I don't think I should leave. If something is needed, perhaps you could handle it?"

"I see. Your presence is *essential*. In my experience these kinds of gatherings tend to orchestrate themselves."

The quickest way to get rid of Tory Venish was to make it seem you've acquiesced. "So where is it, this wrinkle?"

"Ms. Wyndl's suite."

My instinct was toward anger — the nerve of him to ask me to enter Ms. Wyndl's private room during her own memorial — but then it occurred to me there was one suddenly obvious place I'd failed to look for Troke.

I grudgingly followed him up the grand staircase to the second floor.

"Quietly," Venish said, opening the door as though he were worried about waking some sleeping person inside.

I followed him into the room. It looked just as it had when last I'd seen it, except that the bed had been stripped to the canvas and the vases that once held Troke's flowers were now empty.

I went into the washroom but found it empty. I paced across the main room and even dropped to a knee and looked under the bed, but the room was empty except for Venish and me.

"Well?" Venish said.

"Well, what?"

"What do you make of those?"

Venish pointed to several pieces of luggage lined up on the floor in front of the closet.

"Suitcases," I said.

"Of course, but whose do you think they are?"

"Tory, I don't understand what you think the big idea is. They're suitcases. One of the housemaids probably brought them out of storage to pack up Wyndl's wardrobe."

"And the tags?" Venish crossed the room, retrieved a small valise, and held it up to me so that I could see the nametag. *Calvo.*

"They probably belong to Myron. I have to get back downstairs."

"Rather heavy for empty cases, I would think." He pressed the valise into my hands.

And it was indeed heavy. I looked again at the tag hanging off the handle. The name Calvo was scrolled in an elegant hand. A feminine hand, it seemed to me, and I could only guess whose it was.

"Annelie Calvo," I said.

"So it seems." Venish nodded, a triumphant look on his face. "And apparently she is going to be staying in this room."

That did seem odd to me, given the fact that the room which had been hers up on the fourth floor remained vacant. Venish stared at me like a child waiting for his parent to hand down the verdict on some crucial decision. I didn't see that it mattered where the girl chose to sleep, but I did feel, standing in the darkness of that room with a piece of her personal belongings in my hands, like an intruder. I put down the valise.

"Well, we'd better get some sheets on the bed, I guess. I'll inform whatever girl's on tonight."

Venish flashed me a look of consternation and walked out of the room. Poor Venish, I thought. He wanted a partner in gossip, but he'd chosen wrong.

There was no reason to add up the presence of Annelie Calvo with the girl I had noticed in the salon. The salon and lobby were walled with people I had never seen before, half of them women. But just before the pastor signaled his readiness to begin the service, Myron gestured me over and introduced me to his niece.

She did not offer to shake hands, and it would have been impolite to insist. At first, we stood in a hollow of silence. Finally, I simply said, "Hello." To which she fluttered her eyes briefly, as though despite Myron's introduction she was only just now aware of me, and replied, "Yes, hello."

There was no time for further chat, because the attendees began to settle. The air in the salon caught that low-humming current that unspokenly signals a general shift in mood. Myron ushered Annelie to the very front row, demarcated for family. Of which Ms. Wyndl had only the two of them.

I slid into a seat two rows back, directly behind Annelie.

I had not known Ms. Wyndl's religion, but apparently, she had been a Catholic, or at least Myron thought so. And it was entirely Catholic of the pastor to hold a full mass service, despite the relative constraints of the Tilde Salon — no altar and thus no altar boy assistance, no place to rest the Bible, no preparation area for the Host, not to mention the prominent placement of the casket which forced the pastor to remain flush to the speaker's podium the entire time. The cadence of the service, which I was surprised to not have forgotten despite so many years' absence from churchgoing, gave the proceedings an element of rediscovery. I knew to follow the chalice lip to lip, knew how to hold out my hands for the small snitch of blessed bread. I even remembered to draw my palm down the side of my trousers to rid it of any residual sweat before the customary handshake of peace to those seated around me.

Which, incidentally, was when I first touched her.

I reached across the interceding row. Her hand was hemispheric with hot and cold, the palm sticky, but the back of the hand cool as a lake. She did not meet my eyes and only surrendered a slight nod of the head when I said, "Peace be with you."

Once the final homily was sung, in that oddly formal manner common to liturgy where song and spoken language merge into a sort of rhythmic chant, the people filed forth, row by row, to pay final respects.

I slipped out of the room at that point and took up post at the salon's entryway, where Myron was putting on the white gloves required to bear the brass coffin rails for Ms. Wyndl's final exit from the Manse. Mine were in my pocket.

"Rather fine ceremony," Myron said absently. He was having trouble getting the rigid cloth over the loose meat at his knuckles.

"I'm not sure she would have liked it."

"She talked a firm line alright, and I never once saw her dressed to be seen on Sunday morning, except maybe in the kitchen. Still, she would have appreciated the turnout, I think."

"Yes, the room was packed."

Myron enjoyed a subtle, triumphant smile. I watched him take in the cavalcade of mourners with a curiously critical eye. He seemed to be trying to determine who was truly affected and who was going through the motions. I wondered if he felt that legitimate grief was owed not just to Ms. Wyndl but to himself, for his efforts.

Myron had managed to convince two attendees to together step into Troke's absent role, and it was a good thing we had the additional set of hands. The casket was much heavier than I had expected it to be, and the handles were so slippery against the gloves I had to use both hands. But I did not stumble or interrupt the general progress, and Ms. Wyndl was delivered onto the hearse's runners without incident.

Before stepping into the passenger seat to accompany the hearse to the cemetery, Myron asked me to make a last check of the desk drawers in the manager's office, on the chance some item of personal appeal, which it might do well to slip under the coffin lid before the burial, had gone unnoticed by his own check the evening before. St. Stephen's was only five blocks away. I could catch up with the procession on foot.

The office was dark. I had slipped quietly past Venish, who was busy with a guest at the desk. As I closed the door, holding the curved handle tight in my hand so as to control the click of the latch, a voice from within the room said, "There's a key to that door hanging on a little nail beside the molding. That raven-eyed cadaver at the desk will be in here in half a minute if you don't lock us in."

The voice sounded almost drugged, but was distinctly feminine. I retrieved the key from where the voice said it would be and locked the door, then I slipped the key into the watch pocket of my vest and turned around.

The muted glow of the desk lamp silhouetted Annelie Calvo like a projection on a screen. My breath caught in my throat. You would think that might have happened when she first spoke, but it was not her presence, but rather her condition, that jarred me.

Her clothing, which I had found reservedly elegant when we were first introduced, now looked like a slept-on quilt tossed carelessly over her body. The limit of the light made the subtle distinction of the blue skirt and gray sweater bleed together into a single dark shroud. Her posture reminded me of that held by Ms. Wyndl when, on the day of my interview, I summarized for her the events of my life, what I had lost and what I had allowed to be taken from me: a limp doll.

I got my first good look at Annelie's face. In the foyer, in good light, I had given her the briefest of glances. Nerves kept me from making eye contact.

Now I stared.

Her nose was long and tipped in a small, dropped bulb, giving her the main effect of youthful strength. Her cheeks were as downy-seeming as before, but were now tear-streaked, splotched in degrees of pink. Her mouth was full, almost pouty. Eyes brown or green, I could not tell, sitting like sandy crystals behind lashes so long as to confuse the upper with the lower. Her forehead was smooth and proportioned, above which her hair stood out like unfurled wings. Despite the frazzle of it, a luminous softness of texture pronounced itself, as if deliberately sculpted into disarray. No one piece of her seemed to belong with any other, but taken as a whole, all aspects threaded into a seamless net of beauty.

"I suppose they're all on their way," she said.

"To St. Stephens," I said. "Your uncle asked me to check if there were anything personal to Ms. Wyndl that might have been overlooked in her desk."

A sniffle, a cough. She drew the sleeve of her sweater across her face.

"You'd better get to it then."

I moved quickly through the drawers, running a hand violently over the contents within each. I was not particularly concerned with finding anything. Frankly, the idea of cracking open her coffin lid to slide in some article of jewelry or photograph was beyond distasteful, and I don't think I would have been able to do it, even had Myron insisted.

In my haste, I was making an undue amount of noise, which landed harshly on Annelie. I caught her in my periphery flinch against the racket.

"It's a fine thing," she said, "invading the personal space of the dead. I take it Myron already did his own rifling. I wonder if he expected you to find something he missed or whether he just wanted to make sure I wasn't crouched in some corner of the room with a bottle in both hands."

I turned for the door.

"Did Lottie tell you about me at all?"

I turned back.

"A bit. Nothing very personal. Just how," I nearly said *how your parents were killed*, but caught myself, my words bearing the briefest pause, "the hotel was founded and what it was like to have you growing up here."

"You wanted to say something else, didn't you?" She sat forward. "You paused."

As the lamplight passed over her face, I saw that a light film had been smeared across her upper lip and cheek when she'd run her sleeve past her face.

"What is it you were going to say?"

"About your parents."

"That they died. Or how they died?"

"Just that they died and that's why Myron opened the Manse."

"I see." She sat back, the smear across her face once more bursting into relief and then fading away.

"You, um, you have something. On your face. From your sleeve, I think." I stepped to her and removed one of my father's embroidered handkerchiefs from my pocket. "Here."

She was embarrassed, so I turned away, back toward the door and waited until I sensed that she had finished.

"Ms. Wyndl also said that you just upped and went away to school like you decided to go for a walk."

"Awful long walk."

"What is the name of the school? Ms. Wyndl never said."

"Prince of Wales College. It's the one that allows women."

"The one?"

"St. Dunstan's doesn't. Men only. That one's called a university, while we women attend a college. I have no idea the difference between a college and a university. Semantics, perhaps."

She held out the handkerchief. I asked her to keep it, in case she wished to use it again. I mentioned that it was my father's.

"Lottie wrote me once about you. Said you were an orphan. Like me."

"They only died two and a half years ago."

"Well, I guess she felt it was important to use that word anyway. Orphan."

"She told me that orphans are orphans no matter their age. That loss is loss."

Her eyes, which in the pass through the arc of lamplight I now noticed were the kind of hazel that contains a thin ring of yellow within the brownish green, glazed over.

"Do you know why I suddenly, how did you say it, 'upped and went away'?"

I was standing straight as a board with my hands clenched in fists in my pockets. I felt like I was standing on a stage, struggling with lines I had not committed to memory.

"Back in 1938 there was a group of women who booked in for a weekend. On the Saturday, they took the Aaron Salon for a late-night party. We hosted dinner for them there as well, which was an exception to how we normally did things. I assume you were given the speech about being flexible."

"It was one of the first things Ms. Wyndl said to me when I was hired."

Annelie smiled, a pursing of the lips that drew creases at the corners of her mouth and pulled the plane of skin at either side of her nose down like a tucked sheet. The effect was a sort of playful sensuousness.

"It was a reunion dinner for their class from Prince of Wales. 1918. Which meant their years there coincided roughly with the Great War. It must have been a troubling time to work out an education. Many of their brothers or fathers were someplace else, fighting. I was able to speak to many of them. There were about twenty in all. What amazed me, and it truly did, was that with only two or three exceptions, these women were all sinking very happily into spinsterhood. They led small lives. Many were teachers, some worked on farms or in shops in Charlottetown or here in Halifax. But their lives were incredibly free. No children, no marital politics. They simply did as they wished, all the time. One of them, a teacher up in Fredericton, attributed her selfishness, as she called it — I would have said self-sufficiency, myself — but she said it came from the fact that she had insisted on becoming educated, and during that time she had discovered for herself what she wanted and what she was willing to do in order to get it."

"It sounds like a lonely way to go about life," I said. I wasn't certain I believed that, but it was the first thing that entered my mind.

"You think those women never had lovers?" That smile again, this time not so friendly. "They had lovers."

I tucked my chin into my chest and sank into the armchair beside her.

"My point is that they gave themselves a choice. I realized, a few weeks after they had gone, that I was not giving myself a choice. I had always wanted to be here at the Manse. It was where I was meant to be. What I was born into. But what if there was more? I couldn't even say what I meant by *more*, and that right there said *everything*. It got me angry, to give you the plain truth of it. I felt I was already playing someone's else hand but calling it my own. And once I figured that out, it was time to go."

"Is that why you didn't come back until now? I mean, not even to visit?"

Annelie shifted in her chair. Her eyes fell on me like a weight. It was an oddly exhilarating discomfort to be stared at like that. Like some form of discipline was looming, but for an action that I did not regret performing.

"That's not a polite question."

I met her eyes and found that she had begun to quietly cry.

"I'm sorry. I'm not sure how people behave in times like this."

"There's no sure way," she said.

Incredible — the dearness of the loss of Ms. Wyndl was Annelie's and yet she was reassuring me.

We were sitting so close as to be nearly brushing shoulders, so it was with very little effort that she reached across the thin eddy of space between us and took the tails of my wrinkled vest and smoothed it over my middle.

Then: A creak, quite loud in the tightness of the dark office, issued from her chair, and suddenly her cheek rested heavily on my chest. The earthy, vaguely flowery scent of her hair dusted my neck. Her hand fell lax across my stomach. The weight of her body settled fully on my arm. Soon a vague numbness came on and the arm began to fall entirely to sleep.

We remained this way. I watched the clock on the wall count the minutes, then the hour. Once, I whispered that we'd be missed at the cemetery, but she replied only with a light squeeze of my hand. I said nothing more.

As the minutes ticked by, my vest would sometimes wrinkle up over my waistline and my tie become screwed up over my chest, pulling uncomfortably at my collar, causing me to retract my body further down into a slouch, so as to relieve the pressure. With each inch given, I would reach up and worry at my neckline, to no avail.

Then Annelie's hand would rise, loosen my tie, smooth over my vest as to calm me from nervousness or bellyache, and I would exhale and again try to rest.

ix. <u>You Can Take One Thing</u>

ANNELIE DID NOT STAY LONG in Ms. Wyndl's suite. Two days after the funeral, Myron ordered Troke and I to collect Annelie's luggage *and* Ms. Wyndl's belongings and bring them up to the fourth floor.

I still had not figured out where Troke had been those two intervening days between Ms. Wyndl's passing and her burial. But when he stepped into the kitchen the morning of our assignment, Doggins catching him up, he was freshly dressed and clear-eyed. He made no explanation for his absence. I accepted his return without comment.

When we entered Ms. Wyndl's room, I saw that Annelie's luggage still sat in a neat row on the far side of the stripped-down bed, but the valise which had been Venish's evidence of her presence was gone.

Troke asked me to run the suitcases up, while he collated the items in the closet and dresser drawers to see how many boxes we would need to retrieve from storage to get it all moved out.

I had by this time been in every single room in the Manse Calvo, except Annelie's long-empty suite. The room traced the exact same layout and arrangement as the other large suites that made up the fourth floor. A short hall, accented by a hip-high table, led into the sitting room, similar to my own quarters but about thrice the size. The windows were large, and opened as French doors onto the cement and iron balcony beyond. The furniture was uniform with that of the Manse's other rooms, but there were more pieces than in the smaller quarters. Two sofas and two armchairs. An ovular dark wood coffee table. The walls were decorated with framed prints of birds, clusters of flowers, and still lifes of common domestic scenes — a table uncleared from a recent meal; a small dog, a schnauzer I believe, at rest on a hearth rug; a smattering of unrealistically ripe fruit.

I was unsure where to leave the baggage. I did not feel it was right to enter the bedroom. The door to that room was closed. I had been conditioned to respect subtle behaviors. A closed door was not a mistake, nor an absent-minded habit. It had its reasons. I instead lined up the suitcases in front of the coffee table where Annelie could not miss them when she returned.

On my way out I took notice of how clean the room was. All surfaces gleaming, carpets soft as if brushed, fixtures absent dust or cobwebs. I wondered — did Annelie have the housemaids in, or had the room always been kept guest-quality on the orders of Ms. Wyndl as a hedge toward a return as sudden as Annelie's exit?

I knew that in asking me to schlep Annelie's suitcases by myself Troke was buying time alone with Ms. Wyndl's belongings. I could even guess that should he find a particular piece of clothing, a scarf or pair of gloves or undergarment, which held a significance for him, it might disappear into his pocket.

What I didn't expect was to find him ludicrously trying not to draw attention to the fact that each of his trouser pockets, as well as the pockets of his jacket and the breast pocket of his work shirt, were stuffed to such a degree the seams were showing. I could hardly believe what I was seeing.

"You can't be serious," I said.

"What do you mean?"

Troke flashed me the same look of bewildered innocence that he had often given to Ms. Wyndl when she asked him a question to which he had only a disappointing answer.

"I don't know what you've got in there, but you can't take it. All of it, anyway."

Troke squared up on me, but not to intimidate; he was finding the right footing on which to make an argument.

"Walek, you don't understand. There was this —"

Just then, Myron came into the room.

Seeing Troke, he said, "You don't need to go to such measures, Mr. Joonblack. You're not auditioning for the circus. I'm sure there are plenty of boxes to be had in custodial storage. If you come up short, I'll vouch a small amount from petty cash for one of you to get some more from Fraser's Moving on Morris Street. In fact, it just might make sense for you to do that regardless. I'd like us to have an account there." Exhaling, Myron checked his pocket watch. "Annelie will be out most of today. There is no rush to clear the room. Let's just say I'd like it completed by the dinner service, yes?"

We nodded and Myron left.

I turned back to Troke.

"One thing. You can take one thing, and it can't be something that Annelie will probably want. Ms. Wyndl was like a mother to her, from what I know of it."

"You don't know all that much."

I could tell Troke was trying to goad me, but I wouldn't bite.

"I know enough. Now, come on. Empty them before someone else comes by."

In the end, after some mumbling self-argument, Troke decided to purloin Ms. Wyndl's perfume atomizer. It was still most of the way full. I assumed it had been a gift from him and felt it was a safe thing for him to take. I doubted Annelie wanted to smell like a sixty-year-old woman.

As we boxed everything up, I kept a close eye on Troke. The temptation to palm something else, something that *would* be missed, was clearly still in play.

He noticed.

"This isn't exactly the first time I've given myself a little gift, you know," Troke said. His eyebrows arched deviously.

"Do you just let yourself into rooms whenever you like, or what?"

"Of course not. But — you went looking for me the other day, so you checked my room? See that crazy poster I've got above the sofa? The one with the kraut shitting himself as the bombs rain in?"

"Yes."

"I got that in '28 from a group of war veterans who staged a sort of 'we made it out' boozer in the Aaron. I took it right off the wall in the middle of their shouting the chorus of their hundredth war song. They never even noticed. They had a dozen different sorts of the things pasted up. But I liked that one."

"Is that the only time?"

"Sure." He passed me a wink.

I smiled, shook my head, and began filling another box.

It took us four hours to have the room down to its base fixtures. We stacked the boxes of clothing and books and sundries in the sitting room of Annelie's suite, in a corner behind one of the armchairs but away from the glass doors to the balcony, so as not to crowd the room should she want to take her time sifting through them. Then we called down for a maid to come up and collect the spare bed linens from the closet.

As we exited, I looked down and saw the clasp straps of at least three braziers peeking from the front pocket of Troke's trousers. I said nothing. Despite my short lecture on what he could and could not take, I admired his restraint.

That was the last task Troke and I shared. It seemed an appropriate sendoff, given the circumstance.

We cleared out Ms. Wyndl's room on December 26. (Christmas Day itself was restrained. We had only a few registered guests and no event bookings. Troke and I stood down for the day.) The following morning, December 27, after a brief meeting with Myron and Annelie, Troke waited amongst the boxed and latched-up accumulation of his more than twenty years at the Manse for the car Myron had hired to arrive.

The foyer was immensely quiet. We both rocked on the balls of our feet like strangers sharing a waiting room.

"So," Troke said.

"How will you get there? Train?"

"Naw, I've got a reservation on one of the bus lines. It's only about five hours, and this way I get a better look at the countryside. It's been a little while since I've seen it. If I don't fall asleep, that is."

"What's waiting for you there?"

"Work, I expect. I send a little money to a local family to open the house up in spring and fall, air it out, and make sure the yard don't go back to nature. But for all that, it's sat alone about two years now, so there'll be that to face. But I'm looking forward to it. It will be lovely, Walek, to fix up something for myself for a change."

The Manse's front windows were open halfway in order to freshen the salons, and a pleasant coolness came into the foyer. It was an unusually temperate day; the gauge hanging outside the windows read 11 Celsius.

I was feeling quite flushed, whether by the awkwardness of a prolonged goodbye or the slowly dissolving stuffiness of the foyer, I wasn't sure, but when Troke wanted a cigarette, I joined him on the front porch.

"Now that Lor's gone, I guess I can have one of these anytime I want, guilt-free." He smiled sadly and pulled so hard on the slim white tube that the flame from his match was drawn slantwise into the funnel.

"Use to be I smoked like a fiend. My ma's words, *like a fiend*. She was one for getting right down to it. She told me once, we were sitting on our little dock, waiting for my da to come back in, that I was a Poor Man's Cagney the way I squinted through the smoke. I was maybe twenty-three."

"Why weren't you out on the boat?"

"It was a good year, as I recall. We were making enough to take on a local boy and I was part-time up at the Pines. It's a resort. Got a golf course and everything. My ma was a laundress there, did I ever mention that? She set it up, that job."

"Pre-empting the inevitable," I said, smiling at my own wit.

"How's that?"

"Just that it prepared you for working here."

"Aye, I got the flavor alright. When I came down to Halifax, it was the one thing I could reasonably claim to do that didn't involve goddamn fish."

"Did your mother like James Cagney?"

"Don't know. I didn't even know who he was. Never seen his pictures. I took it in stride, figured it was a joke. But she didn't stop there, no. She said that when I was smoking, I looked like I wanted everyone to know the wheels in my head were turning. I was sizing you up and rendering judgment, she thought."

I must have looked stricken, because he began to laugh.

"All in good fun, for Jesus's sake. The best thing for you, kid, is to learn how to read the tone on a voice." He paused to light a second cigarette off the near-corpse of the first, which he then slid into the smoker's friend perched behind us against the brick wall. "Besides she wasn't wrong. I plowed through them. Days were when I reached for a pack in the morning to find it was already done. That alarmed me, but it didn't make me stop. Another time, my ma asked if when I was alone I ate them."

Troke laughed out a fug of smoke. Then he dropped the cigarette, nearly unsmoked, absently down the friend's long narrow neck.

"Ah," he said, looking out over the hotel's front lawn, "I've got a pretty piece of quiet waiting for me. A pretty piece."

We again rocked on the balls of our feet, until the car arrived. It was an American car, a

Cadillac, with a large, aggressive-looking front grill and a nice shine to the coating, even in the filthy dampness of late December.

"I'll write," Troke said, once his baggage was safe in the car's boot.

"I would like that."

I gave it a fifty-fifty chance that he would. He talked a good game, but I wondered if he had the patience to write out his thoughts with the same detail he spoke them.

He held up a hand to the driver, a signal to wait. Then he mounted the curb and came back up onto the porch. He stood directly in front of me.

"I like you very much," he said. "That sounds like weak tea, but it's not. You're a real lad."

We shook hands. My life seemed to have become a succession of leavings. First my parents, then Dr. Hapstrath, Ms. Wyndl, and now Troke. There was variance of impact; admittedly, Troke's leaving was the leanest. But the plainness of my being, in his estimation, "a real lad" affected me in a way I did not quite understand but enjoyed the feeling of. I told him, lamely, that I would miss him, that I would miss his stories, too, which was true.

I stayed on the porch until the car turned onto Coburg Road and was gone.

Later, in the quiet of my room, I was grateful for having heard his last little story. I laid down on top of the bedspread and pictured a woman, ruddy and russet, happily egging on her boy over a habit she may or may not have actually disapproved of, as the sky shimmered on the water, and the waiting for husband and father was almost as good as the eventual arrival.

x. <u>Solo</u>

I WAS QUICK TO SET A ROUTINE FOR MYSELF. I rose at six and was in the foyer by half past. Behind the registration desk was a clipboard on which the day's bookings were listed, along with a list of addenda to be addressed on a weekly rotating basis: checking the integrity of the fire exits and the bolted glass doors of the main dining area; walking the exterior walls in search of cracked mortar between the bricks; passing an eye over the trees on the property's back lot for the presence of rotted limbs; investigating the grass for patches of creeping Charlie and burgeoning fleets of dandelions; testing the veracity of the heating conduits; running a periodic check on the boiler. Attached to these addenda were what I mentally referred to as "the suddens" — issues called down to the desk overnight. These were the rare occurrence that a heating register was offering weak heat or was rattling somewhere beyond reach and keeping a guest awake, or that a minor bit of damage was noticed, either to a room or to one of the common areas, and the caller was simply phoning the information in as a courtesy. Most days, there were no suddens.

Typically, I worked from 7:00 a.m. to 2:00 p.m. straight through, then broke until around 4:00 p.m., taking my lunch in the galley over a book, unless specifically needed. Or, if the morning had been taxing, I would retreat to my room for a rest. Thereafter, I aided Fenella O'Dwyre's staff in setting the dinner service, which began promptly at 5:00 p.m. and ran through 7:30, during which time I was expected to make myself available should the sideboard need refreshing or a table switched out to accommodate a large number of people wishing to sit as one group. I left the breakdown and cleaning of the dining area to the kitchen staff. Until 8:30 I arranged the seating areas of the Aaron and Tilde Salons and stoked their respective fires, which were kept up even in summer for those older guests whose crispening constitutions were sensitive to evening drops in temperature. I wiped down the cushions on the rear patio furniture, swept the walks, made certain the door to the patio remained unlocked and gave a final check to all tertiary exits. If it had been a dry day, I watered the flowers, occasionally spreading crushed egg shells over their beds, which Fenella insisted strengthened the soil. My supper was late, often 10:00, which was when my shift officially ended. A covered plate was left to warm in the oven and I ate alone in the galley or brought the food and a bottle of beer up to my room, if I preferred a quieter bookend to the day. Any events or meetings ongoing were supervised by the overnight clerk and the detritus left until morning.

I had been hired at a rate of $12 per week. This was upped to $16 per week after Troke left. With no social prospects, and my food and lodging provided, I spent very little, except on modest pleasures — books, the odd piece of clothing. I bought a few war stamps; it was considered the least one could do. That aside, I built up a savings. I had much ground to cover in that regard, after the miserable accounting of my college years. I was set on never being that stupid again.

Once a week, I took in a late show at either the Capital Theatre or the Orpheus. Both venues changed out their marquee every Tuesday, and they always got the first-run films. The sight of the ushers' red felt jackets and blue cotton pants and beribboned pillbox hats gave me the sensation of stepping through a shimmering rift in the world into the not-so-distant past, a past where a movie was not preceded by newsreels about the state of the war. I particularly enjoyed the general murmur of expectation that would swoon through the false ceiling of blue cigarette smoke before the houselights flickered and the great room grew dark.

On the nights I did not visit the pictures, I often sat up late, reading. No matter the weather, I kept a window cracked open so as to allow in a steady flow of air. I especially liked feeling a cold current or one infused mistily with rain reach across the room toward where I lay beneath the duvet. There is something wonderful about being wrapped up tight and warm in a space that is cool, and I felt my concentration on such nights was all the crisper for it, too.

That spring after Troke left was as rainy and cold as the previous summer had been inordinately sweltering. On the few humid nights there were, I did not keep to my room. I could never seem to find rest; no book could leaden my eyelids. I instead chased physical exhaustion. In slacks, trainers, and an A-shirt — for who would see me in the dark? — I would walk determinedly to Point Pleasant Park, and there stalk the winding pathways until I felt rung through and ready for sleep.

My quarters, incidentally — I see now that I've yet to describe them — were nicely appointed, if slightly acetic. There was a small sitting room that fed with no intervening door directly to a bedroom that held a double bed and two small nightstands. There were windows in both the sitting room and bedroom areas which opened by crank-handle and provided a fine breeze off the North-West Arm. Each had a small sitting ledge fitted into its molding. What passed for a closet was simply a pair of metal racks bolted into the wall of a short hallway, about three measured steps, that led to the WC. There was also a three-drawer dresser made of unvarnished wood, its drawers lined with paper. There was no kitchenette area, but on a sideboard in the sitting room sat a plug-in single-burner heater that could be used for soup or coffee. It was a very fine room, I felt, from the first moment I entered it the day I was hired. I liked the fact that my truncated belongings fitted well into the space allotted for them. I stacked my suitcases on the sitting room floor and used one of the sitting ledges as a shelf for my books — temporarily, at least. The space beneath the ledges turned out to contain heating conduits, and so the next morning, I moved my books to the sideboard in the sitting room, where they displayed much more nicely.

For the most part that spring, the Manse Calvo was vacant. No surprise there; tourism had become a collateral victim of the U-boat threat outside the harbour, but special bookings were also down. No one seemed to think much of it; ebbs and tides are a hotel's reality. What's needed is a sound footing to weather them, and the Manse Calvo, which had come neatly out of the Depression years, certainly had that.

Then late May saw a sudden turnaround. Perhaps the winter and unpredictable spring had driven folks a bit stir-crazy in their homes. For those in need of some kind of abstention from routine, a night in a hotel can be a fine substitution for an actual holiday away. We were at capacity each weekend and weeknights were full enough to keep staff on its toes. Moreover, because local leagues and guilds associated with various aspects of war production had begun to spring up in litters since the previous year, the salons were booked for meetings several evenings a week.

My work days, or more directly my work nights, began to stretch.

These longer shifts did not affect me alone. The kitchen staff was expected to stay on the clock as much as two hours past their regular shift times, a complication for those who were the wives of soldiers away on duty and had their own homes and children to tend to. Fenella O'Dwyre, who'd had a hand in hiring most of the kitchen staff, was particularly sensitive to their concerns, and began herself to work double shifts, so as to mitigate others' overtime.

Around this time, Fenella and I began a casual habit of listening to broadcasts on the wireless late at night, as a means of unwinding. We sat in the kitchen, over beers or highballs (sometimes both), huddled to either side of Fenella's radio, which she would bring down from her room. We both enjoyed Jack Benny. We couldn't imagine who would not. Fibber McGee and Molly were lesser pleasures but we always laughed heartily, as that program often began when Fenella and I were on our second or third round and thus susceptible to fits of humor. But it was the sober reports of Edward R. Murrow and

Lorne Greene we really wanted to hear. Fenella would toggle the dial between the CBC, which carried Greene, and a fainter New York-based signal that brought us Murrow. Their broadcasts kept us glued to our seats even as the accumulation of the day's efforts and the drink began to settle. It was our impression that these two men were giving it to us as it was, leanly, absent any adjectival bombast. Little of their news was good. We even sat through local reports, many of which were poor, often overexaggerated rehashes of Greene's broadcasts, hoping for some mention of activity in an "east coast port," which (a poorly held secret) referred to Halifax. But nothing that was reported could qualify any speculation as to when, or if, the dark reach of war would scrape its dirty nails over the Maritimes.

Fenella believed that the ramp-up of civic organizations and pseudo-military resource guilds, both categories of which comprised a large percentage of our salon and meeting room bookings, was a simple effect of the city's role as a military hub for the building of naval vessels.

"No one's getting themselves in such a tizzy in Sunny Brae, I can tell you," she said one evening. "Maybe New Germany, but then the folks there might think they've got a point to prove. A name to live down."

I wasn't sure what to think. I suppose I did not think much at all, except to note what was consistent in the broadcasts. Both sides seemed to be pressing forward and simultaneously retreating. My geography was poor, and so most of the towns and villages named in the reports meant nothing to me. I was, however, hooked by the tense description of troop movements and skirmishes (for they were often called that, "skirmishes," rather than fights or battles). There was nothing romantic about it, but an undercurrent of adventure could not be denied. (Any man actually engaged in this "adventure" would have firmly rejected this idea, of course.) I was aware that mine was a place of certain privilege, and I was grateful for the extra work that made a flurry of my working hours, but strongest of all was my gratitude for the company I kept on those exhausted nights, what Fenella called our "wireless midnights."

When the broadcasts grew repetitive and her attention wavered, Fenella would unveil little slivers of what her life had been before she came to the Manse Calvo. Over the course of several weeks, these slivers resolved into a loose narrative of her life.

She had attended Saint Mary's School for Girls, which, she said, was the standard Catholic girls' school in Halifax. I had never heard of it, but then (as she said) there was no reason I should have. Her parents were municipal employees. Her mother was part of a typing pool and her father drove supply trucks all over Nova Scotia.

"We were poor, I guess you could say," Fenella said. "But my parents thought that made life more interesting. How dull, they used to say, if you could just have anything you wanted any time you wanted it. You'd never know what it felt like to really want something. And you would never appreciate anything."

Out of high school, she had waited tables, but despite her friendly nature, she had a rough time faking her way through the last hours of the night when the men got frisky and the women mouthy.

"I stuck it out at a few places longer than I ought've, but it was good money for us, and my brother had a real shot at St. John's."

Fenella's younger brother, George, was something of a prodigy. His interests lay in the sciences and in mathematics, at which he was notably gifted. But though he was an impressive interview for the college boards and scored well on his exams, he could not drum up the type of fellowship dollars that would entirely remove the financial burden from his family, and without doing so, there would be no university for him. So, Fenella sweated through a string of dissatisfying jobs, until two years out of school she caught on at Moirs Chocolates near ("Funnily enough") George Street. Hired as one of dozens to work the quality-control lines, she ascended to shift supervisor in a matter of months, after catching a batch of chocolate-drizzled pretzels that had somehow gotten small metal shavings mixed into the syrup.

"One of the machines had thrown a gear or rod or something. I don't know machines, but there was this smell like someone was burning tires all of the sudden. So, I ran to the packing room and checked a few boxes. I had to bite into one piece from more than ten boxes each! Metal in every single one. George was on partial fellowship then, and after I got promoted, between my parents and me we got him where he belonged."

This was in the summer of 1938. By that October, Fenella had met a young man named Samuel and fallen in love.

She only spoke about him to me once.

We had just turned off the radio on a recording of a local orchestra grinding its way through a series of popular dancehall songs. It was nearly 3 a.m. We were both soundly drunk and less than four hours from the following morning's breakfast service. The orchestra had just concluded a rendition of an older song, *You Took Advantage of Me*.

"Sam loved that song," Fenella said, leaning heavily into the kitchen island. "He had a recording of it by the Mole Faces or Miffy Molars or whoever, and he would put it on and sing along without singing. You know, the way people do when they hear a song they like."

Fenella closed her eyes, as to feel the phantom weight of her words. I asked her who Sam was.

"Have I never mentioned him? Gee, I wonder how come." She gave a morose little laugh. "His father was a fishmonger. Still is, I mean. I assume he's still around. Sam liked carpentry. No blame to be had there. Not many people who are born into fish really like it. They just know it and little else besides. Sam had been on the line at a textiles plant about a year when we met. And he took odd jobs on the side, fixing folks' window frames and door hinges, building bed frames for their kiddies and the like. He was figuring it out for himself. No real training, nothing formal, but he was pretty good. I'll say it like this, he made the bed frame we slept on and it was a fine, strong thing."

"I don't know that you have to give me those kinds of details," I said. I had taken our glasses to the sink and was giving them a turn with a soapy rag.

"Don't be a prude, Walek. This is a love story."

"Fair enough. Go on."

"What I'm saying is he did for himself. And not just the bed. He made all the furniture in his

171

apartment. The chest of drawers, the coat and hat rack, even this little wood steamer trunk where he kept mementos from our dates, ticket stubs and that sort of thing. Not all the angles were true, but they had been made with his own hands and he was proud of them. I think that's a lot."

I smiled at her. "I think so too."

Fenella described the timidity of their courtship, how Samuel at first would only take her places during the daytime, in the hours between when his shift at the plant ended and evening arrived.

"He actually cared about propriety. Who even knows what that means anymore?"

I wanted to tell her that I knew, simply as a means of commiseration, but it wasn't the place.

"It wasn't until after the Germans were already into Austria that we went to bed together. That's almost a year. That kind of patience got sucked up by the war, don't you think? Just last week, I saw some fat pale thighs jiggling over a uniform, right out in the open, right in an empty doorway. In the *street*. Near *homes*."

"You might have seen a transaction. You know, an arrangement."

"You have a funny way of saying whore, Walek."

We both smiled. The conversation was going off its rails a bit, and we were both growing tired. But I wanted to hear the rest of her story, so I suggested we walk a bit in the garden to clear our heads. The night air would help us sleep, I reasoned. She agreed.

We frightened a few foraging animals as we stepped onto the back patio. The rear lights had to remain off, in deference to both the guests whose rooms looked out onto the wood and to blackout regulations, but the moon was almost entirely full that night and gave enough light to walk by. We both knew the route of the garden path.

"Did you live together?" I asked, to get the ball rolling once more.

"No, we never did. I spent a lot of nights there, but I still lived at home. I wouldn't call my parents terribly old-fashioned, but my mother would have keeled over if I shacked up with a boy full-time."

"Are your parents still in Halifax?"

"No, not since that September when Poland was invaded. It was just a coincidence, that news coming and my father getting a job in Dartmouth. But that's how it happened. I think they moved because my mother didn't want him taking the ferry every day. Not that U-boats are lurking in the water. There're those nets across the harbour so they can't get in. But when she gets a thought in her head, there's no talking her out of it. Anyway, they have a little house just outside the city. It's actually only four blocks from the dispensary where my father works. He's in charge of the supply trucks now. Routing, schedules. He doesn't drive them anymore."

"How often do you visit?"

"Every few weekends. My mother doesn't like me taking the ferry either." Fenella's voice dropped, as though she had caught a chill, even though the night air was warm, and felt to me warmer still because of the drink. "I don't much like being on the water." She looked up at me. Her eyes looked almost ferocious in the scant light.

"Okay," was all I could manage to say.

Fenella exhaled, a long and drawn expulsion that brought her hands over her midriff as for support.

"All right, it was like this. He signed up just before the holidays in '39 and was assigned by the next spring. Everything takes time when you're so far away, so I didn't think much of it when the time between letters got strung out. In November of '40, Sam's father came to see me at Moirs. He had three letters for me. Two from Sam and one from the RCN. Presumed lost at sea. A lot of blustering about his bravery, but no details of what really happened to the boat he'd been on."

"I'm sorry, Fenella."

"I sometimes think he's not dead, but that he's living in some shack with an African or Egyptian woman. Gone native, as they say. Sometimes I picture him walking across Europe, trying to find his way back here. I used to think about it a lot, but less and less now. When we're really busy here, I don't think about him at all. And then *that* hurts like hell later."

Companionable silences are difficult for people who do not share either a prolonged history or a mutual disinterest in bridging the gap between one another. Fenella was not visibly upset, she was not crying, but I sensed there was much to organize in her mind, snapshots of Samuel to develop and collate, so as to refresh her memory of him. I have heard that over time you begin to forget precisely what a person you've lost looks like. I figure it relates to the person, because my parents were as clear in my head as they had ever been before my eyes, whereas Theodora Roth, whom I had lusted after briefly but vehemently, though she was not "lost" to me like Sam was lost to Fenella, had become a sparse collection of uncertain physical details.

I let a few strangled minutes pass. Sea birds out across the Arm cut the quiet, their calls echoing in a rapid fade. The cooling air had begun to unravel the tightness in my temples. I was sobering.

"Is that when you came to work here?" I finally asked.

"Almost. When I didn't show up a couple of days at the factory, they fired me. Those were scary days. Of course, by then George had been called up. But he got home service. He works in Toronto. The mathematics, I suppose. I don't know what all he does. His letters are either vague or filled with little black bars. Ms. Wyndl hired me when I was truly desperate. There weren't even waitressing jobs."

"But it worked out."

"In a manner of speaking."

We turned back and returned to the house through the kitchen. I took up her wireless and carried it to her room.

I set the radio down on the side table just inside her doorway and wished her a good night.

"A good two hours' sleep, anyway," I said.

"Do you know what the sweetest thing Sam ever did for me was?" she said. "I'll tell you and then you can go pass out. One afternoon, he took me to the library at Dalhousie and showed me the origin of my name. Fenella, it turns out, means 'fair-shouldered'. I don't think my parents ever knew that."

"I think it suits you," I said. "Philosophically speaking."

Fenella laughed. "If not physically." She turned her left shoulder away to offer in full the wide plain of her strong, broad back. Then, unexpectedly, she rose up on her toes and kissed me quickly on the temple, then stepped inside her room and closed the door.

For many weeks after, through further wireless midnights, though I did not broach the subject of Sam with Fenella again, I wondered at the various coping mechanisms at play within the Manse Calvo. For me there were my parents and, to a lesser degree, Dr. Hapstrath. For Annelie there was the towering void of the parents she had never known and the loss of the stand-in she had. Fenella had her Sam. Even Myron, at a greater remove, lived with a form of irretrievable loss, though his I imagined was easier to carry now that he had become a success in his own right. We were all victims to lost time and questions doomed to go unanswered. In time I figured Fenella would sort the pieces. Mend her heart. Hers was not a generally stolid outlook. The last thing she told me about Samuel was the finest gesture he had made toward her. Therein resides hope.

xi. Truro

JUNE 21, 1942 WAS CLOUD-COVERED but warm
and breezy, somehow bright despite little actual
blue in the sky. I sat in the passenger seat of the
Manse's sedan, a forest-green Packard One-
Twenty, as Annelie steered us toward the farmers'
market in Truro. Our goal: to secure as much
fresh fruit and vegetables as the car's boot and
back seat could hold. Customarily, Fenella would
have been my partner on this trip, but she was on
a double that day. Tory Venish, who sometimes
accompanied her, was ordered by Annelie to man
the registration desk for the day. Venish had not
been pleased. He had insisted that the houseman
ought to stay, reasoning (admittedly not
unreasonably) that he could not be expected to
deal with any problem ordinarily assigned to me.
But I knew that Annelie found him a bit
insufferable and very much a bore.

"Two hours alone with him," she said,
shaking her head. "Don't get me wrong, he's good
at his job. I depend on him. I'm glad he's here, but
—"

"So long as you don't have to speak with
him."

Annelie laughed.

The airport, which marked Halifax's inland
city limits, slid away behind us, and as the road
broke through a vast stretch of arrowhead-tipped
trees, Annelie drew in a deep breath and, apropos
of nothing, said, "We ought to get rid of those
poinsettias on the front desk. Christmas is six

177

months past. People might think we don't pay attention to the details if that's the first thing they see when they step through the door. Deal with it, could you?"

"What would you like in their place?"

"Unpoinsettias."

"I'll see what I can do."

"And the guild coming tomorrow is expecting the draperies in their room to be swapped out with some that are being dropped off in the morning."

"Do you know what time they are expected?"

"Unfortunately, no. But these women, we've had them in before?"

"Not this particular group, but groups like them. The Central Magazine Depot and the Canadian Women's Club hold a joint monthly chapter meeting in the Tilde the third Wednesday of every month."

"Why did I not know that?"

"I suppose it depends on who signs the registration. Venish always uses the name of the person who calls to verify the details. Fenella lists the name of the group. You can guess who gets most of those calls."

"I suppose you know all their names now."

"Folks do seem to like the familiarity."

"Perhaps some gratitude to Tory is justified. As to changing out the draperies, Christ might tell us why it matters so much. The fixtures are perfectly fine as they are. I think they're quite lovely, myself. That sort of purple that looks entirely black in dim light but bright when the sun hits it. What's replacing it is, apparently, what the woman who phoned called 'glory mustard'. Is that even a real color?"

"Mustard is. Glory sounds a bit —"

"Put upon."

"Yes. Exactly."

"Apparently, it's *their* color. They also wear sashes, I believe."

"We'll find out tomorrow evening. It's a small thing, really. I've had worse."

"You'll have to tell me about that sometime."

"Well, we've got a drive to get through. But you don't really want to hear about it anyway."

Annelie held a sigh. Tilted her head toward me, a concession.

"I sometimes wish I had Lottie's way of keeping a firm distance from things. But my mind runs to places unfit for management. That's what she would have said. 'A place unfit for management'."

"She was a very fine house manager."

"You think I'm just like her, don't you? I can tell from your tone of voice. You think I'm Mademoiselle Loretta Wyndl to her Madame. Not everything about her was all that great, you know. I loved her, of course. But by the time I left for school, the pillar I'd made of her showed its cracks."

"All I said was —"

"I'm just teasing you. Not every word I utter needs your total attention."

"How else do people talk to one another?"

"Well, some give as they get."

"You want me to tease you?"

"If there's a point where you come up with something, sure."

Talking this way was drawing attention to the way we were talking, and I grew uncomfortable. I had read into the night of Ms. Wyndl's funeral an intimacy Annelie, I believe, did not. In the weeks following, as she began, with growing confidence and at the behest and allowance of Myron, to assume the post of house manager, seizing her entitlement to the Manse Calvo, I accepted the painful surprise that the quiet hour we had shared was not a preamble to something more. Rather, I would be seen by her as I had been seen by Ms. Wyndl — subordinately. I assumed she lived contentedly in her reclaimed flat on four, but it was not my place to ask about the degree to which she did or did not assimilate Ms. Wyndl's material life into her own. Given the fact that what she knew of me was clouded by our working hierarchy, she almost certainly would have found such a question an impertinent invasion of privacy. We were ever in one another's periphery, but direct contact had to do with work, not casual acquaintance, and certainly not friendship. Our proximity in the car thus unnerved me.

After a minute, Annelie said, "What I meant was … okay look, I met a lot of different people out there who didn't feel hemmed into what they had been born into. A lot of really poor people attended Prince of Wales, for example. Smart people, but with not one salty dime. Wearing clothes short in the sleeves and hems. Bits they'd had for years. Were they embarrassed? Maybe. But they were in class each day, and took their place at the study carrels like everyone else and went to matches and film nights and all that stuff."

"And well-to-do hotel heiresses? Were there enough of those?"

Annelie's brow fell. We passed two kilometer markers in rapid succession, then a third, as she pressed her foot down on the gas.

"Was that not the right place for me to come up with something?" I asked, smiling. It felt good to cast a shot across her bow. I did not want to aggravate her, but to draw her out.

"Just because a woman has had certain advantages does not mean that she is not entitled to choose her own path."

"And yet here you are."

Annelie said nothing, but it was not an angry silence. Her expression drew flat and she began to nibble lightly at her bottom lip.

"I considered going back, you know. That first night, after we met in the office, I went up to Lottie's room and sat on her bed and just looked around at all her stuff and how she had the room arranged. It had been a long time since she had allowed me into her room. I must have been twelve the last time. But nothing was different. Maybe a new nightgown over the peg in the closet. New towels drying over the radiator. But everything else was exactly the same. Right down to how she organized her vanity. It was like by stepping through the door to her room I was stepping out of the time machine from that book. Do you know which book I mean?"

"Yes. H.G. Wells. *The Island of Dr. Moreau* is my all-time favorite novel. He wrote that, too."

"I don't know that one."

"Would you like me to tell you about it?"

"I would just feel obliged to read it."

"That's alright."

Annelie turned her face to me in full.

"Are you interested in what I have to say? All I asked was did you know what I was referring to? Yes or no question."

"You're right. Go ahead."

Annelie turned her eyes back to the road. "I chose to stay here because Myron asked me to. That's what I told myself. Because Myron needed me to run things for him. He's my uncle and I had to help, right?"

181

"It makes sense. I don't think Myron would much like doing it himself."

"No, he would not. So, I caved. But not really."

Annelie looked back over her shoulder to check for cars behind us, then signaled us to a stop at the side of the road. She depressed the parking brake but left the engine running.

"Myron's asking me to stay is not why I have. I agreed because what I discovered at school was that I did not want another kind of life. I did not wish to teach or work in an office or become someone's homemaker or run a boutique or anything else. I wanted to run the Manse Calvo. I had to go all the way over there to finally, really figure that out. The future waiting for me was precisely the future, it turns out, I wanted. And everything I absorbed while I was away was meant to — now don't laugh — it was meant to enrich me. To open me up to things I could take pleasure in and have regard for, like art and books. But also the life I wanted to come back to."

Annelie paused and looked out the window.

"I was a semester from graduating when Lottie died. I was coming back here after I graduated anyway. I had figured things out already. I saw little reason to go through the motion of risking the ferry back to PEI for a slip of paper. I'm not particularly afraid of all that business you hear about U-boats shelling passenger ferries, but I know it happens, or has happened. Besides, going over there in the first place was never about getting a degree. Which, if you recall, I explained the night we met. It was about the opportunity to make a decision."

The thin ring of gold in her hazel eyes flickered like a hint of light off water. I was bespelled. I don't think that's a word, but it is correct nonetheless. I was bespelled by her. All I could say was that she had made a very good decision. That seemed to satisfy her. She shifted the car into drive and regained the road.

We passed the next half-hour in agreeable silence.

The Truro market was busy when we arrived. Such markets commonly open at sunrise and we were hours past that. I was concerned there wouldn't be much of a selection left to us, but Annelie had mooted that before we even left the Manse by putting in a few phone calls. We stopped at four stalls, one after another. Annelie introduced herself, shook hands, and almost immediately palettes of crops were wheeled to our car. Annelie paid each of the sellers from a fold of money she kept tucked in the front pocket of her slacks. In all, the business took an hour and we were then free to stroll around the village.

"There's a little shop on the main road that has a luncheon counter," Annelie said. "We just have to make sure we're on the road no later than three so that we return before the dinner service prep."

We walked through the rows of tents and tables, crossed a gravel-packed road, and passed through a recently razed field, beyond which lay a paved street of one- and two-story buildings.

The luncheonette was the size and shape of a large hut, paneled in clapboard painted bright yellow. Inside, the counter was a raw wood board overlaid by a panel of thick glass and fronted by four stools bolted in a row into the tile floor. We were the only customers. The menu was a blackboard hanging by a nail over the counter. It listed six plated dishes, as well as coffee and bottled Coca-Cola.

"What do you recommend?" I asked as we took our seats.

"I recall their coffee being pretty good," Annelie said. "I've never had their food, but if you like coffee I don't think you'll be disappointed."

Annelie ordered a ham and egg roll, and I chose the fish sandwich with pepper mayonnaise. We both ordered coffees. The woman who delivered our food left us a small metal carafe by which to refresh our cups ourselves, then removed herself to the far end of the countertop, where a smoldering cigarette and fanned-open newspaper waited.

The fish sandwich was quite good and I was finished before Annelie had gone half way through her roll.

"It's like you solved a puzzle with your mouth," Annelie said. "That's how you get indigestion, you know."

"I missed breakfast this morning."

"Order another. We're on the Manse's dime. This time chew it properly. You might enjoy it."

"I enjoyed it just fine. Haven't you ever been so hungry that you didn't realize how hungry you were until you finally ate something?"

"Of course." Annelie looked into her coffee. "I don't mean to be punchy. I'm just used to not caring if someone dislikes what I have to say."

"I think you enjoy being argumentative."

Annelie smiled. "Could be."

"That's not a compliment," I said. "Conversations end when they turn into banter."

"Now who sounds like Lottie?"

I laughed.

"All right," Annelie went on. "No banter. Direct question. How come you didn't sign up for service when the war broke out? You were of age. In decent shape, I assume. Is it because they would have taken you?"

"No." The truth was more embarrassing than cowardly. "It never occurred to me that military service was ever an option. I was going through some things and I guess I was lost in my own little world."

"It's a *war*. There are no little worlds anymore." Annelie cut her eyes to slits. "What were these things you were going through? Was this when your parents died?"

I had forgotten that Ms. Wyndl had made mention of my situation in her letters to Annelie. I said so.

"Just the fact of it," Annelie reminded me. "She didn't fill in the details."

I wanted to forge a closeness with her, yet I did not want to use the story of my parents' death to insinuate myself into her graces. Perhaps that's being too hard on myself. How else do human beings interrelate, after all, if not through commiseration?

I left out some of the starker details — the flecks on Abigail Evry's dress in the *Herald*'s photograph; the supposition of what propelled them there — but I did go further than the event. I described the months of solitude that followed, and the intervention of Dr. Hapstrath, which led to my attendance at Dalhousie.

"It's funny to think, but if Dr. Hapstrath had recommended I join up rather than go to college, I probably would have done it. He wasn't a particularly persuasive personality, but his kindness was persuasive."

"I knew him," Annelie said. "Well, of him anyway. My uncle was an acquaintance. They were both members of the same social club. The Collier Club."

"I've never heard of it."

"It's very hoity-toity. Knife-creased trouser-wearers only." Annelie refreshed our coffee cups. "My father was a member, too. My grandfather was sort of one of the founders. The club, so it goes, had been around for a decade and wasn't taken very seriously. Then Morton Calvo was asked to join. The Great Morton Calvo. His name and the money he put into making it — I don't know what the right word would be — *gentlemanly*, I suppose, turned the place around. Its blue-blood heart has been beating ever since."

"I can't imagine Dr. Hapstrath as the type."

"Well, he was your father's contemporary, not yours. It's not the sort of thing someone discusses with a teenager."

"Fair point."

"Do you think your father was a member, too?"

"I doubt it. He never would have been able to justify the dues to my mother."

"I could ask Myron."

"I don't really want to know. It wouldn't have any bearing on my memory of him."

The waitress sauntered over to us in a faint cloud of cigarette smoke and asked if we wanted anything else. Even though the shop was empty but for Annelie and I, her tone suggested that unless we were still hungry, it was best to pay up and leave.

Annelie deliberately ignored the woman's wearied expression, but thanked her with saccharine politeness, asked for a Coca-Cola to go, and paid the tab just the same.

We stepped outside to the tinkle of the overhead bell. I checked my watch. Half past two. What heat the day held had now vanished, leaving the air brisk, accenting the coffee hum jangling my nerves.

"Where to next?" I asked.

Annelie grabbed my wrist, turned it over, and checked the time.

"Back to the car. The food will start to smell if we don't get it back. We'll have to drive with the windows down awhile as it is."

"Thank you for lunch," I said. "The sandwich was very good."

"It must have been, you ate it fast enough."

"Tell you what—ask me something. Anything. Something I couldn't possibly be clever about."

Annelie rolled down the window as we moved off the gravel road out of Truro and onto the paved highway. The wind tossed a lock of hair across her neck like a scarf.

"Alright. How do you remember your parents? I mean, what do you think about when you think of them, since —?"

"Since I don't have memories of them. Of being with them."

"Is it from photographs? I suppose Myron and Ms. Wyndl told you a lot about them."

"They did, but it's difficult to separate what's true from what's the best thing to tell a little girl so she grows up thinking her parents were really good people. Not that they were bad, or that Lottie and Myron lied to me. But no one's a saint. My father was a bit of a social climber and was always worried about proving something to my

187

grandfather. He never got to outgrow that part of himself. Of course, no one told me that. I learned how to read between the lines as I got older. My mother knew what she was doing by marrying a Calvo. She certainly loved my father, I'm sure, but the money and privilege must have made it that much easier.

"I was maybe eight when I began to invent things about them. Call it a coping mechanism. Odd that I would need to cope with something I never knew I was missing, but that's how it was. I would imagine what they were like. Not based on how they looked, but how they looked in my mind, which was a little different than in pictures. I gave them the voices and opinions I wanted them to have. At night, I carried on whispered conversations with them under the blanket. I played all three sides. Made up meaningless and easily solved arguments, shared details about school, told them about the odd-looking guests we had. I also let them know I was healthy and that Lottie and my uncle were looking after me and all that. I liked to imagine they were concerned about that a lot, because I somehow never felt they could *see* me. It all felt very normal. Some children have imaginary friends, right? Most only-child children."

"I did, until I was about nine."

"What was his name?"

"Henry. I called him Hank. I think I just liked saying Hank."

"Did you go on adventures together?"

"We mostly talked about books."

"I can see that! Little Walek tucked under the covers, book on his knees, talking to the wall about whether the writing was any good."

"Under the brave eye of the flashlight."

"I think it's wonderful."

For a beat, a single second, she took my hand in hers, gave it a tight squeeze, then let go. I felt a sudden ache at how unfair it was that I'd had a relative lifetime with my parents, while she was left to dress up ghosts.

"I didn't have an imaginary friend," she went on. "I had imaginary parents. I could not have *the* Aaron and Tilde Calvo, so instead, when I needed them, I made *my* Aaron and Tilde. They were as real to me as the clothes on my body."

"Do you still, you know, talk to them?"

"I'll never tell." A smile. An eye arched in mischief. She pushed her elbow into my side, as we buzzed across the steel-grid bridge over the Stewiacke River. "Hey, by the way, that book you mentioned before. The one by the guy who wrote about the time machine."

"*The Island of Dr. Moreau.*"

"Can I borrow it sometime? I'd like to know what the big deal is with it."

It had always been my impression that sadness betrayed the truest beauty in a woman's face. Perhaps it was the result of seeing so many cinematic melodramas. Every actress knew how to break off a facile, gleaming sparkle of happiness. Big teeth, wide eyes, the whole thing. They all could do it, even the poorly trained ones. It didn't seem so hard to do. But break the heart, close the little shop, murder the lover or father or, hell, the dog, and what poured forth was a shimmering rawness almost lewd in its desperate honesty.

In this I was suddenly wrong.

The face before me, inquisitive, eager, fully aware of my attraction (it was impossible she didn't see it), lit the very air around us.

The kitchen staff was in action when we arrived back at the Manse. Fenella came outside to meet us.

As we stepped out of the car, Annelie whispered, "Could you handle this?"

I nodded. After two coffees and a Coca-Cola, I figured she needed the WC.

Annelie and Fenella exchanged a few quiet words, punctuated by a brief chorus of laughter, then Annelie disappeared inside.

"So how was it?" Fenella asked.

"Nice. The drive was nice. Truro isn't much, though."

"And Annelie?"

"We talked quite a bit."

"And is she much, would you say?"

I scoffed. "I don't know where you get your ideas, Fenella. We'll need a wheelbarrow for this corn. I'll run and get it."

"You do that, but you're not fooling anyone. Find a mirror when you get inside. You're red as a beet."

xii. <u>Messages</u>

ONE WEEKEND IN OCTOBER 1942, the Manse
Calvo half-booked and absent any event requiring
a houseman, I took a few days' leave in Parrsboro.
I rented a small waterfront cottage. No particular
reason impelled this little holiday. I had yet to take
a planned day off in the term of my employment
and simply felt it was time. Fall seemed right. I
wished to read and walk, to sleep at odd hours if I
so chose, and to generally not be responsible for
anything at all. Those anonymous four days
fulfilled my every criterion.

Upon my return, I entered the house via the
rear galley door, in search of an iced tea after a
parched five-hour bus ride, to find a short stack of
white cards sitting on the kitchen counter, each
reading:

> IT IS FORBIDDEN TO MENTION SHIPS OR
> SHIP MOVEMENTS, AIRCRAFT, TROOPS,
> WAR INDUSTRIES, OR THE WEATHER
> DURING LONG-DISTANCE TELEPHONE
> CONVERSATIONS.

Beside the stack was a note addressed to me
that read:

> *Please swap the old ones out when you have*
> *a chance.*
> *By order of HMG, ha ha ha.*
> *Thnx, Annelie*

191

At the outset of the war, such cards had been installed in every room and beside every telephone in the Manse's public areas, as well as in the manager's office, by direct order of Myron Calvo. That earlier iteration, however, had been simpler, stating almost playfully: LOOSE LIPS SINK SHIPS — REMEMBER! It took me a moment to figure out that HMG stood for His Majesty's Government, a jab at the British sovereignty of Canada. My next thought was, *well, I guess we allow long-distance calls on our guest phones now*, something the Manse had theretofore restricted as we had no reliable means of tracking or assessing the associated charges to a given room.

The door from the dining room opened and I was greeted — well, less greeted than accosted with brief salutation — by Fenella O'Dwyre.

"Hey, glad you're back," she breathed at me. "Venish's gone. Annelie sent him packing."

I set my case down on the floor and looked at Fenella in vague disbelief. I had never heard of a single person having been fired in the Manse's entire history. Had there been, Ms. Wyndl no doubt would have informed me of it at my interview.

"Don't pull a face. I'm telling you, *fired*. And you won't believe why."

"I'm sure I won't. But tell me anyway."

Fenella was flushed and grinning expansively. She looked as I imagine she might have looked as a girl after having been kissed for the first time.

"Bootlegging! When Annelie came into the kitchen and made the announcement, I thought it was some sort of prank. You probably don't know this, but we've been having to up our booze orders the last six months. At first it wasn't much. A case here, a case there. Sometimes whiskey, sometimes gin. Sometimes beers. I figured some of the staff were pouring too generously, and of course everyone has a sip of their own. I don't judge them for that. I do it, too. It's to be expected and a smart manager plans for it. But this past month we had to order in twice as much as usual and bookings haven't exactly been stellar, you know. There were none while you were on holiday."

"That's sort of why I decided to go," I said.

"Funny then that two cases of scotch and a rack of bottled beer were consumed."

"So, he'd been selling it?"

"From the registration desk on overnights. I guess Annelie told him to consider what he took as severance."

"I wish I had been there to hear her say that."

"Me, too. I'm sorry I missed it. And he was such an idiot about it, too. It takes us months sometimes to go through a full case of scotch."

"So, what are we going to do for an overnight clerk now?"

"Search me. Annelie said something about leaving the desk unmanned overnight and just having the desk phone redirected to her room. For emergencies, you know."

"I'm surprised she would go for that."

"Ditto."

"This is actually the second strange occurrence I've witnessed since I stepped through the door."

"You *just* walked in, Walek."

I pointed to the stack of cards on the countertop.

"Oh, right," Fenella said. "Annelie wanted those put up. They're in all the rooms. I took care of it for you. Public areas, too. These are extras, which you should probably hold onto, in case they're needed. I guess we're a little behind the times. These should have gone up last year. Not that it's even a big deal. A little sign by the phone telling people something everyone already knows. The old ones at least a kid could understand."

"I'm surprised we allow long-distance from our phones."

"Right! Since when do we do that?" She shook her head. "What a valuable use of time putting all those up." She made a feigned gesture to pull the sign down from the phone but then dropped her hand into the pocket of her blouse. "So, how was your trip?"

"Parrsboro is very quaint. I read two books, cover to cover."

"Sounds like so much fun," she teased. "Are you hungry? I can throw something together for you."

I thanked her but declined. My legs were stiff from the hours on the bus. Now that I had been standing for a bit, my muscles began to rebel. I forgot my desire for an iced tea. I wanted my room, my bathtub, and my bed, in that order. I agreed to meet her in the galley that night per usual to catch Lorne Greene on the wireless.

I took up my suitcase and shuffled up the back staircase to my room, where on the coffee table in the sitting room area, an old friend awaited me.

A piece of hotel stationery that showed inky thumbing at one of its edges was affixed to the top cover edge of *The Island of Dr. Moreau* by a small metal paperclip. It read:

> *I liked it fine. The chase scenes were terrifying. Those dark woods. That*

*stretch of beach must have felt like a
shooting range. I can see why a boy
would come to love this book.*

*I have now read two books by this
author (the time travel one was not
nearly so entertaining as this), and while
I am not an authority on the merits of
storytelling, the sentence underlined (in
pencil, please don't be mad) sums up
what I feel he was really getting at.
What maybe all writers are getting
at…? I don't think he expects us to buy
the science, but then he's after the soul
anyway, wouldn't you say?*

*Thank you for loaning it to me for so
long, and for not bugging me to give it
back until I was ready.*
　　　　　—Annelie

I turned through the pages and found, on
page 106, the following line underscored by a faint
trace of lead: "Sometimes I rise above my level,
sometimes I fall below it, but always I fall short of
the things I dream." It was a curious choice. A
piece of dialogue spoken by Dr. Moreau, referring
to the plethora of near but not absolute successes
he had made of transmogrifying animals into
humanoid versions. It was a heady and cruel
remark, spoken with the whimsy of a poet
reflecting on the insufficiency of language to carry
the weight of his artistic ambition.

I sat down on the bed and held the book open
on my lap, wondering what Annelie might have
really been trying to tell me. I did not think it was
merely that this bit of dialogue served as

synecdoche for, as she alluded in her letter, "what all writers are getting at," though it served nicely as a synecdoche for the book itself. My first impulse was, of course, to superimpose a romantic tint on the language, but this I quickly quashed in favor of an alternate possibility: that what she meant to show me was not that *she* had unattained things for which she yearned, but rather that *I*, in her estimation, did. And this thought drove me back to the romantic question I had only just dismissed. In short: Annelie was telling me she was aware of my affections — and what's more, she did not wish to dissuade them.

But I could not speak with her of this, I felt; it would violate the bounds her method of communication had established. She had not spoken to me directly, but left a note. Put her mark in an object she knew to contain particular meaning to me. Yet, this swatch of text *was* some kind of overture, was it not? An arrow of intent?

I looked out the window. The leaves were gone from the trees, and the ground was littered, meaning much of this molting had occurred during my time away. As I was technically back on the clock, I decided I had better get going on the collection before the winds picked up, as they would come night.

Leaving my case unpacked, I went directly to the shed, retrieved the yard implements, and gave the afternoon to a good rake-up.

That night I met Annelie in the manager's office. Our conversation was friendly and fairly on the surface. She was direct and forthcoming about Tory Venish; I didn't even have to bring it up. She asked about my trip and I gave her a bare-bones account of Parrsboro's landscape, forgoing mention of the two books I had completed while there as it might too readily segue into a discussion of her note. Leaving it at that, I went to bed.

In the weeks that followed, as I fell back into my workaday life, there seemed, day by day, less of a pressing need to cleverly respond to Annelie's overture, if that's even what it was. I grew, by the day, less sure.

This lack of surety was eliminated altogether, however, when I finally discovered, two months later, her second message.

The New Year's weekend's lone booking was a small family reunion in the dining room. Fifteen guests. Single table setting. The food had been prearranged from a local delicatessen, which I was informed was owned by one of the attending family members. The kitchen staff was dismissed for the night. Fenella and I simply served and cleared. The group was gone by 11 p.m., I assumed to celebrate the chimes of midnight in their own homes, and our few rooming guests had by then gathered in the Aaron Salon, where Fenella oversaw a small complimentary wet bar.

Annelie was off-grounds. She had decided to spend the weekend at Myron's house, where her uncle was recovering from a surgery to correct some degradation in his left knee. Annelie volunteered to assist him in his recovery exercises and to more or less keep house until his regular girl returned from her own holidays after the start of the new year.

Once the dining room was put to its usual rights, my responsibility ended, both for the night and, really, for the year. I shared a drink with Fenella in the Aaron and watched the clock count down the final seconds into 1943. (We shared a chaste, thin-lipped kiss.) Then I excused myself and went up to my quarters, where I planned to devote the twilight hours to a small project: the cleaning of my book collection.

My personal library then ran to fifty-three books. A modest collection, about one-half of which had been saved from my liquidation of the house on Pepperell Street. The other half had been acquired piecemeal and with deliberation since I came on at the Manse Calvo. I was a habitual re-reader. I adamantly believed that true reading lay in reengagement with a given story. (My father used to say, "Better to know ten books intimately than a thousand superficially.") Thus, I was careful about what books I accumulated. I had read nearly all the volumes held in the Tilde Salon, and that limited collection acted as a sort of testing ground, much as the Sackville Street Library had in my youth, for titles I might wish to add to my permanent collection. A Modern Library edition of Bram Stoker's *Dracula* I acquired in Parrsboro, which became book fifty-three, is a perfect example. The Tilde held an illustrated edition of the novel, which was, as to be expected, abridged. But I had read it, found it excellent (despite its prolixity), and it whetted my appetite for the real thing.

I had had a limited list of people to gift during the recent holidays — Myron, who as scion of the hotel would expect a gift from every employee (I bought him a fifth of scotch); Fenella, for whom I purchased a portable record player secondhand and a copy of Rachmaninoff's recording of selected works by Frederic Chopin, which I felt might relax her at the end of a long day; and Annelie, to whom, knowing she loved books, I gave recent printings of Virginia Woolf's *To the Lighthouse* and Edith Wharton's *Custom of the*

Country, which I myself had not read but knew of. (She gave me a copy of *The Time Machine* in a fine jacketless faux-leather edition that retained W.A. Dwiggins' unusual art-deco illustrations from the 1930s.) Because of this modest taxation on my budget, I was able to justify giving myself a gift, too. An extravagance, but the outlay would, I felt, yield rewards in perpetuity.

From a local shop I purchased a small bellows meant for cleaning out the inside of a camera, basically a miniature rendition of a traditional fireplace bellows, and at an extortionate premium from the manager of the Capital Theatre I procured ten pairs of white usher's gloves. I suppose I might have found something comparable at a men's shop for a fraction of the price I paid, but I bought them "in the moment." Finally, I purchased from the shop in the Dalhousie University Art Gallery a compound called Absorene, a putty-like substance that the label promised was a gentle but effective means of removing dust, dirt scores, mold, and larvae from book pages, covers, and bindings, all without leaving a trace of action. I bought three tubs.

These items, along with a half-pound of ground coffee and a small container of baking soda I pilfered from the Manse Calvo's kitchen, were laid out like a surgeon's implements on the coffee table of my quarters. I set my books in discreet stacks of ten and one of three, and got down to it.

I figured my project would occupy my free time nicely through New Year's Day and night, and hopefully into my birthday the day after. Dull though it may seem, it was my ideal way to ring in the new year — solitude, a fresh and curious task, the presence of my books, and an absence of responsibility.

This was my process, which I am unsure even now is the *correct* methodology but which has nevertheless kept my books in fine shape and given me a pleasurable routine in the years since I first began it: All of my books, with the exception of two, were hardback editions, many with dust covers, and so, as I worked one book at a time, I removed the cover and laid it as flat as possible, without compromising its natural folds, across a dish towel; then I inspected the hardback itself for traces of dirt scoring, the development of mold, or possible mites or larvae; if any were present, I took them away best I could with a torn strip from one of the usher's gloves, then I gently ran a die-size snitch of Absorene over it; if that didn't do the trick, a slightly damp piece of usher's glove followed immediately by a dry piece of the same usually did the trick. Then I searched the book, page by page, for the same invasions. If I found any on the pages that Absorene could not handle, I used a controlled sprinkle of baking soda followed by a draw of dry cloth. This was invariably a success. Once every page was vetted, I laid open the spine and used the bellows to shoot away any accumulation that may have rested between the glue-bind and the interior of the hardback. A few times I had to follow the bellows with a pinky finger wrapped in usher's glove, but this was only to scour the very ends of the binding ribbon. As for the dust cover, I simply went over it, regardless of its visual state, with the Absorene, followed by a draw of dry usher's glove. If a book had an odor, even a slight one, I placed it in an empty shoebox which I had sectioned in two by a wax paper-covered piece of cardstock, the other section of which contained an ounce of coffee grounds milled through an ounce of baking soda.

An hour in the shoebox, lid firmly on, and what odor there was disappeared. In none of my books did I find mold, thank goodness, but I was generous with my criteria for using the baking soda just the same. It was my first try at this discipline and I was, as anyone might be in a trial run, overly cautious.

The first night I cleaned seventeen books before I was too bleary-eyed to continue.

On New Year's Day, I made my rounds and then — since the weather was little more than a chill with neither snow nor sleet and nothing much in the way of wind — gave the afternoon to a prolonged walk through the neighborhoods that skirted Point Pleasant Park. The park itself was empty when I turned into its unlatched gate. The hour I spent strolling the park's unpeopled lanes carried a surreal aspect. I let my mind ooze into a brief disuse, and ran my fingertips over the skeletal branches that framed the walkways. When my nose began to run from the cold, I returned to the Manse Calvo.

I enjoyed a hot bath before appearing downstairs in preparation for the dinner hour. Fenella and I ate our supper together — bologna sandwiches and salads. Our conversation was a loose, lazily hopeful tennis match of resolutions neither of us were certain we would keep in the coming year. We laughed a great deal. I did the washing up so Fenella could take control of the front desk, and after doing a final check of the exits went up to my room, where I resumed my project.

This sequence of events I pretty much mirrored to the minute on my birthday as well. By the time night fell on January 2, 1943, I was cross-legged on the floor of my quarters, with only two books yet uninvestigated. The copy of *The Time*

Machine Annelie had given me required practically no effort; it was a fine copy. I gave it a cursory wipe with a dry piece of usher's glove and set it bedside. I planned to begin reading it that evening.

That left only *The Island of Dr. Moreau.*

All the books that preceded it had required in total only one pair of usher's gloves, a third of the box of baking soda, and about half the coffee I had purloined, the other half of which I planned to quietly return to the canister in the Manse's kitchen pantry. I had also discarded approximately one-half of one tub of Absorene. The tubs were only about the size of coffee cups; I was gratified that the stuff could be made to stretch its usefulness so well.

I had purchased a bottle of pinot noir as a means of toasting what I hoped would be the success of a well-done project. It awaited me on the sideboard as I set the dust cover of *Moreau* on the tea towel and went about my usual process.

There was no accumulation in the space between the hardback and the glue-bind and ribbon, and the page ends, though thumbed to an almost waxy smoothness, remained fairly white, taking on a mild creamy aspect, but not so as you might notice, unless you were scouring the book for flaws, as I was. On my page-by-page examination, I began at the back and worked my way forward. As a left-hander, this was simply the means by which I could exercise the best control over the turning of the pages. Because of this back-to-front process, Annelie's inscription, which was made on the blank side of the book's title page in the same faint pencil lead as her underlining of Dr. Moreau's dialogue, came as a complete surprise — and a final one, for though it was the first leaf of the book, it was the last page I flipped to.

What she wrote was: *I know I can tell you, but if only I could.*

I had no idea what to make of this. She knew she could tell me what? And so knowing, what kept her from doing so?

I turned these words over in my mind until I could no longer keep my eyes open. I eventually drifted to sleep on the couch, the wine forgotten on the sideboard. Before I succumbed, though, I concluded that whatever the intent of her inscription might be, we were now, albeit in an awkwardly removed manner, engaged in a courtship.

xiii. Bit of a Hash is All

DURING THE SPRING AND EARLY SUMMER OF 1943, the business of the Manse Calvo ground nearly to a halt. We were far from alone in this regard. Grocers' shelves throughout the city were close to bare. You could read the desperation on faces in the streets. We had to remove sugar and cream from the tables; we began to provide them only upon request and then in single servings. Bacon and pork all but disappeared, as did sausage. Biscuits were served with every dish, so as to augment the smaller, lighter portions. There were more than the usual number of fish offerings from the Manse's kitchen. It was almost fortunate that we had so few people to feed during those months; revenue was lax, but then so were expenditures. Most of the housekeeping staff was furloughed, and corners were cut by keeping only one oil lamp lit in each of the salons and in the foyer after dark. By the end of April, Myron cut off all advertising. "That well," he said, "has no more echo."

I was left with little to take charge of that summer, except to maintain the status quo of the property, which was easy enough, though I suppose the grass got a bit yellow, the flower beds a bit wilty, and the bocce pitch accumulated more gravel than it ought to have. But despite the stagnancy of this period so far as work went, beneath the surface of hum-drum hours lay my own personal piece of wartime engagement: my aforementioned courtship of Annelie Calvo.

I must explain what I mean by courtship. We went on no official dates. We never kissed. We never so much as held hands. What we did was talk. The strands of friendship, which, no matter what anyone says, outlast the gossamer threads of passion, were woven first. We approached one another with no angle to play, doing things in the proper order. As our conversations moved closer, whispers were sometimes shared, fleeting touches of the wrist, a guiding hand at the small of the back through doorways and around corners and at the cusp of flights of stairs. It was a slow, nervous, and silent dance to which there were no practiced steps.

Funny that I should have no notable exchanges to reconstruct, even though we spoke daily. More than not, it was of work that we spoke, or at least work prefaced the eventual segue into something else. We spoke often of guests and rooms, of course, and the sorry state of our cache of food stuffs, but not always such things. As much as that, we talked over reports that came in both over the wireless and through the current of gossip (*the wind*, my mother would have said) of troop movements, the growing dangers of the seas, of towns seized and towns annexed, as well as local developments — elementary schools that put on renditions of Shakespeare to raise funds for supplies; churches that stopped locking their doors at night to offer sanctuary to the unhoused; shops that closed and were replaced within the week by an entirely different business, yet were still owned and operated by the same undaunted people.

I was as much glad for the gradual pace of our relationship as I was its advocate. I wished more than anything to be near her in whatever circumstance she deemed comfortable. I was desirous, of course. I hoped only that when she was ready, Annelie's signal to me would be clear and strong and deliberate (in a way her *Moreau* messages were not). I was willing to be told how to do things, how to court. One advantage I had was that my ego had no lines to draw.

The first Saturday in August, in a welcome boon, we hosted a wedding reception for the son of a business friend of Myron's.

The day went off without a hitch. It was nearly five in the morning when the last guests finally staggered up to their rooms, and Annelie and I sat at the kitchen island, whiskey sodas nestled in our hands like torches in danger of going out. Annelie had let the rest of the staff go at two, Fenella shortly thereafter. Beyond the dining room window, the pre-dawn sky was a burnished post-rainstorm orange, a striking sight.

The alcohol, rather than temper my nerves after the previous hours' activity, enervated me. I was suddenly more awake than I had been all evening, and so out of the blue, with a casual confidence I was rarely able to summon, I brought up the phrase Annelie had underlined in my book and what she had written in its flyleaf.

"It's pretty late," Annelie said, closing her eyes.

"Or pretty early, depending on how you see it," I said. "I can never seem to find a good time to bring it up, but I'd like to understand, so I'm choosing a bad time, I guess."

Annelie opened her eyes, smiled. "Fair enough. Top us off and I'll tell you."

I replenished our glasses. Annelie sat quietly a moment, as though holding her breath for a deep dive. Then she began.

"I entered Prince of Wales expecting it to be like some kind of novel. Learning for learning's sake. A lot of serious people who didn't waste their time on frivolous things. I don't know where I got that notion. I suppose it was the result of my actually having *no* notion, just a sort of fantastic idea in my mind. And yes, because I can feel you thinking it, I did take myself too seriously. I didn't know any other way to be. Low enrollment made it so that everyone got her own room, which didn't help me break out of my shell. I went the whole first term and through the holidays pretty much floating around in my own little headspace. I liked my classes fine, but there's a difference between getting by and really getting on. So, when the spring term began, I was determined to be a different person, to the degree that I could. I joined a couple of groups, including one that met Friday evenings in a study room in the library basement to plan the end-of-term picnic, which the whole school tends to turn out for, so it was a big deal. All we really did was drink wine we smuggled inside our bookbags and gossip about our instructors and guess about the boys at St. Dunstan's. Obviously, it became my favorite thing. I made a few friends, and it turned out I even shared classes with some of the group. I was becoming part of something. I still had tons of alone time, though. The other girls had their own stuff. I had never been as happy as I was that spring and summer and fall. I felt it was going to be the time I would always turn back to when anyone asked me how I got on at college, or what things were like for me at the start of the war.

"It didn't last, of course. If it had, there'd be nothing to tell, except to gush on about how good it all was. A month or so before the holiday break between terms — this was my second year, now — a few of us broke curfew and took a cab into Charlottetown for a pub hop. You probably don't know Charlottetown but for every shop there's three places to get a drink. For every house, probably, too. Anyway, we eventually wound up at a crummy little place that was tucked into what looked like an old fishing shanty. We met a pack of boys. Locals, not CFAs. At first, we sort of condescended to let them buy us drinks. When I say condescended, I mean it literally. We floated down from our elegant little plinths and deigned to sit with them. We continued to see them occasionally as the term passed, times we snuck away from campus. And we never had to pay for a thing, which we liked. It might not say good things about us, but that's how it goes, right? It's not like they were pouring booze down our throats so that they could convince us to join a church.

"Anyway, I'll get to the point. One of the boys was named Anton. He was shorter than me, with a light raspy voice and really short yellow hair. Not blonde. Yellow, like a doll's. The girls and I privately called him Pooh, because he really did resemble that bear from the children's book. Not too bright upstairs, but sweet-natured. On the Saturday after finals, we were all cutting looser than usual. I had missed supper and it all went to my head pretty quickly. I agreed to take a walk with Anton. It was a warm night and I was feeling a lot warmer from the drink and so the cold air outside was wonderful. Anton got talkative when he drank. While we walked, he gave me a rundown of pretty much his entire life. A sort of summarized version, which ended with the fact that he worked as an apprentice for his father during summer breaks and most weekends while classes were in session. His father was a smith. According to Anton, he was responsible for every pair of handcuffs and leg irons used by the Charlottetown police.

"I admit I was being flirtatious. And why not? I was in control of myself, in my estimation, and he was too nervy to pull some kind of stunt with me. I was a girl away at school and it was my right. I asked if I could see where he and his father made all those shackles and cuffs and whatnot. The smithy was something like ten blocks from the pub, but we were already most of the way there by the time I asked, so it was no big whoop to keep going.

"It was a little storefront that opened out the back to a big wood-framed tent, where all the equipment was kept. Despite the space of it, the air felt very close. It was the kind of denseness that comes with hot metal, I suppose. You can sometimes smell it on a car or train that passes on a really hot day. A burnt smell, but not quite burnt, more like the residue of a burning. Well, whatever that smell is, it was *everywhere* in that shop. After three minutes or so, I couldn't take it anymore and asked to leave. Anton just laughed about me being a sissy and said he wanted to show me something. I followed him into the back of the shop. What he wanted to show me was the door-sized crosshatch of bars his father was making for a paddy wagon. He seemed really proud of them.

"I didn't see a thing of it. My vision was swimming. My head was hot and felt like something soft had broken open. And that was it. I blacked out.

"What woke me up was a clock on the wall striking six. I was lying on the floorboards, curled into a bit of a ball, and right away my head was screaming, but otherwise I didn't feel I was hurt. Not even a bump from falling. My clothes weren't messed up, either. I sat up, expecting to find Anton asleep in a chair. But he wasn't anywhere. The front door was cracked open. Light was coming in the windows. It was morning. I was suddenly terrified about what that meant, his not being there and that door being open. I closed my eyes and tried to bring back what had happened between the time we had walked into the smithy and the moment before I passed out, but my eyes were burning and I couldn't think. He probably just got scared and left when he couldn't snap me out of it. Or so I told myself. Or maybe he went back to get my friends. I couldn't remember how late was it that we left the pub. Maybe it was late enough to have been close to morning, and he would be back any second with the girls in tow. Then all of us could drag our heavy heads to a cab stand and go on back to school.

"I stood up and that seemed to help my head a little. But then I felt it … running down. And I knew.

"I've never been so scared, Walek. Never in my life. I threw up right there on the floor. I used the smithy's filthy toilet to clean myself. I found a towel in a cabinet and used that. When I was done, I cleaned myself a second time. Then I threw up again. That seemed to kill most of the headache. I didn't bother cleaning up the mess I had made on the floor. I would let him explain that to his father, if he could.

"My friends all assumed that something had happened. Something deliberate, I mean. Deliberate on my part. I didn't correct them. I didn't want to talk about it. I was slated for two classes that summer, because perpetual enrollment let me keep my room year-round. I was also meant to work in the administration office, typing forms and putting together the fall mailing list for new students and alumni. I didn't change anything. I let the summer pass like it wasn't part of the regular flow of time. At night, I did my reading and wrote my papers. For about a week, I tried using liquor to get to sleep. I thought I would need it from nerves, but it didn't work. It just kept me awake, and annoyed that I was awake. So, I stopped drinking altogether. Sleep returned. I suppose there was a numbness there I wasn't willing to pick at, like a scab you just know will bleed if you fuss with it. In an odd way, I didn't even really feel violated. I didn't remember *anything*. There were even a few nights when I felt like nothing had happened at all, that I made the whole thing up in my mind. That it had been sweat drooling down my leg that morning. Those were weird nights, let me tell you. Lying in bed, wondering why I was making such a big deal of everything in my mind. I can't believe I ever really thought that.

"Before fall term started, I took a bus into town and went to the smithy. I was finally ready to confront him. I figured that since St. Dunstan's had not started up yet either, there was a good chance Anton would be there. But he wasn't. Turns out he wasn't even on the island anymore. He had signed up and gone to Sheffield for training. I spoke to his father. When he told me about the enlistment, Walek, the pride on his face — how could I tell him the real reason his son had suddenly acted on a swell of duty and honor? I told him I was a friend of a girl who was too shy to come herself. I gave a fake name and left.

"On the bus back to the college, I had a good cry, and I'm not one for that. But by the time I was back in my room, whatever anger I felt was gone and sadness had taken its place.

"A couple nights later, I told a girl named Marne what happened. She belonged to our little group. She was also, if her stories were to be believed, the most experienced with boys. I thought she might be my best chance at empathy. She was patient as I went on and on, like I've been doing tonight — I thought it was patience anyway. But then I caught her looking at the clock on my nightstand, and I knew she neither cared nor was surprised by what I was telling her. I said so. And she said, 'Bit of a hash is all,' and cocked her head to the side, the way you do when you're trying stupidly to talk to a dog or a baby.

"What those six words were meant to impress upon me was that what had happened was not important. Nothing to be concerned about — to have *ever been* concerned about. I couldn't remember anything and so what was the point of even thinking about what I couldn't really, actually think about? It practically didn't happen. She promised that she would help me find someone nice the next time we went out. As though the solution would be to have intercourse with my eyes *open*."

Annelie took her drink at a draught and let the glass almost fall from her hand onto the table. It landed with a hollow thud on the tablecloth.

"Do I need to explain she and I never spoke again? I dropped out of that group, too. I went back to the life I had led my first year. Going it alone. Keeping focused on my studies. It worked. I felt self-possessed again. As for visits and holidays and all that, I wasn't afraid, or ashamed. I just wished to keep on going with the life I was living. The life I had control over. In my letters to Lottie and my uncle, I used the U-boat danger as an excuse. It was perfectly reasonable. Neither of them questioned it. I wanted very much to tell Lottie everything, but a letter was not the place for it. As I think I told you already, I was planning to come back once I graduated. I figured I could tell her then, personally. But of course, that didn't happen, and maybe it's for the best. She would have raged, but it would have made her feel useless and that would have been cruel of me.

"On the ferry coming over for Lottie's funeral, everyone sat silently out of fear that a lot of chatter might be picked up by a submarine lurking below. I thought about my time away, and how what Marne had said would stand for everything that would *not* define me. I would not deviate from my intentions. I wouldn't shy from feeling my awkward way through things. I would not be defined by bad things. I would define myself. That's really, I guess, why that phrase in your book spoke to me. I saw striving in those words, a never-ending struggle for self-truth. I know Moreau was mad, but there's a little piece of me, maybe of everyone, that's mad, don't you think? I think hope is mad. Regret can be mad. Maybe I was hoping you would ask me about it and I would have the guts to tell you all I just told you. You waited *so* long. I suppose I'm grateful for that. You are important to me, Walek. I found a little part of something important to you that spoke to me, so that you would know this about me."

I moved not a muscle, raised not an eyebrow or corner of the mouth. I just looked at her. More fully than I ever had before. I tried to grasp the singularity of the moment. It was in more than the story she had told.

Finally, I said, "I know you don't want pity or melodrama, but I will say, for that phrase you chose, for why you chose it, I know that feeling too. I know it very well now, and I agree."

Few are the arrows we take in life willingly. The most welcome I ever allowed to pierce me was the expression of affection and relief that held Annelie's face after I spoke those words.

xiv. <u>A Known Secret</u>

MYRON ARRIVED AT THE MANSE on August 9, 1943 in dapper form. He wore a fine gray worsted suit, offset by a bold red tie and matching suspenders, which flared like ribbons beneath his unbuttoned jacket. His shoes held a shine. A curiously mischievous glow hung about him as though he had just trounced merrily from the bedroom of some friendly local spinster. He even wore a hat, unusual for him, because he was so plainly vain about his thick brown-black hair.

"This is a day not to be wasted indoors," he declared, standing before Annelie and me at the reception desk, a few minutes past eight in the morning. "Both of you, slap on something smart and be back down here in ten minutes. I will speak to the kitchen girl, what's her name, about taking care of things up here for a little while."

"Fenella is her name, and since I am in charge of this desk and this house, I don't see how you can walk in here like the last person to leave the party and tell me what's what."

Annelie kept a thin smile as she spoke. It was not a show of covert anger, but amusement spiked with her usual readiness.

Myron smiled broadly. "Go and get changed. I will speak with Ella."

"*Fen*ella," Annelie repeated.

Myron, ignoring the correction, moved swiftly away, in the direction of the galley.

Before Myron stormed the foyer, Annelie and I had been going over the day's planning. We had gotten no further than *follow up that breakfast has been broken down and the dining room readied for the lunch service*, which was scribbled in a slanting, slashing hand on a slip of paper that lay flat atop the reception counter under the palm of Annelie's hand. But something about Myron's mood got hold of me — the presumption of his order to us, that we would willingly follow it. I slid the slip of paper away from her, picked it up, and folded it into a neat square that fit into the breast pocket of my work shirt.

"If we don't talk about it, then does it really even exist?" I said.

"Right. I'm that easy?"

"You tell me."

Annelie held a sigh, then blew it across the desk in mock frustration. "I can't imagine what the big deal is anyway."

"It must be something specific. Not just a walk through the Gardens."

"Can't guess."

"He's not losing his marbles, do you think?"

"There's a better chance of you losing yours."

Annelie thought a moment then gave her head a little shake, as to clear her ears of a sudden ringing sensation.

"Fine," she said. "We'll tag along, though what the hell he expects me to look like, I don't care about. I'm wearing this. If I decide my time is being wasted by this whatever it is, I can come right back here, right to this spot, without stopping. You can go powder your nose if you like." She softened the tone of her words with a brush of her fingers over my nose and mouth.

I went upstairs and changed out of my work clothes. I didn't own anything that would stand up to Myron's standards, so I figured I might as well be comfortable. Flannel trousers and a blue sweater over a plain white oxford. I ran a wet comb through my hair.

When I returned to the lobby, Myron was already leading Annelie out the front door.

It was a typical Monday in Halifax. Lots of foot traffic. The Birney rail cars hooting, sliding past. A general sense of doing was in the air, everyone with a destination, someplace they needed to be. Even, it seemed, us.

On Water Street, the remarks began to pour from Annelie.

"We're not going to a pub, are we? Or to some handshake-and-smile gathering for your little men's club? It's too damn early. Coffee is what's called for, yes? ... Have you bought another hotel? Is that what this is about? ... If this is some kind of nostalgia visit, I'm going to kick you ... Myron, have you met a lady friend? Because you can just tell me. I'll be happy for you no matter what."

To each, Myron shook his head but did not break his gait. I kept quiet, happy to be out of doors. It was a fine morning with very few clouds, and the breeze off the harbour, though it carried some of the day's rising warmth, brought also the briny smack of the sea.

Then, as we turned off Water Street down a narrow alley and onto the wood-planked walk of the wharf, Annelie's patience timed out.

"All right, uncle, I'm done walking. What's the idea?" Annelie's forehead was sheened in sweat. I was holding her discarded cardigan sweater. Her shoulders set back as she spoke, like a bird in preparation for flight. "Explain what in hell we're doing, or Walek and I are going back. Whether you know it or not, there is actually a lot

217

to do today, and I don't like having one of my staff taking the brunt of my responsibilities on a whim like this. Fenella probably thinks you're still in charge, the way you slammed into the kitchen and told her how it is."

Before either Myron could answer her or she could renew her harangue, we emerged from the alley to the sight of a large steamship that had taken slip dockside. The plank had yet to be let down, and from our position on the far side of the walking path, I could see that the water was only just starting to calm. Painted in bold black along the upper side, the words *QUEEN MARY*.

It was the most immense object I had seen in my life. The forecastle alone seemed as voluminous in area as a soccer pitch. At quick count, there were eight visible levels within the ship, or at least eight had windows or portholes running the line of the port side. Above the uppermost deck, flanking the three enormous steam vents, were rows of lifeboats, strung like holiday lights, covered crisply with thick tarpaulins. I supposed there were unseen decks as well, where the machinations of the ship's propulsion lay. I could only imagine what bestial workings were hidden deep in the ship's guts, but three huge cylindrical vents, painted in red and white, rising out of the ship's decks and breathing a dragon's breath of steam and burnt coal, gave some indication.

"Now do you forgive me?" Myron, standing erect as a minister, had to shout over the static activity of the ship and the sudden chorus of cheers from the dock workers and gathering throng of uniformed sailors as the plank began to slowly be lowered.

Annelie burst out laughing. I caught the transformation of her face just as it broke, and the moment turned into an occasion of pure joy. It was the kind of unselfconscious display that life weans you off of as you grow older. Here was a glimpse at what I believed to be a ten-year-old Annelie, through whose eyes registered a new toy or an arrangement of clouds that suggested a shape known only to her. This amalgamation of childlike and mature made me feel that perhaps youth never really leaves us; it just gets a bit stubborn about what's worth stepping out for.

A group of men passed before us and walked briskly down the dock toward the ship, coming to formation alongside the plank as it settled on the platform. A young man stepped forward in attention at the hatch above. He produced a small silver whistle and gave it one long draw. A few seconds later, passengers began to emerge from the exitway. Military officers for the most part, their uniforms looking newly pressed, their bodies composed and moving with confidence.

A dozen such men descended the plank and were milling about on the dock before the true purpose of the *Queen Mary*'s presence was finally made clear.

His wife descended first. I knew from the papers her name was Clementine. She appeared every inch the aristocrat. Her clothes were very fine, if slightly ostentatious. Her hair sat in coils pinned up into a lacy hat accented by bright pink flowers. She was not exactly pretty but there was an energy to her face that seemed both difficult to look away from and slightly discomfiting to take in. She guided her daughter, who wore her father's famous brooding set of mouth and lumbering roll of the shoulders, down the plank and took the

219

hand of an officer as she made the final step down to the dock.

Then — Winston Churchill, like a director who only steps onstage once the players have soaked in their applause, stood at the mouth of the ship's exitway, turning his eyes to the city rising in front of him, before finally, preceded at each step by a thin black cane, descending. He was a striking figure. Fully a head shorter than the least member of his contingence and with a stocky body that seemed to swim slightly within his clothes, Churchill nonetheless exuded an imperial confidence, meeting with a flash of barely restrained curiosity each set of eyes he passed.

The three of us became swept up in the crowd of passersby which developed now that, like a strike of lightning, word got round of who the *Queen Mary* had brought into port. We moved into the flow of bodies, and once the Churchills' envoy had everyone corralled and heading away from the ship to a row of cars that stood ready off Lower Water Street, we found ourselves shoulder to shoulder at the very front of what had become an impromptu receiving line.

As they passed, the Churchills gave off respective attitudes. The young girl looked exhausted, perhaps a bit sea-sickened. Clementine Churchill held her nose in the air, but she did not give off an arrogant caste; rather, she looked full of pride, a poised and practiced politician's wife. I caught Myron in the corner of my eye and saw he was beaming with flushed cheeks at her. And that was when the prime minister himself passed us, close enough to see the wind-scored end of an unlit cigar, like a bit of frayed rope, clenched in his maw, and Myron's eager flush met with Winston Churchill's amused, unruffled demeanor. Here was a man used to having other men blush in the presence of his wife. A man who knew how to accept such behaviors as a passive form of compliment, who had conditioned himself to observe trivialities with the wink-and-nod they deserved. A little smile drew up his pudgy face, and he gave Myron an almost imperceptible nod of the head. Then he passed on and was gone from our sight.

No one would learn of the reason behind this brief layover until more than a month later, when the Churchills were safely back in England. The September 21 edition of the *Herald* would run a front page trumpeting HALIFAX HONOURED and the details of the conference between Churchill, Canadian prime minister Mackenzie King, and U.S. president Franklin D. Roosevelt would be made plain. Guests of the Manse Calvo would awe over the supreme execution of the secret transatlantic voyage, speaking of how "Churchillian" the whole thing was.

After the hurrah calmed, we headed back up Morris Street, more ebullient than on our trek from the Manse. My arm was hooked comfortably at the elbow through Annelie's, and I enjoyed a genuine rattle of pride and enthusiasm and hope.

Annelie was in such a fine mood she allowed Myron to divert us from returning to the hotel. Instead, we were his guests for an early luncheon at the Collier Club.

xv. <u>I Said I'd Write</u>

WHEN LT. GENERAL EDWARD CORNWALLIS founded Halifax in 1749, he represented more than 2,500 souls. A thrice-removed descendent of one of those settlers, Winston Allen Collier — husband of Marian Rose Collier, for whose fellowship Dr. Hapstrath had unsuccessfully championed me years before—founded the Collier Club in 1859, and since that time the club had catered quietly to a select roster of the privileged. After a period of decline in the late 19th century, the club accepted Morton Calvo into its fold in 1904, soon followed by his sons, and as a result of the Calvo largesse enjoyed a renewed period of fortune.

Given the vaunted social arena I assumed Myron courted, I expected the Collier Club to be every inch a histrionic keep fortified by money old and new. My expectations were somewhat met, but mostly not.

The atmosphere was remarkably muted. A dozen faces turned to meet us with passive observance as we stepped through the doorway. The members in attendance that day were each slightly older-looking than Myron, certainly no younger, and all were dressed similarly to him. Most cradled, despite the early hour, a glass of liquor. All wore the expression of belonging.

We had come into the club's main parlor, known amusingly as "the rumpus room." It was about the size of one of the Manse's salons and furnished expensively, its bits and ends of furniture arranged in segregated clusters of matching fabrics and styles. (I have no eye for furnishings; there could have been authentic antiques everywhere, for all I knew.) Much of it looked to have been there since the club's founding and in that time been only casually regarded. There were smoothened patches on the pillows and seat cushions. Cigarette and cigar burns stood out like exhausted eyes. The floors were exposed wood overlaid with massive rugs trafficked to near-pointlessness. Along the leftmost wall was a series of large windows, shuttered in slats of black wood and operable by a row of brass-handled turncranks along the lower moldings. The view beyond the glass was of a pair of small boat docks jutting out into the water of the North-West Arm. Along the opposite wall were six apertures fronted by tartan curtains. From behind one of these curtains came the boom of choral laughter.

"Private dining alcoves," Myron whispered, noticing the turn of my eyes. "Perfect if you aren't in the mood for the open air of the rumpus room. Usually, you have to reserve one in advance, for guests and the like, but I've brought a trump card today." I assumed he meant the story of our attendance at Churchill's "secret" embarkation.

Hanging on the wall between each dining alcove's aperture was a large, framed portrait of a different, and I assumed passed-on, member. One of the portraits was of Otto Hapstrath. It was a very fine likeness; the artist had chosen, kindly, a middle-aged version of the professor. His hair was a sweep of golden brown and his eyes held the same amused, pointed curiosity I remembered them having in life. He was depicted in a suit of dark blue, a plain white shirt, and a yellow tie. I found this muteness to be wholly correct, for Dr.

Hapstrath had never been much for ostentation; moreover, the relative dullness of the suit amplified the liveliness in the eyes and face.

Turning from the portrait, I noticed we had drawn the attention of a council of jacketed servers, each of whom looked somewhat shocked. At first, I couldn't figure why. But then I looked at Annelie.

I leaned toward her. "This isn't your first time in here, is it?"

"Oh yes," she whispered in barely concealed giddiness. "It absolutely is. He's never tried to bring me in here before. Now I see why. I think a couple of those old men's faces are melting down because of me." She took my hand in hers. "Just when I thought this morning couldn't get any more interesting."

I gave her hand a convivial squeeze and turned back to Myron, who was now engaged in a muffled but tense discussion with one of the servers.

"Honestly, Mr. Calvo, this is unprecedented, though I can hardly call it surprising." The server's posture was board-stiff. He was perhaps a half-dozen years Myron's senior and looked unaccustomed to accepting guff in any form.

"You make it out to be the end of the world," Myron retorted. "I promise it is not. In fact, the end of the world will be averted yet, if who we saw this morning has any say in it." Though his expression was placid, I could feel Myron itching to make some kind of declaration. "Besides, this young lady is my niece. Her father is remembered here, as is her grandfather." Myron held up a hand conspiratorially. "Not to put too fine a point on it, my good sir, but you know how to solve this little problem in a cat's blink, don't you?"

I understood immediately what, or rather who, the trump card was and what purpose she was meant to serve.

The swiftness with which Myron's ploy worked was like something out of the movies. The server snapped his fingers and two others immediately set about preparing the rearmost private alcove.

Two minutes later, we were seated, myself opposite the pair of Myron and Annelie, at a cozy, dimly-lit table.

"A perfect way to punctuate a perfect morning," Myron said. "I'm always too lazy to take a lean on one of these rooms. I never really have a reason anyhow. It would be looked at as absurd if I reserved one just for myself."

"More absurd than the little parlor trick you just pulled with me as the object of distraction?" Annelie looked pointedly at her uncle, but her words were soft, pleased.

"Oh, I'll be forgiven for this stunt in a week. Some of the others will use it to rib me a few weeks more, and then it will become a mild bit of legend."

"Well then, I suppose it all worked out," Annelie said. "Of course, this means I'm ordering something obscene from the menu."

"We all should. The present has no substitute. It has no conflict with the past and is inquisitor over the future. So, let's take advantage of this moment, yes?"

"Uncle, I'm happy to be here," Annelie said. "But I would like to know exactly what this has all been about. How did you know that ship would be docking at precisely that hour?"

"And," I added, "did you know what her particular, um, cargo would be?"

"I can't really speak to that, Walek." Myron smiled. "But as to your question, dear, the rolls of the Collier Club boast a great many successful men, one or two of whom belong to the local Admiralty. We have a sort of unspoken rule here that a secret divulged within is not really a secret divulged. That's about all I can tell you."

"So, you knew Churchill would be on that ship?" Annelie pressed.

"I knew only that a representative of importance would be arriving, no more. I suppose I owe a certain someone a few rounds next I see him." Myron threw up a finger and a server ducked his head into our alcove. Their eyes met and the server whisked away, the look serving as instruction. "What a wonderful experience! Extraordinary to see the man in the flesh. Who would have thought?"

Annelie and I shared a glance. It had been extraordinary, but it had also happened with the dexterity of a planned military exercise. Churchill and his party in our sight less than two minutes — and in that narrow breadth of time, a feeling of constant motion. The car waiting. The mysterious rendezvous to make.

I asked Myron if he knew the purpose of Churchill's visit but he shook his head.

"If I didn't know it would be him," he reasoned, "how could I possibly know his purpose?"

The server returned with a silver platter bearing a bottle of Jameson whiskey, three tumblers, a small canister of ice, and a board of sliced cheese and bread. Myron sat back and watched the goods be delivered, his face drawn into a slope of lazy thought.

When the server left and the curtain drew closed, he said, "I suppose I expected a celebrity, possibly an American. I had tried last night before nodding off to figure out who would be a good shot in arm to our people, a sort of public morale booster. A lot of those American film stars and even sports players are now in uniform. Of course, what we got was, let's face it, the *ultimate* morale booster."

"He seemed very heavy," I said. "Not in size, I mean. He was actually shorter than you'd expect from seeing him in photographs. But in personality, maybe. Presence. You could tell he carried the weight of someone who gets the final word about things."

"What a starry intelligence you have," Annelie chided me. I suddenly felt the light abrasion of her stockinged calf against my trouser leg. "But you're right. You could tell he just loved the attention, and knew exactly what the people expected of him."

"Yes," Myron said. "There is something to be said for being bodily close to a person who you know has been in it up to his neck and is still swimming for the ribbon."

"I read once that he served as a soldier in the First World War," I said. A footnote gleaned from some now-nameless history text, one of the myriad haphazard volumes curated by my mother into our Pepperell Street sitting room shelves.

"Yes, that's true," Myron affirmed. "A lifelong servant of the people. A writer, too. Columnist and historian. Remarkable." He sat forward and poured the drinks. "I think that once you realize just how unimportant you, a single person, are in the grand scheme of things, the rest of your life is thereafter spent simultaneously struggling against it and slowly, cripplingly coming to terms with it. These contradictory impulses are how most folks pass the time until time runs out. This contradiction, however, does not exist in all men. We saw one of those blessed exceptions today."

Raising our glasses, we made a toast to imminent peace.

Lunch was a fine spread of Chesapeake rockfish dressed in scalloped potatoes and steamed lentils, followed by a tureen of lemon custard with whipped cream, which we all shared. Except for the fish itself, every single thing we consumed, down to the cream in our after-meal coffee, was on the general ration list. Yet when Annelie asked for an extra plate of potatoes, the server brought them directly. No fuss, no tsk-tsking, no disapproval. They arrived in a cloud of steam with an ellipsis of halved grape tomatoes and deliciously glistening sweet gherkins rounding the edge of the plate.

As the food and drink settled within us, we grew laconic. From somewhere in the rumpus room, a clock tolled the noon hour. I drew open the curtain and looked out onto the shivering water of the Arm. I wondered, despite what was said and written, filmed and broadcasted about the war, how a world could manage to sustain such carnage and bloodshed in one place and in another the solemnity of the family of brown-feathered ducks that presently waded into view. This was not poetic meditation; I'm not really capable of that sort of thing. I was simply stuffed to the gills, a bit tight, and unable to reconcile the variegated wideness of humanity. I wondered if when victory came, if it ever would, such luxury as I was now enjoying would vanish from the world, or be made manifest as a result.

My eyes grew heavy. I was a second from drifting off. But then Myron sat up with a thick cough, rocking the table between us, and when I looked over at him, a thin white envelope, shredded open at one end, was held out to me by his manicured hand.

The letter, written and signed by Kyle and Sarah Dixie, acting proprietors of the Digby Pines Resort, had been received at the Manse Calvo on July 18.

Troke Joonblack was drowned either late May 25 or early May 26, in what is called the Raquette, an inlet of the Bay of Fundy. Kyle Dixie had been helping Troke rebuild the sea-facing side of his house, and so had come to put in a few hours' work on the afternoon of May 26. He did not, as he usually did, find Troke already at work. Instead, Doggins sat alone at the house's front door, shivering with his usual energy and nipping lightly at the misty air, as if, according to the Dixies, "trying to call out but unsure where he ought to call out to." Shivering perhaps more than usual, because Kyle Dixie found him soaked through and with traces of moss and other ephemerae of the drink matted to his coat.

Troke's boat was never found, but Troke himself was eventually discovered at the mouth of the Raquette. The Raquette was not a spot of known danger. It was shallow, almost bare, when the tide is out, though high tide is known to come swiftly. The Dixies hypothesized that Troke's boat had accidentally run aground on the basin's floor, and that when he tried to veer back into deeper water in order to make it back to his own dock, there was a breach in the hull and he didn't make it.

After Troke was buried, the Dixies adopted Doggins. They reported that he now lived well, if melancholically, on a pile of Troke's old shirts lined over a wooden box beneath the Pines' front registration desk and had become something of a mascot for the resort.

Accompanying the Dixies' letter was another, addressed to me. It was dated May 23.

Dear Walek,

As promised, a letter. A long time coming, eh? But better late than never. I said I'd write. This is a letter. I am writing it. Sitting at my kitchen counter with the sea air taking the curtains into the room like a young woman tossing her skirt.

Are you enticed now to come visit?

I think I've just about pulled myself together here with the property. And with all the rest, which I'm sure I don't need to explain in words. You are welcome in Digby anytime you wish to have an actual conversation. I got no phone. Just make your leaving Halifax chase a letter letting me know by a week and that's fine by me.

— Troke (& Doggins, who remembers you)

I stared almost through the sheets of paper, as though fearing some invisible ink had been used to addend its horrible summary. My fingers caused ribs to form. Small damp waves.

When it was clear I had nothing to say, Myron said, in a tone that felt to me a bit forced, "Troke was a fine man. He kept us afloat for a lot of years. Even if Ms. Wyndl was a perpetual prod in his backside. He was of a jovial demeanor."

230

I turned my eyes to him. "They were in love."

I don't know why I said it. In the moment it seemed a perfectly simple fact to state. But I could see it had never been made plain to Myron. He never realized what had been going on right under his nose, so to speak.

"Did you not know that?" Annelie asked her uncle.

"I suspected she had someone," Myron said. "But her personal affairs were fathoms below our level of familiarity."

"I knew," Annelie said.

"Of course." Myron smiled.

"What I want to know is," I said, looking at Annelie, "did you know about this letter?"

Myron and Annelie exchanged a look.

"For how long?" I pressed.

"Only since this past weekend," Myron said.

"My uncle was feeling very guilty for keeping the letter to himself, and he wanted to tell me quietly," Annelie insisted, "so that I would be the first to know, and also to ask my advice for how to tell you."

"What advice did you give him?" I asked.

"I asked him to let me tell you. But he didn't want me to."

"It was not her place to answer for my actions," Myron said. He went onto explain that it was coincidental that he rather than Annelie should have opened this particular piece of post.

On July 18, Myron had come around to the Manse to have lunch with Annelie. A random decision, as such things usually were with Myron, and he had agreed to cover the desk while Annelie tended to something or another in the house. The post arrived during this interstitial and, slightly bored, Myron had opened much of it. He had pocketed the Dixies' letter for fear that it might upset Annelie.

A glass of whiskey was slid quietly across the table. I ignored it.

"Do you suppose I might have wanted to retrieve the dog? That I might have wanted that option? I mean, who are these people anyway? There's not even a goddamn photograph. How do we know any of this is real?"

"It's real, I promise. Every word." Myron leaned into the table edge. "I called that resort they operate the day after opening the letter and spoke to Kyle Dixie. We spoke for some time."

Now that I was not looking at Annelie, but at Myron, my anger refocused. It was not a common emotion for me. I could not decide how best to act it out.

"This 'fine man' was, I guess, actually one of the unimportant, right Myron? 'In the grand scheme of things.' As am I. I must be. I'm just a boy shuffling under the weight of a man's job. I certainly cannot be approached as though I am anything other. As though I have not already handled loss worse to me than this."

I stuffed the letters into my shirt pocket and slid out of the booth. Annelie hitched, as to follow me.

"Don't bother. I'm just going to go. I may be awhile coming back to my shift. I will make up the hours this evening, if need be."

I drew the curtains, but before walking away I brushed them open once more. "I am not going to be like this for much longer. At least, I don't think I will. You were both doing what you felt was best."

I released the curtain, took a last glance at the portrait of Dr. Hapstrath, and made my way through the room and out into the air.

My arches ached terribly by the time I returned to the Manse Calvo. Fueled by street-vendor coffees, I had been moving at a brisk pace for several hours over cement and brick-laid roads, weaving through the packed blocks of the downtown business districts and then branching out to the sparse row houses that lined the North-West Arm down from Connaught Avenue, near Halifax Airport, all the way back to the frontage road that skirted the Manse's rear grounds.

I used the fire exit at the far east end of the house and went directly up to my room.

Closing my door, I sensed right away I was not alone.

The bedside light was on. In my bed Annelie lay on her side. Her fists were clenched and tucked inward against her neck.

I could not tell if she was asleep or in that half-sleep that is cognizant of sound but too heavy to make movement worth the effort. I sat on the couch and removed my shoes and socks and made gripping motions with my bare toes until some of the stiffness in my feet began to subside. Standing, I thought about removing my sweater, beneath which I was perspired, but I knew that once I lied down, the heat of my body would begin to exit the fibers, and I would grow cold unless I kept the layers on.

Annelie was still in the same outfit she had been wearing at the Collier Club. She had not even removed her shoes. I wondered if she had come directly here from the club to wait for me and simply grown tired, or had returned to the hotel, assumed her regular duties, and only then come here out of exhaustion, trusting that my eventual return would wake her. Each scenario seemed as likely as the other, and I did not discern a difference one way or another. I did not feel that, if she did go back to work after our lunch at the club, she was somehow less concerned for my state of mind. She was, after all, in charge. I could imagine no patron who might be patient to the absence of the manager on the grounds that one of her staff members was having a tough day.

I took in the whole length of her, and when I reached her face found her eyes open. She smiled but said nothing. One of her hands untucked itself from the hollow below her throat and drew a small circle on the empty space beside her.

I lied down with my back to her, my hips pressing into her belly.

Above us, the ceiling fan whirred an insistent sibilance. Annelie draped one leg across me, leveraging the weight of her body against me, and reached across to unlatch the window next to the bed. The air was cool, a breeze moved in from the water, tempering the humidity that had settled since early afternoon. The sun was a sliver of intense orange at the horizon line. In moments it would be gone.

The double bed fit us perfectly. Annelie hoisted her leg off me, and I felt it tuck like a pet into the contour made by my own legs. The very ends of her red-brown hair were scattered about my pillow. I had a split-second fantasy of Annelie's long-fingered, fair-skinned, agile hands reaching across my chest, going under my sweater and oxford, and swimming over the skin beneath. But it was only an instant, this desire, before the warmth of our proximity superseded and I grew incredibly tired. Before I succumbed, I felt Annelie's arm come to rest across my chest and her body slide fully against mine.

The night passed. No touch toward or untoward, not even a kiss, but an intimacy nonetheless. The beauty of being held.

xvi. <u>Briefly, 1944</u>

MOST WEEKENDS THROUGHOUT 1944 WE WERE
FULLY booked and better than half the rooms were
taken most weeknights. Myron, ever the shrewd
operator, lowered the hotel's rates by twenty
percent for rooms and salon bookings alike
through the end of the year, balancing this
reduction with a reduced kitchen and custodial
staff, essentially eliminating the hotel's part-time
positions. As such, I adopted some custodial
responsibilities.

Weather-wise, that summer came on with
uncharacteristic strength. The sun was bold and
fixed most days, and the nights were damp but
without any real demonstration of rain, more like
the moisture that would ordinarily become rain
was instead suspended in the very air, thickening
the lower atmosphere. I placed electric fans in all
of the Manse's common areas, and even though
blackout regulations remained in force I was able
to keep the windows in the salons partially opened
at night by placing restraining cords across the
curtains to keep them from billowing outward and
thus leaking the salon's inner light.

My courtship of Annelie Calvo maintained its
measured gait. The night we slept beside one
another in my bed released us from all timidity,
and we became fully agog in stolen embraces. The
kind of grappling kisses that leave clothing all
twisted up. Yet our passion had a chasteness to it.
It remained, literally, clothed. In this I was
content. Annelie had not, since the night she laid it

236

all out before me, brought up or even alluded to what happened in Charlottetown. Nor did I. I could not appreciate the malevolence of what she went through, an ignorance aided by her own lack of certainty, which I considered a kind of cruel blessing. We more or less played the days as they came. We favored long walks and went to the movies as often as we could. Our first official date happened on my twenty-third birthday, when Annelie took me to see the 1932 adaptation of my precious Wells novel, *The Island of Lost Souls*, starring Charles Laughton, at the Gaiety. It was a very fine feeling to sit in the dark with her hand in mine, her stockinged ankle bobbing gently against my calf like a low pulse. We alternated theatres week by week, so as to get in as much variety as possible, though we made an exception the last week of July and first week of August, when we went to see John Huston's *The Maltese Falcon* at the Capitol Theatre six times running.

By summer's end, everyone at the Manse Calvo knew about us. We were at first anxious that Annelie's authority might be called into question, but there was a remarkable lack of concern. In retrospect, we had Fenella to thank for the absence of gossipmongering, I suppose. It was a measure of the respect the staff had for her, surely, that coaxed them into following her outward example of not caring about our relationship one way or another.

Fenella's and my late-night sessions over the wireless fell to the wayside for a while that year, circumstanced by how busy the hotel had become and the surrender of my free time to Annelie — but also to Fenella's having begun to date a man who worked for Keith's Brewery down on Lower

Water Street. I learned of this from Annelie, who, quite by accident, had met him.

She had gone with Fenella down to the brewery to make a change in our standing order in advance of winter, knowing that things were likely to level off. While Annelie finalized the change in our account with the shift foreman, Fenella slipped away. Annelie later found the two of them sitting atop a pair of wooden barrels in the brewhouse.

"He was wearing a long apron and a dirty cap, but underneath the apron his clothes were pressed and he was even wearing a collar and tie," she told me. "I considered pretending that I hadn't seen anything, but that's no fun. I marched right over to the two of them and introduced myself. Fenella about died! His name is Nathan, but he insisted on my calling him Nate. He's decent looking, not what I would call handsome, but you know how some people have an innately trustworthy look to them, like they were born to be a grandfather? That's what he looks like. He was very polite, but not fake about it. He didn't let go of Fenella's hand the whole time we spoke. I made an excuse that I had one more thing to finalize with the foreman, even though I didn't, and left them to themselves."

"I think it's good she's met someone. She's entitled by now."

"It's crude to say, but nothing will undrown Sam. You know about him, right?"

"She told me."

"Grief ought to have a limited shelf-life. Especially in wartime."

Come fall, Fenella and I began once more to meet in the kitchen after shift-end to listen to the radio. Annelie joined us when her duties at the front desk permitted. Reports remained uniformly desperate, but now there seemed an undertone of optimism to the voices echoing in from the ether. The Americans were making significant progress, and this had, after years of struggle that preceded the American intervention, stimulated the British Empire into rousing, decisive campaigns. One declaration I recall: *Allies Hammering Toward Siegfried Line, Germans Rolling Back Like Empty Barrels.* Names of villages captured, places none of us had ever heard of, poured through the speaker. It seemed that each week there was another piece of ground gained, another body of water conquered.

In early December, a report came through from an American wire service declaring that in an effort to shore up the northeastern coast of both America and Canada, a contingent of American seamen and soldiers would be dispersed at select eastern sea ports along the Atlantic coastal region, so as to prevent German submarines from making further efforts to cripple arteries of shipping and export, arteries that both countries would need in order to see the war through to the end.

The three of us had taken the radio into the dining room and were listening over a late supper.

"I can't believe they actually reported that," Fenella said. "The man even said 'eastern sea ports.' That's code for us, isn't it? Nate told me he'd heard some sailor bragging on about it at the pub one night. How Halifax's industry is so important that any time an eastern sea port is mentioned now, it's us. Not just *any* sea port, but *us*. May as well have come right out and said 'Americans will be in Halifax, so come on out, Jerry, if you feel like taking a poke at them'."

"There's a reason we don't really get the American broadcasts," Annelie said. "They sometimes forget that the whole world can now listen in."

"It's not going to stop all those submarines, however many men and ships they send. They're scary *because* they don't attack every day. When they blow up a ship, it comes just when you think it won't."

"Maybe the tide has turned in our favor," I chimed in. "Maybe the war is going to end soon."

"Nate thinks we're looking at another year, at least."

I turned to Fenella.

"How's he figure?"

"It's just a feeling he's got. He sees a lot of RCN around the brewery. They like the pub there, I guess. He's quite the eavesdropper, my Nate. I suppose there's something to say for puzzling out an informed opinion." Fenella paused, thinking. "You're not going to ask me who Nate is, are you?"

I smiled.

"Sorry, Fenella," Annelie said. "I had to tell someone."

"I never said he and I were private. It's just fun watching Walek's cheeks burn. He looked exactly that way the first time you came back from shopping in Truro. How could I remember that, right? I remember because I thought it was plain adorable how you couldn't play off how smitten you were. What about me, Annelie? Was I burning up too when you saw us that day?"

"You certainly looked happy."

Fenella looked deeply into the table in front of her. "We all get by, and it's fine. We do what needs doing and all that. But what is it to be happy? Actually happy? I'd forgotten that I was able to be like that."

"I know what you mean," Annelie said. Her knee gave mine a little bump under the table.

"Me, as well," I added.

"I can't believe you two haven't been an item all this time," Fenella said. "I just assumed. Every time one of you had to rush off on a moment's notice, I thought, 'Oh, they're having it off again'."

"You know," Annelie said, "I have this feeling, it's a bit sick, maybe, but I have a feeling that there are some people who will look back at the war with a lot of fondness. People like us who are not right in the thick of it. Life and love's being lost every day all over the world, but not for us. We get to have it. This is a selfish thing to admit, but I sometimes think the war could go on forever and it wouldn't bother me in the least, so long as I could keep the life I have now. I would only say this to you two. It makes me sound awful, I realize. But it's true."

Confederates in this particular selfishness, neither Fenella nor I reproached her.

xvii. <u>Yellow Only of Bruises</u>

EVERY ROOM IN THE HOUSE WAS BOOKED for New Year's Eve 1944 — the entire property, in fact — by a single patron: The United States Navy.

Annelie was concerned. On the evening she learned of the commitment Myron made on the Manse's behalf, I was sitting on the couch in her suite, while Annelie paced before the fireplace. It was rare to see her so anxious.

"What really irritates me is Myron won't tell me what we're getting for all this. I mean, *every* room and all public areas. Basically, the whole grounds, up and down, in and out. Even the unused servants' quarters. And there was some mention of cots. I'm supposed to ask you if we have any cots tucked away in storage that could be made available."

"We have some in the rear garage, and a few in storage under the main staircase," I said. "But they're only fit for children. I thought soldiers were used to sleeping on the ground anyway."

"These are sailors. They get bunks."

"Where are we going to put cots anyway? In the hallways? In the kitchen? Fenella would love that."

This conversation took place at the end of what had been a very long day, comprised of me out in the cold rebuilding a wind-wracked section of the back fence. My participation now was facile at best; I certainly had no energy to talk her down from a rant.

"Myron won't tell you how much we're being paid. Okay. I'm sure it's because there are still details to hammer out. It might be that he wants to wait until he knows for sure. *For sure* for sure."

"Like a surprise? A New Year's gift?" Annelie scoffed. "Please, Walek. You don't close down an entire business to the fancy of one patron without nailing down every detail first. Myron's smart enough not to get wrapped up in patriotic generosity that would amount to a financial gutting. Especially not after how close we came to ruin last summer because of him. We're getting paid. I would just like to know exactly *what* we're getting paid. I am co-owner, after all."

"What do you mean, ruin?"

"It's a bit beside the point right now."

"You brought it up."

Annelie exhaled loudly. "We were in pretty deep water for a little while, that's it."

I was taken aback. "We were slow for a while, but I figured that's how it is with hotels sometimes. With all the cautions and rationing, I honestly didn't think much of it."

"The place was ghostly for months. How could you not have suspected?"

"I suppose I figured a business has to be able to anticipate the occasional dry spell."

"It was worse. Much worse. Myron insisted on keeping up 'standards', as he called it. Crisp linens, polished flatware, full oil in all the candle wells, the back lawn manicured like it was the Queen's croquet court from Lewis Carroll. Which meant spending more than we were taking in. A good deal more. Myron was convinced that without maintaining everything people were used to, we might lose all our business through bad word of mouth. He never convinced *me* that would be the case. I mean, have you seen some of the other hotels in Halifax? Some are really nice, the Waverley, the Lord Nelson, but most are shitholes, if you ask me, compared to the Manse Calvo. But no matter how I tried to reason with him, I was countermanded."

"Luckily, fall was flush," I said. "And this year's been busy straight through."

Annelie set her fists into her hips in the style of Ms. Wyndl.

"Myron's not a lazy businessman. Overzealous sometimes, but never lazy. He's had time to gnaw over last year and figure out where some of the fault lies."

"And this Navy thing, you figure he's trying to refresh the accounts?"

"Something like that. Our margins are thin as Bible-leaf some months, even now."

All I could do was encourage her to take it up with Myron again and not let him walk away until he came clean. It seemed a meek thing to suggest, but Annelie pounced on it. She pulled on her coat, gave me a peck on the cheek, and was out the door.

Exhausted, I slid off my shoes and stretched out on the couch.

I must have fallen asleep, because when I next opened my eyes, the sky outside the windows was black, my reflection in the glass was clear as still water, and a small fire was stoked in the fireplace. Annelie sat in the chair beside the grate. Occupying the rug between us was a room service cart, topped with several covered plates, and a bottle of white wine in a sweating silver bucket.

"Good, you're up. Now we can eat."

Annelie was dressed in a long flannel robe from beneath which showed the collar of a satin pajama shirt. She removed the plate covers, revealing a steamed lobster with claws intact, a small tureen of scallop and mussel stew, a basket of assorted breads, and a plate of roasted broccoli.

I looked around for the clock before remembering that it was in my own room that a small clock stood on the sitting area window ledge.

"What time is it?"

"It's four hours since we last spoke."

"It took you all that time to wrestle it out of Myron?"

"No, that took about ten minutes. I came in thundering, like an *idiot*. Turns out he was ready to tell me everything. Afterward, we took a Birney car down to the wharf and I helped him sort out deliveries with a few local fishermen for the 30th. Then we went for a drink. It was so frigid my bones feel bruised, but it was nice to see all the Christmas decorations, even if there were no lights strung up."

Annelie wheeled the cart over to the couch and plopped herself down beside me.

I poured the wine. "Well," I said. "Let's have it."

"As far as money goes, we're getting twenty percent under the going rate for each room, and thirty percent under the standard wedding reception rate for the salons. But an added deposit of $600 for general property access."

"And is that good?"

"Considering the fact that a third of the rooms would probably have otherwise been unoccupied and the salons been ostensibly free of charge, I think it's not too bad at all. But the money's not what's interesting."

Annelie drained her wine at a draw and gestured for me to pour her more.

"You are going to have to completely clear out the rear grounds because the USO will be staging a live show on the patio. Brass band. Local girls hired from the clubs downtown to dance and sing. A pair of bagpipers who usually play for change by the wharf are coming in, too. The Navy intends to film the whole thing for newsreels celebrating the alliance of American and Canadian forces, or some such thing. Myron says it's free advertising for us."

"We're doing that for free? The concert and all that?"

"That's what the deposit is for, pretty much. But what's got Myron really excited is the fact that they want to interview him for the newsreel." Annelie paused to sip at her soup. "His ego is like a hot-air balloon right now. I'm talking Jules Verne big."

"That all sounds like it's going to be quite a lot of work." I spoke generally, but of course I meant a lot of work for *me*.

"Actually, that might be the best part of all. Aside from making sure the yard and patio are ready, you and I have been instructed to basically stay out of the way. Myron will be doing all the face-to-face stuff. And the Navy is sending in a crew to deal with the show. The setup, the striking, all of it."

"Are they leaving the next day?"

"Supposed to be out by check-out, eleven sharp. Not that we have any rooms booked on the first."

I was dubious. We had never thrown a big to-do for the New Year before. Hosted some large groups, sure, larger than the normal run of things, but ones that for the most part went their way after midnight. Now the entire Manse would be at the beck and call of a single group, and for the whole night. I had practically no direct experience with military types. Aside from the occasional shoulder rub in the narrow seats of a movie theatre, I had never even been in close proximity to a uniformed person. Now I would be answering to them.

Annelie, I noticed, was studying me.

"You really don't like this whole thing, do you?"

"I think it's fine. We've just never done something like it before."

"And likely won't again, if what we're hearing on the radio is true. All the progress and that." Annelie began scissoring into her lobster. "What don't you like about it?"

"I said its fine. I'd just as soon have a quiet one this year, that's all."

"Well, we're stuck on the same life-raft. Believe me, I would prefer that to this, but it's only one night. It'll pass like a blink. Besides, we don't really have to do anything."

"That'll change."

Annelie smiled. "You may be right, but regardless we won't be responsible if things don't go off the right way. It's Myron's cherubic face they want on their newsreel. The price of that is owning up to the deal he made."

I took a sip of wine. "I would never describe him as cherubic."

"Oh, he'll be glowing like an angel. You wait and see."

Late morning New Year's Eve, I stood on the front porch and watched two parallel lines of uniformed men march up Lemarchant Street. Each carried a dark blue duffel.

This is what Americans look like, eh? I imagined Troke remarking, a hock of tobacco nested in his cheek, eyes squinting in evaluation. *I suppose we ought to make ourselves impressed. Looks to me like they're used to that.*

All told, thirty-seven men trod through the Manse's front door and were greeted by a pressed and dressed Myron. All fourteen guest rooms plus the two vacant servants' quarters, were "double-bunked," leaving five short straws to deal with the child-sized cots I set up on the second-floor landing. (Unlike its equivalent on the third floor, it bore an alcove off-set by a narrow wall that offered something close to privacy.) I expected those relegated to this sad billet to hem and haw about it, but instead they each lashed together two cots, end to end, with spare belts from their duffels, making for a still-narrow but now long enough place to repose. I was impressed by the quick fix. To help them further, I retrieved some metal clamps from the storage cabinet beneath the grand staircase and used them to better secure the adjoined legs. For this I was asked my name, slapped on the back, and thanked with a casual enthusiasm that made me blush.

As the evening proceeded, I was pleased to find that each man I met, if only in short salutation, was the epitome of politeness. And I met pretty much all of them. More than I didn't, anyway, though I cannot say for certain. They became after a time a single morphing expression of gratitude.

Around nine, Myron announced that everyone should start making their way out to the rear patio. The show was underway by quarter-past. I did not stay to watch it, but rather joined Fenella and Annelie for supper in the relative quietude of the kitchen. The beat of the band and the hoots and cheers of the men penetrated the walls only slightly. It was like standing outside the padded doors of a theatre in which a film was playing.

"This place was certainly built well enough," I said, taking up a chair. "That's a brass band not a hundred feet away, but it sounds like they're playing on one of the docks out on the Arm."

Fenella turned in her seat and looked blankly at the wall. "Well, damn." She turned back to Annelie and me. Eyes glassy. She leveled them woozily at Annelie. "What is this stuff and where did you get it?"

"Rye. We don't serve it because Irish is easier to get. Cheaper, too. I've been saving this since my birthday."

I now noticed that standing on the table between us like a centerpiece was a squat, round bottle with an unassumingly bland beige label that read *Templeton – Small Batch*.

"Myron has a funny idea about what it is a girl wants on her birthday," Annelie said.

They were both happily tipsy. Not exactly drunk, but hovering in that delicate space where liquor is friendliest.

I got up and went to the cupboard and took down a small enamel mug. Returning to the table, I saw that they were using proper whiskey glasses, and so waving the mug in the air I made the droll statement, "You don't mind sharing with the common help, I hope."

"I'm here, aren't I?" Fenella said, laughing with a squint to one eye, as though it were a better way to see clearly.

249

"You might want to ease back," Annelie said. "It'll be just your luck my uncle comes bursting in here with something he needs you to do."

"Oh, supper is already set. The cisterns are hot and the trays, too." Fenella took a deep sip from her glass. "It's New Year's and this place is crawling with lonely young men."

"And Nate?" Annelie said. "What about him?"

"What about him? I'm *mad* for him. Can you believe something like that!"

Annelie and I shared a look. Fenella noticed.

"I'm not talking about getting off with one of these Yankees, Annelie. But they *are* lonely and far from home and drinking. Oh, are they drinking. I fully expect my cheeks to be pinched purple before the plates are cleared off, and I'm not talking about the ones on my face. I can deal with that better if I'm, you know."

I helped myself to three fingers of the rye. There was an infectious aspect to their growing inebriation. I was about to call for a toast to the beginning of a new year, one that would see an end to all troubles, when the kitchen door whooshed open, and standing in the aperture were four skinny, ruffled boys. They each gripped empty beer bottles in their fists and wore expressions of desperation, which matched the asperity of their cowlicked hair and rumpled coat collars.

Immediately I saw their eyes roam over Fenella and Annelie's bodies.

Annelie noticed, too. I could tell by how the light of laughter dissolved quickly from her eyes even as she assumed a pliant expression.

"Can we get you boys some more beers? Or maybe you could just help yourselves. They're in the icebox to your left." She spoke with casual but distant courtesy.

"Maybe grab two rounds," Fenella added, still smiling gaily. "That way you don't miss any of the fun out there."

"Plenty of fun right here," said one of the boys. An awkward reed of a person. I was certain to have spoken to him earlier in the evening, but I could not place where or when. Was he one of the unfortunates I helped with their kiddie cots?

"Oh, aye? And just what sort of fun do you imagine we're having?" Fenella said. Her lips were wet with whiskey, her tone playful, and her eyes gleaming, all of which projected a picture out of step with a guarded change in her posture, by which she folded her arm protectively over her chest and hunkered into a bowed slouch over the counter's edge.

Annelie reached across the counter and laid her hand over Fenella's shoulder.

"If any of you young men are dissatisfied with the show that has been arranged, you are instructed to take it up with either your sergeant or with Myron Calvo, who is the proprietor of this hotel." Annelie's tone was unwavering in its polite conclusiveness.

"We don't got a sergeant, doll. We got a Master Chief." This from another of the boys.

"Well then," Annelie went on without missing a beat, "your Master Chief can surely address any concerns you gentlemen have. In the meanwhile, you may help yourselves to more from the icebox, but then I will have to ask you to return outside. The galley is for staff only."

"This isn't a galley." A third boy now speaking up. "It's a kitchen. Boy, are you precious." He had a rather angry-looking,

251

horseshoe-shaped scar running in an inverted ellipsis over his dimpled chin. "I got a girl back home, about as sturdy as you, so I'm saying we could have a particular kinda fun. Fun I can vouch for."

Annelie affected a wistful tone. "It has always been my romantic ambition to be someone's second choice. But sadly, I have a skinny little runt of my own just like you and I don't think it would be fair."

The three who had thus far spoken and whose bodies were blocking the doorway now stepped fully into the kitchen. A fourth, older-looking than the rest, with a tinge of graying hair at the temples, held back.

"Knock it off, Stag." This senior man chuffed the scarred one harshly from behind. Then, straining his head upward so as to speak above the crowns of his comrades, he addressed Annelie. "We'll get our drinks and be on our way. Thank you, miss."

The senior man retrieved as much beer from the icebox as his arms and coat pockets could hold. Then he crossed the room, bottles clutched close to his body, and took a position between the three boys, and Fenella, Annelie, and me.

"Alright, fellas, off we go. Come on. That band's almost finished and I hear there's dancers coming out next."

He began to prod them with his elbows. It took a minute — a heavy minute, laden further with unbroken stares — but finally they relented, and all four disappeared out the doorway. A brief holler echoed from the hall, followed by the brief slam of the rear patio door.

I turned back to the counter. I felt nervous sweat at my underarms and the inside of my elbows. My cup felt heavy in my hand. Placing it on the table, I found that I had been gripping it rather tightly. The skin of my palm was bleached of all color.

I exhaled.

"Skinny little runt?" I said.

"Oh, cool it," Annelie said. She gave my hip a playful pinch.

"Maybe we should cut off their drinking at the dinner service," I said.

"An open tab was part of the barter. I can't do anything about it."

"I'm thinking of Fenella. She's the one who'll have to deal with any," I struggled to find an appropriate word, "rowdiness. Her and her staff."

"I appreciate your concern, Walek, but I think I can outwit a bunch of hammered teenagers." Fenella smiled at me.

"I guess I could talk to Myron," Annelie said. "Then he could take it up with their, what did he call it?"

"Master Chief," I said.

Annelie looked at the clock on the wall above the door. "I'd better do it now. The show's going to be over in less than an hour." She buttoned her sweater up to the throat and left.

Fenella and I craned our necks to see out the window that looked onto the patio, but the spidery ribs of the shrubbery gave our already limited view the effect of looking through broken glass.

"Think she'll make a fuss?" Fenella asked me.

"Probably not. She talks hard sometimes, but this means an awful lot to Myron. Being able to be in that film they're making, I mean."

We sipped our drinks quietly, enjoying an equable hush, waiting, listening to the reverberation of the event outside.

After a few minutes, Annelie still away, Fenella asked me, "Did you listen last night?" referring to the CBC over wireless.

I told her I had not.

"I guess the Allies have practically taken control of the Siegfried Line. Or close to it. The Germans are retreating."

"That's very good news, if it's accurate. What about the Japanese?"

Fenella screwed up her face as might a young girl who was about to admit a minor indiscretion. "I don't really pay much attention to what they're doing. I know it's all one in the same, the Axis Powers, but the fighting in Europe hits me harder, I guess. The Pacific, all those little islands out there, I never know where it is the reports are referring to. At least French towns sound French and German towns German."

A few seconds later, Annelie slipped back into the kitchen, her face red with cold, and took up her seat once more.

"How did he take it?" I asked as she drank a mouthful of whiskey.

"Incredibly well," she said. "In fact, he marched me right over to the Master Chief guy and made me explain all over again. He said that while our house was at the Navy's disposal, the safety and security of the females on staff was to be respected. He demanded that the Master Chief address what I told them immediately. That's not what I wanted, of course, but this Master Chief is not the mess-about type. He asked me to point out the three who were giving us a hard time and then apologized on their behalf. Said he hoped that would suffice because those three would not be allowed near me again to make personal apologies. I said it was fine and Myron cooled down, too.

And that was it. I came back inside and here we are."

"Well, I'm glad that's settled," Fenella said.

It was then that the outside door swung open and Myron walked in. First thing, he noticed the bottle on counter between us.

"Pour me a small one, will you, Walek?"

I hopped down from my stool and retrieved an enamel cup identical to mine. I poured two fingers' worth. Myron drank it at a draught.

"Glad you saved this, dear," he said to Annelie. "Boy, that helps. I wanted to let you all know that those three young men are, as Master Chief Holland put it, 'sequestered to quarters' for the remainder of the evening. I have been asked to have a member of kitchen staff run up their meals. A male member of staff, is what I feel is right."

"We've got one, though he's not on the kitchen staff," Fenella said.

"No problem," I quickly agreed. "Glad to be of some kind of service."

Myron, smirking, asked me, "And was that a veiled criticism of my keeping you away from your assigned duties?"

"Sir yes sir," I said, snapping a salute. The rye had begun to form a great brown cloud in my head, lifting me up to a slightly higher plane where witticism has more buoyancy.

Myron smiled, then looked into my own mug and seeing an inch of liquor snatched it up and gulped it down.

"Put your drinking on pause until you've completed this little errand. Then you can take a bottle of whatever you like up to your room as far as I care." He turned for the door. "On second thought, better that you switch to coffee now. As Ms. O'Dwyre so succinctly put it, you are the sole male member of staff here this evening. Your presence, if not your skill, might come to use later in the evening."

With that, Myron exited.

Once the door had swung shut, Annelie sidled up beside me. Her arm curled under my side, caressing my ribs, my lower back. With her free hand, she slid her glass in front of me.

"Go ahead. But after this one, you'd better listen to Myron. I don't think it's just a possibility he'll want you around later tonight. He just designated you crowd control." Annelie placed a soft kiss on my temple. "I'm going up to bed. And I'm taking this," remanding the half-empty bottle of rye to the collar fold of her sweater. "Sorry, Fenella. Looks like its coffee for two."

Once the show outside came to a close, and the men were seated in the dining room, I pushed a rolling cart bearing three covered plates and three small carafes of coffee out to the foyer. I had been instructed that no more alcohol be doled out to the sequestered sailors. I expected resistance on this point, but hoped they would be cowed by the dressing down they received from their Master Chief, along with a sense of dereliction of standing, if not of duty.

Two of the boys were in respective rooms on the second and third floors, and the third was cotted on the second-floor landing.

I made the third-floor delivery first. The door opened, a feeble voice thanked me and asked that I leave the tray on the floor outside the door, then the door closed. I suspected the early onset of a hangover. In the scant light from within the room, I saw the shadow of a scar over the boy's chin and knew he was the one the senior serviceman had called Stag.

Given this innocuous encounter, I returned to the foyer for the other two trays confident that their deliveries would be just as muted.

One boy I found lying on the lashed-together cot. He was out of uniform to the waist and flipping distractedly through a copy of *Life* magazine. Even at a glance, I could see that he was taut and muscled. I was unfamiliar with the kind of bodily confidence that would allow for such open comfort outside of private space. I, myself, tended to keep a shirt on even in my quarters, unless I was just out of the bath.

I set one plate down on the uppermost step before the landing itself, and carried the other carefully in both hands around to him.

"There's coffee, too," I said. "Just let me drop the other plate and I'll come back with it."

"I don't really want coffee," the boy said.

"I could bring water or tea. We also have Coca-Colas."

"You know I want a drink. Come on, pal. Tuck a bottle of something in your little jacket there, and no one'll be the wiser. Consider it a favor to the war effort."

His face, blanched as unbaked bread, became equine as he smiled. The jaw elongated and a row of surprisingly pronounced teeth showed themselves like piano keys.

"I can't do that," I said. My voice did not waver. "Excuse me, please, while I deliver the other boy's meal."

"We're men, you fucker." He slapped the magazine down on the carpet. "Do I look like a boy to you?"

Clearly, he was not suffering any tightness of the head. And his punishment, such as it was, hadn't made a dent in his demeanor. I felt it wise not to rise to the bait, but to deliver the other serviceman's food, which I did.

Or almost did.

After retrieving the covered plate from the step where I had left it, I saw its intended recipient traipsing lazily up the hall toward me.

There was something unnerving being alone with them like this, though neither, despite their behavior and mutually heightened conditioning, seemed particularly threatening.

"That for me?" he asked. A cigarette dangled from his mouth, unlit, and he swung his elbows in a disjointed manner while his hands swayed in the folds of his trouser pockets. "I could eat a whole hog, hoofs n'all."

He seemed the youngest of the three. Short sandy hair, a pug nose, freckles, and a chin that ran so smoothly into the narrow trunk of his neck it seemed he had no chin at all. I handed him the plate. He accepted it gingerly, with both hands, as though he expected it to be piping hot.

"Thanks for this, and hey, we didn't mean nothing before. Not a lot of girls for us, day to day. We're used to 'em being better able to take a joke." He looked at me quizzically. "I can't tell if you're pissed off or afraid." He looked over my shoulder at his friend. "We get that a lot. The uniform, I guess. Has to be the uniform, really. If I were back in Illinois and you saw me in my coveralls, you'd stop squaring your shoulders. Hell, we might even get along." He broke a brief smile that revealed a row of burnt biscuit ends where one commonly found teeth. Then he moved past me toward the landing.

I was unaware that I had "squared my shoulders." But as I turned back toward the stairs, with a mind to retrieve their carafes of coffee from the foyer, I realized, in the sudden motion, how stiff and tense my entire carriage was. A small pinch registered in my right hip at the torsion of my body. I became aware of a knotted hillock of muscle bisected by my backbone, just where my ribs ended and my shoulder began. And it hit me: I was, in fact, scared.

Once I realized this, a flood of whatever hormone cools the nerves against tension or anxiety hissed through my body like a gas, and I laughed, aloud, with no pretense or awareness that I was going to until the sound had left my mouth.

"Something funny?" the equine one asked. "Something's funny, Frank. I wonder what it is."

"Cool it, Stolley." The one called Frank turned his face to me. "How about that coffee I overheard you got for us?"

I walked slowly up the hall toward the stairway. I must have kept, like rigor mortis, an idiot's grin on my face because the one called Stolley sneered openly at me as I approached.

I paused at the drop of the top step. This was the tipping point. There was no reason for me to say anything. There was nothing that needed saying, nothing required by the situation. All I needed to do was return to the foyer, take up the carafes, and re-ascend the stairs. But some devil had infiltrated my blood, and somehow I couldn't resist.

"You might want to head back to your room," I said to Frank. "Your Master Chief wouldn't like it if he caught you jail-breaking."

"You say something else, pal, and I swear," began Stolley, but Frank did not seem to hear me.

In the flicker of my eyeline, I saw his jaw working greedily over some roasted chicken.

I fashioned a smile. I expected them to smile along with me, I really did.

But then I realized their attention had zeroed onto a space beyond me — something behind me.

I turned to look.

Annelie stood poised at the far end of the hallway, dressed in a long argyle-patterned flannel dressing robe that despite its density could not hide the truth of her figure. Her hair was loose over her shoulders and the top of her chest. Her face was slightly flushed, and I knew — a private detail, and I knew it — that she had only just washed her face. Her bare feet were like nightlights in the dim hall. One foot rose, itched at its opposite's calf, the movement defining the tracery of bone and artery along the pale, smooth top of the foot. All in all, she made the picture of desirability.

"Well now," said Stolley. "Looks like we weren't barking up a dead tree after all. What do you say, Frankie?"

"I, um," began Frank, his mouth stuffed with food. To his credit, he was plainly unnerved. "We'll take that coffee now, pal, so you can walk the lady out." He may have looked at me, but I never took my eyes off Annelie. His voice seemed to fall out of thin air.

All that registered on my consciousness was Stolley's snide undercurrent, its assumption that the one called Frank was party to its subtext, which presumed Annelie's presence in the hall to be some kind of silent physical overture.

I couldn't bear it. I spun, as on an axis, toward them.

"Just take your lesson," I said. "We don't have a whatdoyoucallit, but there's a garage out back, and its doors have locks."

"The hell are you saying? The hell's a whaddayoucallit?" Stolley stood up. "You mean brig? Is that what you mean? That you got no brig? Why would that matter, houseboy?"

"Sit down already." Frank shook his head. "That girl is watching us. We're already in for it."

"Well then, if we're in for it, how about we make it count?" Stolley glared at me. "We don't take well to being threatened. You were threatening us there a second ago."

"I was giving you a friendly warning, is all. Before you both forget what we're doing here on this landing."

"Well then, I suppose I ought to go apologize to that young miss personally. That's being friendly, too."

I put up my hands, palms flat, like someone waving down a car. I did not think either of them would mistake my posture for anything but the demonstration of caution it was. But the gesture was too quick, and Stolley took it for a deliberate move.

Before I realized he had gotten close enough to bridge the space between us, my cheek was smacked flat, an explosion of fire, and my teeth dug into the side of my tongue, causing an instant, liquid warmth to leak into my mouth, the taste like an oily coin.

I staggered back. Vaguely I heard the soft, hurried tread of Annelie's feet coming up the hall.

"Jesus Christ!" In the teary-eyed periphery of my vision, I saw Frank jump to his feet, and I thought he was coming for me, too. So, with as much displaced weight as I could muster, I lashed

261

out, blindly. It was luck that I caught Stolley on the ear, a contact that clanged like a bell up my arm, biting into my shoulder as my fist ricocheted backwards off his head. I stumbled back once more.

My punch had practically no effect on him. In a flash, he was on me. I don't suppose that Frank had stood up with the intention of joining in, but rather to stop things getting worse. However, now that I had become an active contestant, he no doubt became duty-bound to support his friend.

The individual motions I cannot separate one to the next. The reign of fists and knees. The posture they took over me. I know only that I was quickly on the ground and that sprouts of urgent pain broke out in numerous places on my back, thighs, and head. I don't know long it all lasted. Perhaps minutes, though likely less. I doubt it took Annelie more than ten seconds to make it up the hallway, for soon I heard the crescendo of hollow metal against the wall (she had flung one of the dinner plate covers down the stairs), followed by Annelie's voice calling out in a frantic scream that was so jarring and operatic that the servicemen's assault suffered a momentary pause before resuming its metronomic consistency.

The air seemed to quicken and there came the sound of approaching bootfalls. Voices calling out breathlessly. A ribald exclamation.

I saw Annelie's bare feet inches from my face. The sweep of her dressing robe. I never saw the two boys being dragged away, whether they were removed bodily or simply by command. I closed my eyes, succumbed to the warm brush of the carpet, and was gone.

I reopened my eyes unaware that my position had changed. My face felt only the smooth fibers of the carpet. But then came a light clatter from nearby and I understood, from the limited reverberation of sound against walls closer than those in the hallway, that I was in one of the rooms. I assumed it was mine. I rolled over, issuing an involuntary groan, and found not the blank wall of my own sitting room, but the stone fireplace of Annelie's, in which a good-sized fire was roiling over a set of logs.

The clatter resounded once more, and was this time followed by the hush of feet across the floor.

"Think you can sit up?"

Though all the lights were out, the only source being the fire, I still could barely manage to open my eyes. They felt swollen, though they did not seem to hurt. My eyelids felt tucked into the skin of my brow, as if my skin had slid to a position much lower on my face than it normally occupied.

I set my hands flat to the floor and slowly tried to push myself up. I found that I could. I suspected that I was only a few feet from the couch and so pushed myself backwards, until my back bumped up against the thin end of the couch's seat cushion. I took a deep breath. A spear pierced my right side, and it felt like a pair of terribly strong hands were at the same time gripping down on the meat between my shoulder blades.

I exhaled and dropped my weight back into the couch.

"Did you drag me up here?" I asked.

"That Master Chief ordered two of the others to carry you."

I detected the faint odor of rubbing alcohol.

"Those two guys, what happened to them?"

"It's taken care of. Now let's try to take care of you."

"I can just lie down for a while," I said. "You don't have to do anything."

"Don't be stupid. Just keep still. Expect some of this to hurt."

Tucking her robe between her legs, she sat before me cross-legged. I closed my eyes and leaned back.

A large ball of wet cotton ran in long strokes over my face, bringing a sting to separate places on my left cheek, left earlobe, right eyebrow, and the space between my nostrils and upper lip. This was followed by another pass of cotton, this one dry, then the application of what felt like small butterfly plasters over the places that had reacted to the alcohol.

"I have a mirror. Do you want to see?"

"I don't know. Do I?"

"It probably feels worse than it looks. Ice would help, but I forgot to get some, and no way am I going back down there when all those guys are still at it in the salons."

"Reasonable," I said.

"What I'm saying is, it will only get better, and probably soon enough after you see a doctor tomorrow. If you look now, you can be sure it won't be as bad the next time you look."

"Then I'll look."

Annelie held up a small hand-mirror.

My left eye was swollen nearly shut and a knot sat beneath the skin on the very outside of my jaw on the right side, near my ear. The skin on my face looked a bit red, but otherwise not very alarming. But on my neck and collarbone, where my sweater and shirt had been torn open by the assault, the skin looked beaten. Black-green, brown-blue, the bruised yellow that is the yellow only of bruises.

Annelie pulled off my sweater and oxford, unlooped my belt, and pressed a very warm, wet cloth into my right side. I took the mirror from her. Further patches of that unique yellow were presenting on my chest and stomach.

"They might have cracked a rib or two," Annelie said. "I'm going to put a lot of white tape on your side here and then wrap a bandage around your chest. Your legs will just have to wait until we can have a doctor out in the morning."

As Annelie administered the tape and began winding the fabric bandage around my torso, she was forced, by the motion, to press her body into mine. Her arms hung about me, hovering in their mode of action, like a planetary ring. Her hair smelled curiously of flowers.

I tried again to open my eyes and found it a bit easier. They opened to slits by which I could see only the bottom half of my normal pattern of vision. At first, I was unsure what it was I was looking at, but then Annelie's arms rose slightly to pass the bandage again across my back, and the loose sway was unmistakable. From the aperture of the robe's unfastened collar were Annelie's breasts. Her skin, in the wavering firelight, held the freckled lineament that accented her face and arms and hands.

How common, a young man bug-eyed at the glimpse of a breast. It's funny, really. I was suddenly in very little pain.

I don't know if it was the rigidity of my muscles that she felt in the quick pass of her arms, or perhaps the catch in my breath, but she noticed that I had noticed what it was I was noticing.

She looked me full in the eyes.

"I pretty much saved your bacon tonight, so this is not some reward." Annelie slid from her robe and placed her full length against me. "This is because it is something I want."

I had never seen any part of Annelie's skin but what was common to the world. Her face, her hands, the slope of her neckline. But now — a landscape of pearlescent belly, a small triangular mole above a pocket of downy golden hair around the navel like misplaced eyelashes, the wide flat hips growing down to legs like pylons. Her fingers pushed into my hair. She pulled my mouth to hers, gentle at first, a brushstroke, then onward, tongues meeting, exploring, exchanging breath. A subtle contortion, a strain of thigh muscles, and the envelopment, pulling me into her as though I were pulled through a hidden sanctuary beneath her skin. For a time, there was a sea-going element, the sofa we lay against undulating as if there were no floor beneath, just the unsteady ripple and chop of water. Then suddenly something became unbridled in me just below my stomach, not unlike nausea, and just as suddenly receded like a passing spirit.

Like the beating I'd taken, I could not say how quickly it was over or how long it might have lasted. As with any moment so long desired, there was a soupçon of hallucination, a tidal element, and I gave myself to it with utter resignation.

We never slept. We watched the fire slowly die and eventually the burnished light of sunrise slip through a break in the curtains. At one point I asked what she had been doing in the hall, but she let the question pass unanswered, from which I surmised her intent had been to visit me in my quarters. What we had just shared was answer enough.

Shortly after six o'clock, we heard the front doors open and a shuffling procession of silent bodies cross the cold wood of the front porch. Then the doors closed.

It was 1945.

xviii. <u>Quasimodo</u>

LEERING BACK AT ME from beneath the ruthless light bulb over Annelie's bathroom mirror the morning of January 1 was a remarkable visage: a topography of pulp. Hues of red and pink, blue-green and that unique bruised yellow ground into the porous texture of my skin. But more remarkable than the state of my face was the smile that played across it. Though I was the very picture of a grotesque, the happiness from which this smile took its source was as rich, total, and profound as any feeling I had seized or suffered in my entire life.

While I'm not a particularly erudite person, I am decently read, enough to know that there is pretty much no new or original way to describe the satisfaction and renewed curiosity that follows a first act of love. So, I say simply this: I had made love for the first time, and in so doing believed I had also found it.

I limped back to the welcoming warmth of Annelie's bed. I draped my arm over the curve of her back and pushed my mangled face through the waves of her hair. A kiss against the soft eave of her earlobe. Then I dropped my heavy head onto her pillow and was elsewhere for the remainder of the day.

I didn't risk a walk downstairs until the following evening. I realized, once I made the foyer, that we remained empty of guests. I spied through the open door of the manager's office Myron lounging amidst a cloud of cigar smoke.

I went in to speak with him.

"Glad to see you on your feet," he said. "I was reticent to bother you up there." A pause — perhaps a knowing one? "I figured you would resurface when you were ready, or at least able."

"The doctor was supposed to be here yesterday but is now meant to come this evening. I felt it was best not to meet him in Annelie's room."

There, cat out of the bag. Bag gone to tatters. But Myron did not flinch. He barely seemed to hear me.

"Doctors all over the city must have their hands full after the New Year. Every New Year, I imagine. It's an argument for medicinal sobriety."

In effort to not prolong pleasantries before addressing the looming issue of what had happened two evenings prior, I said that I would not pursue charges against the two young sailors. I saw no point in it, I said, nothing to gain.

Myron, characteristically prepared, produced a letter typed neatly on official U.S. Naval letterhead.

"It's signed by a Vice Admiral," Myron said. "I don't know the system of rank and file and all that, but *admiral* sounds awfully up there, doesn't it?"

I sat down and read the letter. Toward its conclusion was the following: *The attendance of an internal disciplinary concern will be addressed in full by the proper individuals within our branch of service, and does not warrant nor invite the testimony of those of foreign citizenry. Moreover, the unfortunate circumstance of this situation precludes our ability to honor the fulsome aspect of our previous agreement.*

Myron, who I felt eying me closely, read my confusion.

"They killed the film they were going to make. The newsreel stuff." He drew massively on his cigar, so much that he expelled a searing mist almost without capturing it in his mouth at all. "I was meant to be interviewed for it, I'm sure Annelie told you, but it didn't come off. They were going to do that bit in the dining room. Me surrounded by America's finest enjoying the decorous hospitality of a Canadian rooming house. That was the idea, I believe. But then, well, you know."

"If only they had clobbered me five minutes later."

Myron's ovular face blew briefly like a full sail before giving up a startled breath.

"Walek, I, — Don't think such an appalling thing, not even as a joke." He leaned forward, wrenching his full weight onto the desk, producing a groan of wood from somewhere within its cavities. "I owe you so much more than an apology for what you've had to suffer. I am proud of how you handled yourself, especially knowing how those same boys had tried to accost my niece and Ms. O'Dwyre earlier. If only I had been firmer when Annelie told me of that. I should have demanded those two little mutts be returned to wherever it is they sleep when it's not New Year's Eve."

Myron's eyes had gone almost rheumy with emotion. He fell back into his chair with a jarring rock. "I allowed my ego to get in the way of my business objectivity."

"It's not your fault, Myron. I probably shot my mouth off a little bit."

"And what of it?" Myron retorted. "You heard the mouths on most of those sailors. There's an adage about having a mouth like a sailor, and for good reason." He began to chew on the end of his cigar.

"Any guests tonight?" I asked.

Myron shook his head. "It was a trying night for us all." His voice was flat and matter-of-fact. "Bookings will open on the fourth." A plume of purple smoke. "For now, some quiet."

When the doctor finally arrived, Myron excused himself so that my examination could take place in the office, no need to trudge back upstairs.

For a fortnight I was Quasimodo lurching about my modest cathedral.

The doctor had verified Annelie's suspicion of a cracked rib. He fashioned an extremely tight poultice out of fabric bandages soaked in some kind of quick-setting paste that made me feel I was supporting a cast, as one would see on a busted arm or leg, beneath my clothing. The weight of it dragged me slightly to the right each time I took a step. I was advised not to move around very much the first day or so.

When registration reopened on January 4, bookings began to trickle in once more, though (and I do not know if this was luck or design) the remainder of the month was absent any salon arrangements that would have required my attention. January is an unpopular month for marriage and a stilted, perhaps even poor one for business in general; it has, in my experience, always been this way.

The doctor returned in two weeks to remove the poultice (with a small clawed hammer and scissors) and assess the healing. I was asked to perform a few slow calisthenics, and he was gratified, as was I, that I could manage a pretty normal degree of movement with only mild discomfort. I was advised to be smart about what I felt capable of doing, and to not lift anything over ten pounds for another couple of weeks.

I took that advice handily. I filled the daylight hours of those heedful weeks with light maintenance tasks. My nights belong to Annelie. She brought a portable record player down from her room, and we listened to Dinu Lipatti's interpretations of Chopin, while Annelie lay on my bed, propped up in a half-nest of my pillows, and read a copy of *Leaves of Grass* she also brought with her. Sometimes she scribbled a few lines that took her in a small black journal that she kept in the front pocket of her skirt. When she grew tired of reading or the record ran out, we gently made love.

Much of winter passed this way. Business slowed, but never altogether dried up, as our peninsular city was held fast in a glistening icy blue.

Then, in April, the thaw — and along with it a loosening between Annelie and I, which itself is not to be confused with a thaw. We had shared a bed every night for three months, wresting the cold from the sheets with our body heat, but I could feel her growing antsy for her own space. Once I was fully mended and back on the job, we stayed together only every other night. This in no way suggests a rift in our romance; rather, we simply both placed a premium on regular intervals of solitude. I was, frankly, grateful to find our natures so conjoined.

I had done very little reading that winter, which was unusual for me. Winter's lax demands on my hours usually made it possible to catch up on books I'd quietly stockpiled over summer and fall. But between having to do sessions of movement and stretching per doctor's orders and the time I gave to Annelie, I was often too tired to focus. When alternate evenings freed up, I dove into a small pile that sat on my bedroom window ledge. I devoured Wells' *The Invisible Man*, which, amazingly, I had not read before; Conrad's *The Secret Agent*, from which, while I ultimately did not like the novel much, I found the following phrase particularly stirring: "Neither his spiritual, nor his mental, nor his physical needs were of the kind to take him much abroad. He found at home the ease of his body and the peace of his conscience…"; a collection of stories by Rudyard Kipling; *Youth*, also by Conrad, which I liked a bit better, along with *Heart of Darkness*, which I did not; and, oddly for my predilection was toward literature (at the expense of almost all else), *A World in Crisis*, Winston Churchill's history of the First World War, which blew out all other concerns for a solid week. In this way I reconnected with myself, with the self that took refuge in storytelling; thus sated, I felt more fully present in the hours I shared with Annelie.

April was, in general, a month of rain, but a few days of bold sunshine brought out the flowers along the Manse's garden walking path. The grass came in lush, and I had to make runs at the back lawn every few days with the push-mower in order to keep it from going feral in its shadier places. Even during the sopping nights there was an absence of gloom. The city twinkled life. We took this as an indication that blackout regulations had softened, that Halifax was now marginally safer, though no official announcement to that effect had been made.

When not working, Annelie, Fenella, and I — and when he was on the grounds, Myron — kept up our habit of huddling over Fenella's wireless, soaking in every drop of reportage we could get, but we no longer did so in the kitchen. Annelie asked Fenella to bring the radio into the foyer, where the grave, faceless voices of trusted men wafted through the whole of the Manse Calvo's ground floor. This soon drew guests in from the salons. I brought out some wood armchairs from the garage and lined them up on either side of the foyer, adjacent to the salon's respective entryways. Nightly, these chairs became occupied by women and men whose faces seemed equal in gravity to the voices speaking to us. Fenella began an evening coffee service, and guests, always permitted to drink in the salons, were now permitted to smoke as well. (I erected additional cisterns.) Children played on the grand staircase, their voices disciplined not by their parents but their tacit understanding that something quite serious was coming through the radio's speaker.

It was in this way, these ad-hoc privately public forums, that we learned of President Roosevelt's sudden death on April 12, of war correspondent Ernie Pyle's death later that month, and shortly thereafter of the American seizure of Bologna on April 24, which it was claimed closed the Italian front of the war. Italy capitulated a week later, on the heels of which came the fall of Dachau — an occasion on which Myron handed out not one, but three rounds of free drinks to everyone.

May arrived dressed in hope. The spring air fresh. Folk wore expressions of pleasure and appreciation long kept dormant. Days of gentle sun and mild wind alternated with days of fat, ground-sopping rain.

On such benevolent afternoons, Annelie and I would sneak out after the lunch service for a walk through the neighborhoods, always intending to call on Myron at his house on Owen Street but then forgetting almost as soon as we were away. Women were out with their hair tied up off their necks to stave off perspiration. Their skirts were now thinner, their thick skin-shaded leggings banished, their shoulders revealed in winter-ivory smoothness. Men's collars opened up; ties could be found sticking half-out of jacket pockets. Sweat-matted hair peeked out from hats tipped back on the head as though unneeded, merely a gesture to style. (Annelie one day commented that every man in Halifax now looked like a worn-out salesman. When I asked what the women looked like, she jibbed me in the ribs and told me not to worry about the women.)

An earned peace was finally imminent. Unfortunately, Halifax had to withstand one final assault before its people were ready to accept it.

xix. <u>Damned Foolishness</u>

MAY 8, 1945 IS SOLIDIFIED in the annals of history as Victory in Europe Day, a tremendous moment in the lives of untold millions. Freedom and liberty triumphing at terrible cost over tyranny. But in the midst of it I saw only confusion and danger.

Fires pocked the wharves. Dancing bodies possessed the streets and parks and quays, their collective voice like a call to some unknowableness they were desperate to reach. From a distance it might have made for a grand gesture to the voracious will of the spirit. But whatever one might at first have seen, little time was needed for the veil to fall and for the riot to present itself as the riot it was. For this was not a celebratory massing — it was a yawp of anguish and relief.

Why was I even in town?

I had volunteered to accompany Fenella down to Keith's Brewery. She and Nate had planned, back in April, a week's getaway, and Fenella, undeterred, meant to see their plans through.

We made it most of the way down to the wharves unhindered, but the crowds thickened considerably near Lower Water Street. There, Keith's sits just steps from the harbour and so was a readymade target for the swells taking control of the harbour walk. As we rounded the rear gates, we could see, through the iron stanchions, ale being handed out by the case and single bottle to assuage the looters from rending irredeemable damage to the factory and warehouse. Men were stationed at each of the brewery's points of ingress, fulfilling requests as though they worked for the Royal Post.

Fenella rose up on tip-toes to see over the heads of the massing people, searching for Nate's face amongst the workmen behind the gate.

"Maybe he's at another entrance," she said.

"But he called earlier, right? To tell you where to find him when you arrived?"

"Yes, but look at all this. Who's to say what's going on inside the place."

"Why don't we just jump on this queue? If he's there, you're set. And if not, whoever is can tell you where to go."

We were being jostled from all sides and I could see that Fenella was having a difficult time trying to think. She reluctantly agreed.

The air was suffused with an energy that, like the potential for lightning during a rainstorm, teetered on the thin edge between joy and mercilessness. There was an anger underscoring the scrambling, the singing.

A riot, by definition, has no bearing. It exists entirely outside the margins of expectation. A single act of violence, no matter how brazen, how terrible, can typically be traced to a point of explicable propulsion, a motive. A riot, however, vaporizes its starting point upon inception. It was no longer about the war for many of these revelers, nor about celebration or declaration or opportunity, or anything but the moment itself, divorced from cause and reason.

The line, fortunately, moved quickly. I watched those who came before us slither their way past, their prize in hand or under arm or balanced atop woozy head. The faces, made up of varying clay, shared an aspect of hunger, not physical but somehow spiritual, as though the potential for violence that blanketed everything fed their very souls.

At the gate, several men were handily at work. I stumbled forward to the metal spires. Right away, I saw Nate was there. He was soaked in sweat, his eyes frazzled.

"Hell of a thing, eh?" He laughed and drew the iron gates open just wide enough for Fenella to slip through. They embraced. Nate whispered into Fenella's ear. She waved to me, wished me luck getting back to the Manse, and ran inside the warehouse, her valise trailing after her like a scrambling pet.

"Here." Nate slipped a bottle of beer into my hand. "It's best you look like all these others."

"How are you planning on getting out of here?" It seemed that the entire quayside was under heavy occupation.

"Left my car on the other side of the ferry port," Nate said.

The person behind me began to jog me in the back, impatient for his spoils.

"You'd better skedaddle," Nate said.

"What's the best way to go?"

"Not the wharf-side," he said. "These lot have taken it all up. Folk are falling into the water, there's naught room down there. Back up into town, I guess. Fighting your way through's really the only way."

"Thanks. Be safe," was all I could think to say.

"Don't you worry about us. I'll have my eyes on nothing but her until we're free and clear. Boy, what a relief it'll be."

Tucking the bottle to my chest, I scampered through the captured streets. Looking around, seeking some slim pocket of escape, the more debauched aspects of the riot became apparent to me. Several shopfronts had their windows shattered, and people were leaping into and out of the ragged glass holes, their arms heavy with looted material. There were broken bottles underfoot, and nearly all planters and advertising stands had been toppled, some of them smashed. Fistfights sprouted in the roadway. Couples fornicated in doorways.

In trying to figure a way around or through the throng, I stumbled upon, or rather burst in on, a sight lost on the rest of the revel. I had slipped into St. Matthew's Church off Bishop Street via the vestry. I followed a narrow wood-walled hall and eventually emerged into the main chapel. There, scattered across the pews, sat two dozen or so people, women all, and I saw immediately each was clasping a child. Their small eyes shone in the dim like the eyes of cats. An intruder, I held up my hands in a gesture of caution, to show I was no danger to them, but only then realized I still clutched the bottle of ale. A few of the women gasped. The wood of the pews creaked under their frightened weight. The sound was enormous in the hollow space. I sensed a presence behind me and turning found, at terrified attention, a priest. In his hands he held a splintered oar. Neither of us said a word, the blunt capability of the oar saying all.

From outside the chapel's main doors, the tumult roared. Since I did not wish to cause any further fright, nor to have my head staved in, I carefully retreated through the narrow hallway and back to the vestry, where I quietly let myself out the way I had entered.

Spring Garden Road was pretty much impassable, so I headed inland along South Street, trying to find a path of least resistance back to the Manse Calvo. Almost immediately, the congestion of bodies made progress impossible, so I cut back to the north via Queen Street and onto Brunswick, skirting the majestic rise of the Town Clock, and darted up the damp knoll of Citadel Hill.

Standing there, catching my breath, with the city spread out before me, I enjoyed an evanescent happiness. I was crawling with sweat and half-delirious with all I had seen. Yet in my exertion I felt very much alive to sensation, to the fresh moonlight above me, the tickle of grass at my ankles, the almost choral static of voices at all points in the city.

This cacophonic rush vanished almost as quickly as it had come on, however, when I looked westward and saw the Public Gardens, inexplicably ungated, teeming with celebrants, and I knew the trees and flowers and hedges were undergoing a terrible destruction for no other reason than that the park's lushness was there for the taking.

As from a cold blast of water, I snapped-to. I still held the unopened bottle of beer in my hand. I dropped it on the grass and descended the hill onto Sackville Street, running with all might past the Public Gardens. I cut through Camp Hill Cemetery and Dalhousie's upper campus, until, pausing for breath, I stood once more on South Street — the Manse Calvo a mere five blocks away.

I was about to resume my run, when I saw, not more than a block ahead of me, a small cluster of celebrants. The street was otherwise empty. They were using a tidy row of great elms opposite the university medical building as, alternately, trapezes and urinals. Empty bottles were flung indiscriminately at houses, parked cars, street lamps. I wondered at how they had strayed so far from the nucleus of the real action.

I kept perfectly still until the group moved on to the next block, then I sprinted toward Lemarchant Street.

The Manse was alight, the front lawn deserted. I went around to the back and there came upon Annelie and Myron scrambling in the near light of dark, hurriedly nailing up wood planks over the ground floor windows. They paused between pocks of their hammers when they heard me accidentally crash through a hedgerow and onto the stone patio.

"There you are," Myron said. Elegantly suited as usual, he was sweating heavily beneath the awkward weight of a wood panel the height and breadth of a doorway. In his pursed lips, a pair of dull gray nails. "What took you so long? The noise is growing, you know."

I tried to describe what I had seen, but was almost immediately cut off with a swipe of Myron's hammer through the air.

"Is Fenella safe?" Annelie asked.

"Yes, I left her at the brewery. Nate let her inside. They are going to leave tonight."

"The staff's gone," Myron said. "We sent them home to look after their own."

"We sent them to the riot," Annelie said.

"You're probably right," he conceded. Then he looked at me and held out his hammer. "All right, now that you're here, you can keep going with this. I want to kill all those inside lights." I took the hammer from him. "How close is it all getting?"

"There's a pack of a dozen or so a few blocks away," I said. "Past that most of what's happening is down near the wharves."

"Well, that's where the pubs are, and the brewery," Myron said. "And hopefully that's where it will stay. What about these people you mentioned? How were they acting?"

"Like the rest, I guess. Just stumbling around. They're drunk, so…" I trailed off.

Myron took out his pocket watch, an odd gesture given the circumstances. "Yes, well. Not much time." He entered the house, leaving the door ajar.

I looked at Annelie, confused. *Not much time for what?* She just shrugged and said, "He's extremely worried."

"He should be," I said, but immediately regretted the tense expression this produced on her face.

We got down to the work of boarding up the windowed walls of the dining room, which was like trying to hide the presence of a greenhouse. We moved in unspoken synchronicity, working with a precision and efficiency that a sober eye might observe as practiced, even though nothing could have prepared us for such a night as this.

When the glass was at last gone from sight behind the sheets of pinewood, we stood a moment, enjoying the carbolic plumb of our breath on the quickly tempering evening air, and remained long enough to see Myron appear on the house's third floor, first in one room, then another, then another, his appearance preceding only by a moment extinguished lights and curtains drawing shut.

We ran back around the house to the front door, where on the porch lay a stack of pine boards for the salon windows. We arrived only just in time to see a displaced pack of inebriated, ecstatic folk stumble gaily over the sidewalk on the opposite side of the street, called in their orgiastic momentum by the burning lights describing the arched entryway of the Manse's façade.

Annelie and I froze, hoping they would not notice us and simply pass by — or notice us and, seeing that the hotel was supervised, pass by anyway. I felt we stood on the brink of something uncertain.

Annelie ran inside and snapped out the salon and foyer lights but too late to distract.

I stepped off the porch onto the stone cobble of the footpath and awaited the madding crowd, exhaustion settling like an accumulated debt in my bones.

I met them blank faced. A smile would invite. A frown could antagonize.

What I should have done was follow Annelie into the house and do what I could to secure things from the inside. I came to realize it only too late as two of the men split off from the rest and hopped over the front lawn fence, raising bottles toward the Tilde Salon's windows.

Though no more than ten feet away, they (thankfully) missed, smashing uselessly against the brick. But in the wake of their shattering, the balance of the mob came on fast. Stunned by their quickness, I held up my hands, but they rushed right by me as though I were nothing more than a turnstile.

The next volley of bottles was on target. The windows of the Tilde exploded, leaving craggy holes like toothless mouths. The front doors were wrenched open so vehemently that one of them slipped its upper bolt.

They rushed inside as one animal. It seemed not a second ago they were all the way across the street. Now they were in the house, bringing a symphonic demolition with them.

I screamed with all the lung I had Annelie's name. I looked up and saw that a light remained glowing on the fourth floor, and at once I tore around to the back of the house and slipped inside by the fire exit, using my key.

I took the steps three at a time all the way up.

The door to her quarters was locked and I banged on it with my fist, calling her name so she would know it was me, and not one of the mob.

A second's pause, then Myron let me in.

Annelie immediately gripped my hands. "Are you alright? I thought you'd be right behind me. What are they doing?" Her eyes were wide as saucers in the glow of the single candle.

"They're inside," I said. "They rushed — it was too fast." I shook my head. "Is anyone else here?"

"Besides me?" Myron was pacing furtively, stopping every few paces to listen to the air.

"I mean in the house."

"No," Myron said. "Everyone else was sent away. I've told you that already."

"Uncle, please," Annelie said. She did not turn her eyes from me. "Should we stay up here? Would they even bother to come up here?"

"I don't know. I snuck in through the fire exit. Back stairwell. If you both want to leave, we should probably do it now. While they're occupied in the salons."

"While they're destroying the salons, you mean." Myron was, I now noticed, in an impotent fury. "This goddamn bacchanal, to what end for it!"

Annelie squeezed my hands in hers, and a sharp sting shot up my thumb, into my wrist. I took my right hand away and found a red gash at the thumbnail. I immediately felt my pulse in that small wound like a somnolent rhythm. How did I get this? I could not account for it.

"Sorry," Annelie said. She stepped away from me, toward the door, twisting the tails of her sweater over her knuckles as though she were drying her hands.

Abruptly, she stopped.

"The office," she said, spinning on her heels. "It's not locked."

"There is nothing that is not replaceable," Myron said. From the shiver of his voice, I suspected him of doing a rapid accounting in his mind of the office's contents. He did not sound entirely sure.

"There's the safe," Annelie insisted.

"It's a safe," Myron said, injecting some confidence into his voice. "Besides, even if by some miracle they opened it, which would require a mind significantly more sober than any of theirs, I'm sure, it's only paperwork they would find. Nothing worth even casting aside, let alone pilfering."

"But it's the ownership papers and acts of incorporation for the hotel."

"All of which exist redundantly at the bank." Myron stepped up to Annelie and took her gently by the shoulders. "Our safety, *your* safety, is more important than any item in this house."

Annelie thought a minute.

"Even Grandpa Morton's portrait?"

I had seen the painting of the senior Calvo in the office numerous times. A decent likeness, but not exactly precious given the circumstance.

Seeing my confusion, Myron said, "Built into the frame of my father's portrait are forty five-dollar coins that were minted in 1843, shortly after the regulation of the Canadian dollar to other North American currency. The portrait was a gift to my brother, Annelie's father, on the occasion of his twenty-first birthday. It isn't the image that matters, you understand, but what is hid in the frame. Over time, old currency appreciates. Those coins are terrifically valuable. Of course, you would have to destroy the frame in order to get at them. A sly reminder by my father to Aaron that he could only reap the value in an act of desperation." Myron drew a deep breath, turning his eyes to Annelie. "Which coincidentally explains why I never ransacked that portrait during last year's dire straits."

"They're only coins," I said. I also looked at Annelie. Her face was inscrutable. "If you're looking for an excuse to go down there and confront these people — and there are at least ten of them, by the way — a money-stuffed picture is as good as any. Of course, it would be completely stupid." I turned back to Myron. "We shouldn't even be here. We ought to take the fire exit and use the hotel car to get out of here altogether. Find a police station. There's one on Jubilee Road."

Myron, having lit an enormous cigar, expelled a combined cough and scoff. "There are no policeman to be found tonight, I assure you. I can't even imagine how beyond their limited capacity this all be. Still, it seems reasonable that we should find someplace else to wait it out. My house is probably the best place. I don't have a key to the Collier Club and breaking in, the mere *idea* of it, would just make me no better than —."

Myron went no further, because, turning from the dark fireplace into which he had pitched the burning match, he realized that the door to the room was ajar. Annelie was no longer there.

I might have caught up with her on the second-floor landing, but I guessed wrong which flight of stairs she would take. By the time I was down the grand staircase and reached the foyer, she had already slipped quickly down the fire exit stairwell and was in the manager's office. She was not alone.

Two young girls were lofting the cushion of the manager's chair between them like a beach ball, on top of which was balanced (but only just) the full desk set — blotter, inkwell, pen station, stamper and pad, the whole lot. They were both shirtless beneath bellhop's jackets, likely purloined from one of the cabinets beneath the registration desk. Cigarette smoke undercut the yeasty fug of beer the two girls exhaled with every breath.

Annelie stood against the wall, beneath the portrait of her grandfather. She was shouting at them as over music, but the girls only laughed and kept on with their game. I don't recall all of what Annelie was saying, but certain words punctuated the air like pistol-fire, words I had never heard her speak, the most jarring of which was *cunts*.

Then, sick of being ignored, Annelie balled her fists and stepped directly in between them.

"*Put my property down right this goddamn second.*"

Sound seemed to stop altogether but for a piercing yelp from one of the girls as the chair cushion broke its arching trajectory and came with precision — the kind of precision capable of a drunk who has found that anger is a useful focus lens — straight at Annelie.

Only a couple of feet before the cushion met her chest, its payload dispersed. The pen in its holder, what one might think was the most dangerous projectile in the group, merely glanced off her shoulder. The stamper and pad did not even touch her body; they faltered like birds with broken wings at her feet.

The damning objects were the Inkwell and, unbelievably, the blotter.

It was a small piece, the blotter, about the size of an A4 portfolio laid open. When the inkwell struck her chest, less than an inch from the soft pit of her throat, Annelie convulsed backward, her arms flying out in front of her, a combination of the shock of impact and the impact itself. Her stomach buckled. Her knees bent, bowing her back. It was this adjustment of her carriage that removed the crucial inches from her height and made the sculpted corner of the blotter's point of impact not her breast — which would cause no more than a bruise, maybe an abrasion to the surface of the skin — but the ridge above her eyes.

Above her left eye to be precise.

Her head did not snap back, as from a punch, nor did she crumple down, not right away. And since neither of those violent reactions happened, I did not at first see how her left eye went woozy, then sleepy, then simply hung unclosed, like a piece of drapery whose catch has grown worn.

Annelie fell almost casually into a seated position on the rug. She seemed unsure what was happening. Her face was drawn, not in fear or pain, but mystery. I could almost see her thinking, *What was that?* She scratched quickly at her eye, as to dispel a small, piercing crust of sleep. And then she collapsed, her left eye still open.

The girl from whose hands the pillow and Its load had slipped, seeing Annelie fall, said, "Shit, I didn't think that would happen." And she began to laugh. A sniveling, fearful sound that suggested the danger of what she had done was recognized but amusing to her nonetheless.

Her friend leaned against the credenza that stood against the wall opposite the doorway, her eyes wide, coming to a realization of what they had done. She began a low, rapid chant, her chin tucked into the collar of the bellhop's jacket. "Fucking shit, fucking shit, fucking shit, fucking shit, fucking shit," on and on.

I stood there in rigor. After taking brief stock of the two girls, I looked down at Annelie and my first clear thought was that she might be more comfortable if she turned onto her side, as she did when we shared a bed.

I don't know what it was that kept me from taking her up in my arms that very second. I must have looked like a stunned child when Myron finally appeared, his bellowing, terrified voice filling the office.

"Get out of here now, you harlots!"

This exclamation ignited them to action and they bolted from the room.

Myron dropped to his knees and took up Annelie by the shoulders and began trying to carry her to the door — a show of strength that surprised me.

"Quickly now," he said impatiently. I took up her legs. Myron looked in my eyes. If there is a purity to fear, I saw it in that moment. "She's only just breathing."

"Your car," I said.

We shuffled through the foyer to the hall that would take us past the kitchen to the rear exit, and then out to the garage — leaving the Manse open and vulnerable to the night, to the continued impulses of the infuriated mob.

In our urgency down the hall, Myron muttered, "Foolishness. Damned foolishness." I couldn't tell if he meant how the riots had touched us, the general carelessness of it all, or his niece's stubborn refusal to stay out of its way.

xx. <u>Assessments</u>

WHILE ANNELIE LAY UNCONSCIOUS IN THE OPEN WARD on the third floor of Cogswell Street Hospital, I made the following assessment of the damage to the property and grounds of the Manse Calvo:

    i.front doors separated from hinges; colored glass in leftmost door cracked but not smashed from its molding.

    ii.front windows describing (respectively) foyer, Aaron, Tilde, and 'mud' room intersecting front doors and foyer — all thoroughly shattered. Will require boarding up and eventual replacement.

    iii.rear exterior = uprooted hedges and flowerbeds. Displacement of four flat stones in the garden path. Bocce court kicked up; repairable with a run of the rake. Overall, disturbance is cosmetic.

    iv.kitchen = eviscerated; every surface scored, every light smashed, both iceboxes gutted and their wire racks tossed to the floor. A lot of broken glass. Pooled liquid in corners of room and around table legs. Cabinets pilfered; some cabinet door hinges pulled away & need replacement.

    v.dining room = undisturbed. Door between dining area and kitchen sustained scoring and divots from thrown objects on kitchen side only.

vi.foyer: lighting fixtures intact on ceiling but ripped from locations on walls. Gashes in wallpaper evident. Floor scuffed superficially. Carpeting on main staircase ribbed at edges and foxed due to what seems, by odor, to be urine. Furniture overturned, upholstery torn, frames broken in multiple places. None salvageable.

vii.Aaron: carpeting shows a patch of oily black; possibly an unsuccessful attempt to start a fire. Furniture overturned, gashed, stuffing strewn. All but one armchair unsalvageable. Wall hangings all pulled down. Rents in wallpapering. Canvases punctured, irreparable but for portrait of Aaron Calvo: canvas intact but frame splintered down entire right length and upper left corner; remanded to MyC for repair and restoration at own discretion & expense. Also: window curtains and rods pulled down; curtains strewn in errant piles but otherwise unmolested.

viii.Tilde: library eviscerated. Shelves removed or broken down to bottom of case-frames. Books: some have split spines and/or loosened pages; some ripped clean in half. A quick accounting shows only eleven volumes salvageable. Thread of grace: one of the eleven is *Dalhousie's Earl: A History of the Life and Occupations of George Ramsay* by Otto Hapstrath. Copy remanded to my quarters, permanently. Other damage to room similar to that found in Aaron. Exceptions: curtains shredded; largest sofa unharmed but for evidence of spilled liquor; wallpaper pulled off in large strips and tossed into the fireplace but not lit; oil portrait of Tilde Calvo lying flat on the floor but otherwise unmolested (now in hands of MyC).

ix. registration area: entire desk and counter splintered all around its edges; all cubby drawers withdrawn, rifled & discarded, many broken apart on ground behind desk (glue may repair them); bellhop stand reduced to kindling, spare uniforms missing (presumed stolen, were not located anywhere in subsequent search); guestbook shredded, unusable but will be salvaged for posterity (seek out bookbinder in town; bill to hotel accounts). Lamps smashed, shades dropped and seemingly kicked through. Top of registration desk raked with scores possibly from heavy edge of lamp or one of the cubby drawers before it was busted apart; will need professional restoration.

x. stairs b/wn second floor & ground level: carpeting ribbed; spots of dense liquid saturation, possibly liquor, urine, or water from turned-over plants on landing. Window curtains still in place but window behind them shattered; the culprit a hammer (found in a cubby?) still wedged into a piece of craggy glass in the bottom of window frame. Traces of water damage on wallpapering at interior corners approx. 2 m from floor.

xi. second floor landing: plants again turned over, stomped upon, dirt and water mashed into carpet & rug. Wing chairs tipped over; legs broken off. Fire hose box broken into, hose run out several meters, but wheel unturned.

xii.rooms 202 & 206 (rooms closest the landing): broken into, contents ransacked, bedding disturbed; evidence on bedding of 206 of intimate contact (staining, odor). Windows intact, curtains unharmed; WC apparently ignored altogether.

xiii.manager's office: portrait of Morton Calvo (unharmed) remanded to care of MyC, along with the following: two small oils depicting wharf landscapes from view of top floor of MC and boat on the harbour, respectively (painted, I was informed, by Careene Calvo); all files relating to MC operations, business agreements, loans, credits, along with contents of small safe hidden behind portrait of Sr. Calvo, which was undiscovered during the assault; two boxes containing printed advertising materials. Desk set in possession of Halifax police. Manager's desk disheveled but largely unharmed; scrapes and scratches, all addressable. Glass cabinet containing past guest books smashed, volumes tumbled to ground but otherwise intact. Cabinet unsalvageable. MyC requests these volumes be kept in my quarters until further notice.

On May 9, the attending staff at Cogswell Street Hospital assessed the cause behind, status of, and prognosis for Annelie's evidently comatose state (paraphrased here):

The inkwell had struck her at the suprasternal notch, the soft hollow at the base of the throat, taking her breath. As she was in the midst of speaking (of screaming at the two girls) she had little oxygen in her lungs, and the blow from the dense glass inkwell caused, in how its impact radiated through her body, an interruption of her ability to recover respiration. This was coupled with the strike from the blotter, the gold-tipped edge of which pressed into a nerve cluster just above the ocular nerve, at the crest where the eyeball itself gives way to a slender space protected only by the muscle and skin of the eyelid and the fold of skin that covers the supraorbital ridge, the area of bone just above the eyeline. This occurred just as the snapping motion of her body, in reaction to the impact of the inkwell, caused an inverse concussive reaction at the back of the neck, in the area beneath the occipital bone where the brainstem meets the spine.

But this was not the most harrowing, or pointed, fact.

While her lungs were deprived of oxygen and thus unable to metastasize the gas to the rest of the body, notably the brain, her arms, flung reactively outward by the rapidly successive impact of the inkwell and blotter, caused what the doctors termed "a borrow." Basically, the blood flow that should have been routed to her brain was instead "borrowed" by her arms — so quickly that the nerve impulse lagged behind the reactive motion. Coupled with the breathlessness Annelie experienced from the inkwell's strike, this "borrow" caused a misdirection of crucial oxygenated blood flow and general deprivation of oxygen to her brain, which then resulted in unconsciousness.

This all sounded well-considered to Myron and I, yet the doctors could not account for why the unconsciousness was sustaining itself for as long as it was. A slap to the face or a splash of cold water ought to have brought her around. As they could not account for her persistent proto-comatose state, they could offer no guarantees of its ever ceasing and her returning to the waking world.

I returned to the Manse Calvo in the late afternoon of May 11, after straight two days at the hospital ward, alternating bedside vigils with Myron, and otherwise uselessly pacing the halls and cafeteria. In no mind to face the wreckage of his business, Myron had left Cogswell Street by cab, bound for his house on Owen Street. I walked back alone.

On Lemarchant Street, there was no evidence anything had transpired two nights before. I expected something, some shred of proof that it had actually taken place. Discarded bellhop's jackets, perhaps. Some blood on the brick. But there was nothing. The street was entirely deserted but for me, an eerily strange thing.

The front doors had been leaned upright into a near approximation of their correct positions, and, mysteriously, a length of twine was looped around the door handles to hold them together. There was no posted notice, which I surmised would have been placed by authorities had what transpired been, by some random circumstance, officially reported. I supposed that, however it shook out, the conclusion to that evening occurred solely under the skewed authority of its participants.

I entered the house, mindful to reset the doors behind me.

The clock read 2:07 a.m. when I finally completed my damage assessment and slid between the sheets of Annelie's bed. I doubt I dreamt. A few seconds later, it seemed, a band of sunlight fell across my face, pulling me from dead rest.

Fenella and Nate returned from their holiday betrothed. Can't say I was surprised. There is a transcurrence that takes hold in a world undone by straits, which can goad people already prone to positivity into making big decisions. (By year's end, primarily as the result of soldiers returning home, the papers would report a great many marriages, including theirs.)

Fenella was floored by the condition of the Manse. I could barely keep her still long enough to give her the details of Annelie's situation once she saw the state of the kitchen. She left her baggage in the hall and immediately set to doing what she could to address the disarray. I watched her attack with systematic precision first the surface mess, then the counters and cabinets, and finally the orderly stacking of broken-off cabinet doors and icebox racks.

In deference to me, I suppose, to not leaving me to sift through the rubble on my own, Fenella stayed a few nights. Once Nate sorted out his flat, which needed a few windows replaced but was otherwise as he had left it, she officially moved out. "Shacking up honest," as she put it. She didn't hand in notice, nor otherwise suggest she was resigning her position, but with the hotel closed indefinitely and practicality demanding that she find gainful work, there was little sense to her staying on.

I helped her pack. Nate brought a delivery truck from the brewery. A regular car would have done, but I suppose he couldn't get hold of one and it never occurred to me to make use of the Manse's house car.

"Nate thinks there might be something for me at the brewery," she said. "There's a lot of catch-up to be done now that pretty much all their stock was handed out to the hooligans."

We shared a look. I can only imagine what my face said to her, because next she said, in a voice strong with self-justification, "It's a chance to maybe learn a trade. Something to really do."

"I might not be here if you come by," I said. "Hospital, you know. But you can always let yourself in. Keep your keys."

"All right, I will."

"Have you gone down to see —"

"No. No, I think I would rather not." Fenella's voice dropped to whisper. "I wouldn't be any help."

"You've been helpful here. Really helpful. The kitchen looks almost new because of you."

"Oh," she chuffed me on the shoulder, "this is nothing. It's just a lot of work. Besides, I've been downtown. I've seen what happened. This place isn't half as mangled as a lot of buildings. There's shops down there that will likely have to close altogether. The looting wasn't even the worst of it."

I had not ventured from the house except to make the walk to the hospital since the night of the riots. Fenella's assurance, though kindly offered, did little to chin me up.

"Maybe come down for a drink soon," she said from the humming cab of the delivery truck.

"Now that we have no excuse to huddle over the radio," I said. I smiled, to soften it. But it was a bitter remark that I regretted immediately.

As they pulled away, I felt that she had somehow been a figment of my imagination, that there had been nothing to pass for friendship at all in the time of our acquaintance. Her exit had been tremendously easy, her destination not three miles away but across the whole landscape of her heart. Love is after all, in its unique way, a form of escape. A cove of protection. I was sad to see her go, especially since I suspected that her ability to check in on me and the Manse would grow thinner over time. I was also envious — my own cove was closed to me.

A crew of workmen arrived at the Manse Calvo on June 9 as I was readying myself to meet Myron at the hospital for our daily vigil. They informed me they were there to take measurements on behalf of the city council. They did not explain why "measurements" were needed, nor what exactly I was supposed to understand as being "the city council." (They did not seem to know themselves.) I kept an eye but let them go quietly about their work, which took about an hour. They drew measuring wheels down the boundary lines of the entire plot, from the brick of Lemarchant Street all the way back to the far edge of the back lawn. They did not seem concerned with the house itself, or its present state of disrepair. I was confused. I planned to ask Myron, figuring he would naturally know what this was all about. But after the workmen left, as I was gathering together a few odds and ends, my eyes came to rest on a single-column story in the *Herald*, a copy of which I'd left among that day's mail on the registration desk. It was one of those write-ups that are tucked beneath an advertisement, as though meant to be overlooked.

Local government, it read, was investing in select pieces of property as both a sop to local business owners and a concerted means of dipping a civic toe into the tempestuous waters of postwar, and post-riot, rebuilding. Suddenly, the workmen's assignment became clear to me.

Twenty minutes later, as we sat in folding chairs on either side of Annelie's bed, Myron looking anywhere in the room except at Annelie, I told him I had figured out that he put up the hotel for the city's restoration program.

The month since Annelie slipped into her coma had carved itself into Myron. His once-bulbous cheeks now had deep folds that ran like tributaries from the dark moons beneath his eyes down to his jawline. What on most men his age is considered crow's feet were on him more like rakes left by the claws of a hawk. His entire profile was becoming a crooked, riven valley of worry and lack of rest.

Deflated, his shoulders rolling down as if in shield from a cold wind, he turned to me.

"What choice have I?"

Stubbornly, I said nothing.

"I know I throw out a convincing line. An affectation I inherited from my father, I suppose. 'Even when you're down, play it like you're up,' he used to say. I always though it affected Aaron far deeper than me, but who's kidding who? The truth is that businesses like the Manse are not all that lucrative. We turn a profit, that's true, and in a time of war that's something of a miracle, but it's

300

no windfall by any means. There have been months these last few years that if my own house wasn't already paid for, I might have possibly had to give it up. You'd have had me living across the hall from you in one of the servant's quarters! And it would have been just the place, because I would have been a servant of the hotel as much as its proprietor. This city program just might bring us out of the quagmire we're stuck in."

Myron paused. He looked suddenly bereft, an unusual aspect for him.

"This only came about in the past week. I haven't had this in my pocket all the while. Truly, Walek."

"I believe you. If it were otherwise, you would be within your rights, too."

"Those stupid kids really did a number on the house, which of course you're all too aware of."

"Yes," I said. "The damage is incredible."

"This program is a necessity, when you think about it. It behooves the government to bring Halifax back from the brink."

"I know you're right. I'm not much good right now, anyway. I've managed to address several things, though. The curtains and rugs. I gave the carpeting a good scrub and repainted the walls in the foyer. And the back patio now looks good as new. But most of what needs fixing is going to require actual professionals. Crews of them."

"This has nothing to do with what you can and cannot make right. Not even the devil himself could have orchestrated what happened that night. It was poor luck, nothing more. And the result — in a hundred years the house will never again see another debacle like that one. You mark my words."

"I have tried though. I really have. To my limits, that is."

I don't know if it was my ego that felt bruised, or whether I had been nursing, unbeknownst to even myself, a now-crumbling vanity associated with the common name of my job, *useful man*. And so, I was mollified by what Myron said next.

"Walek, what you expect and what I expect will hopefully someday meet. You are the business's caretaker, that is true. But I do not expect you to become proficient at any, let alone all, of the vast number of specializations that will need to be employed in order to bring the house back to its former state. It is not for you to take on. It is for me. And I am neither ready, nor in a position, to do so. Not yet anyway, as you pointed out with regard to the city's restoration initiative. Keep up the general maintenance as best you can. Keep our visitations here. And try to keep your head above water, as they say. I am comforted to know you are there, in the house. I feel it is safe with you."

When I returned to the Manse Calvo that evening, I immediately opened up the windows of all the guest rooms to freshen them with the outside air. Then I took a pair of hedge clippers onto the front porch and began to sculpt the surrounding hedgerows.

It might seem a lie that July 1, 1945 was the first time I set foot on Pepperell Street since surrendering my family's home those years ago. But it is true. Nothing in the way of my duties pulled me in that northwestward direction, nor did any casual stroll I might have taken, my primary points of interest being the Public Gardens on a more easterly route and Point Pleasant Park further south. I had, so far as I was aware, no aversion to the sight of that house. I never imagined over the intervening years, when I pictured in my mind, that shame or guilt were scheming behind the curtains, as it were, barring me from passing visitation. Pepperell Street was simply easy enough to avoid.

On this day, I went out of my way.

I chose a diversionary tack on my usual route to Cogswell Street Hospital, eschewing the peaceful sobriety of Camp Hill and its cemetery, as well as the fragrant current that would surely be coming off the Public Gardens on the late morning breeze, in favor of a northbound, car-choked Oxford Street. Why? For the same reason that a beer drinker will on occasion order a whiskey. An impulse.

At first blush, I almost didn't recognize the house. The driveway, crushed stone before, was now paved black, and the front lawn, formerly accented with daises and small bushes, was now nude grass, not too well tended. The eggshell blue my mother had so appreciated when she and my father first examined the property, and which had always been well-maintained during their lives, now lay beneath a heavy-looking coat of brown that I likened in tone to well-worn shoe leather. It made the house seem a dormitory — an allusion I found to fit perfectly once I crossed the stone-laid path to the front door and saw not one but four doorbells corresponding to four different person's names. The bank, or whatever entity now owned the property, had converted it into flats. A fifth nameplate (which bore no doorbell) read *REAR* after the surname. I looked around to the back and realized that the space above the garage had been converted into a flat as well.

303

I backtracked toe-heel to the apron of the driveway and just stood there. It was still a very fine house, I thought. Respectable. Impressive, actually. But it did not feel dear, though I wanted it to. Looking up at it, there was no pang of posterity, no called-forth memories, not even a surge of anger or self-remonstrance at the ugly fecality of its new façade. It was just a house I once lived in that I remembered being very different than it had become.

I have said it was an impulse that brought me there. Of course, that's not so. As a sad child will run his arm over a rough piece of rock or a deranged person will make bloody use of a bit of broken glass, I had hoped that purposefully causing myself some pain might unleash something raw and misshapen and true within me. I wanted this something to remain etched upon me while I sat beside Annelie, and to aid me in unzipping the sheath of my own self-pity in order to appreciate, if I could, the weight of what lay before me. Not just the fact that the woman I loved, though within my reach, remained sequestered in an alternate realm of unresponsiveness. Not just the tenuous, tremulous nature of what I had done with my adult life. And not just the semi-squalid loneliness of my solitary nights in the Manse Calvo, which were not like my time alone in the house now standing before me, but were boring and damned-feeling and meant I was no longer attuned to solitude but wanted my peopled life back.

I hoped to appreciate, if I was even capable, the ways I would be better when Annelie woke up. I could not even say what those ways might be. I felt a potential for betterment, only I could not seem to wrest it out. Revisiting Pepperell Street, the site of my worst and most inexcusable failure, ought to have done that. But I did not see a lost home; I saw only a place of business.

As I walked away, proceeding toward the Common, beyond which rose the hospital, I did, however, appreciate (and at all not sadly) that the place of business I now laid my head each night was, without reservation, home.

July in Halifax is commonly when summer drives its shoulder into the ground. Heat amplifies. Humidity sustains the salt in the air. A cramped sort of feeling gets in beneath your clothes, even as the fabric slips and slides over your damp skin. There are days when it feels like you simply have to get through on faith in that first swirl of fall wind. Days when it seems nothing very good will happen.

Until it does.

xxi. <u>Hold It Together, Please</u>

THE FIRE ALARM, AMAZINGLY, DID NOT WAKE
HER. Nor did the transfer of her body from bed to
portable cot. Nor the jostling of the two orderlies
who lifted and carried her down the stairs, through
the hospital's ground-floor halls, and out into the
open air.

It was the rain. A patter, unworthy of shelter.
Beginning not two minutes after the building had
been cleared and all patients and staff alike stood
or crouched or lay inanimately scattered along the
Common.

The cause of the emergency clearance was an
explosion at the naval magazine across the
harbour on July 18, about 9 p.m. Some flint or
spark, perhaps a carelessly discarded cigarette
butt, took up with the heat and produced such
tremendous fire that the ammunition dump began
to go off, piece by combustible piece, in a
crescendo that would continue, like a threatening
display of poorly orchestrated fireworks, until four
the following morning, when there was nothing
left for the fire to eat.

I imagine the first tentative drops hitting her
cheeks, her brow, absorbing directly into the
thirsty skin, pasting down the wispy hairs at her
temple. A gentle but urgent pressure coming from
what drops made ground on her closed eyelids.
The insistence of the gathering wetness, pooling
perhaps in the hollows near her eyes before
running down and away. I imagine also how the
rainwater doused her lips and how, once she was

aware of being awake, she may have parted her lips and taken this moisture into her mouth, which like her skin had known no such refreshment for weeks.

Why it was felt the hospital needed evacuation remains a mystery to me. Though photographs in the next morning's *Herald* testified to its magnitude, the event at the naval magazine was more of a danger to Dartmouth across the bay than Halifax, and if a danger to Halifax, then more to the quayside than the buildings shadowed by Citadel Hill, of which Cogswell Street Hospital was one. Perhaps in the drydown of the riots, overt caution was preferred over scrambling too late against potential catastrophe. The evacuation did not last very long, in any event. Some intelligent authority must have finally realized everyone was by far safer indoors than out.

Returned to her usual place in the general ward, Annelie, with the motion of a single raised finger (so I was later told), announced her return.

At 11:12 p.m., I took a call in the manager's office, where, having been restless in bed, I was trying to work off some nervous energy by doing a redundant reorganization. I was bedside at Cogswell ten minutes later.

When I saw her open eyes, the lashes clumped together, wet with what I took for tears, I sat heavily in the folding chair beside the gurney and wept with all the love my heart could stand. Arms folded across my chest as against a sudden sweep of fear.

Once I got hold of myself — it took some time — I saw Annelie was frowning, and also that she was trying to say something. I leaned forward, assuming it was the effort that so crimped her features. Her tongue darted briefly out and

307

dampened her lips, and she said, "Hold it together, please." A smile played across her face.

Annelie's next week was a protracted series of tests. Blood pressure. Blood draw. Cognitive assessment. Muscular manipulations. Nervous tension estimates. Ocular response tests. Auditory tests. Over and again. And questions, questions, questions. As though Annelie had been to the limits of the stratosphere and what intelligence she gathered was crucial to the fate of the world.

I don't know if it was Myron's intervention or simply the kindness of the hospital staff, but a cot was made available to me so that I could stay nights. Though she spoke very little, seeming to stockpile her energy in this regard for the next battery of questions, Annelie's mood was not dower. She seemed content to be awake, lying in the open ward, with the summer sun reaching through the windows on the opposite side of the room. When I gave her a summation of what the VE Day assault had cost the house, she took it in calmly, betraying her dismay only in a slight flush of her cheeks.

I do know for certain that Myron tried to secure her a private room once he was told of her recovery, but there were no rooms to be had, not for cases other than of dire need, not even if the subject's uncle was comfortable with and adept at wielding his public stature like a cutlass. Unsuccessful though he was in this regard, Myron struck a mineral vein when he threatened to remove her from the staff's care altogether, her status as patient be damned.

Remarkably, that idea was suitable to the doctors. The open ward was crowded, and not every patient had what could be considered dependable at-home care.

Once her discharge was agreed upon, Myron had Annelie's fourth-floor suite outfitted with a run of parallel bars to assist in gait training, the rigorous process of learning to walk again. The WC was also renovated so that her shower would no longer be within a claw-footed tub, but in a flat, tiled, newly-fabricated corner of the room, with drainage feeding into the same piping that opened a general flow of returned water from the rooms on the floor below. The tub would remain, however, its drainage diverted by new piping, because it was suggested that the occasional soak would aid recovery of mobility. (This was all accomplished at Myron's personal expense.) Past that, her rooms would remain as before. Furniture would not need changing, not even in arrangement.

As to my living in Annelie's quarters, Myron barely blinked. "That will make it simpler. I can inform them we will not need a live-in," was his response.

So, with the assistance of a nurse and an orderly, eleven days after her inexplicable spell was broken, Annelie was bundled into Myron's sedan and brought back home.

As July became August, Annelie improved in line with expectations. She neither exceeded the norm for her type of recovery nor fell behind.

Those weeks were the most intimate time we had yet shared. She could not venture downstairs without being carried and the fourth floor had no proper hallways to speak of, so our movements were curtailed to the suite.

Consequently, we passed most of the hours in conversation. I would sometimes press her for details of what dreams she may have had during what we decided to call her "away time," but she could not offer me any. She wasn't being withholding; she simply didn't know. And once I realized how much this ignorance bothered her, I left it alone.

But then one afternoon, Annelie told me this: "I doubt this counts as a 'memory' of the coma, or whatever I'm meant to call it. God, it's frustrating that the doctors can't even give me a proper name for it, they can only tell me what it *wasn't*. Anyway — do you know how birds sometimes hover on a current of air, like they're suspended in one place? Well, there was a time, and it could have been a week or thirty seconds, I really don't know, but there was a time where I was floating above everything, on a current just like that."

"How did it feel? Was it how you imagine flying would feel?"

"I've never really had a fantasy about being able to fly. I felt free, at first, but then something about it got terribly lonely. Maybe that's why it ended. When I woke up, I knew I had not snapped out of the sky all of the sudden. I just felt like I usually do when I wake up in the middle of the night. First thing is to look for the clock to see the time and decide whether it's worth it to just get up and get on with it, or quickly pee and try to get back to sleep." She laughed. "When I realized I was outside and that it was raining and I couldn't do anything about it because my body was not in my control yet, I was just *furious*."

That was as close as we came to something resembling concrete evidence of what constituted Annelie's away time.

On August 22, she took her first unassisted steps, crossing the room from the bed, laying a small and completely unnecessary fire in the hearth, then returning to her place beside me beneath the sheets.

"I wasn't going to light it," she said, when she saw my expression of disbelief. "I wanted to prove I could, is all."

"And now you have."

"And now I have."

xxii. <u>Restorations</u>

JUST AS MY PARENTS HAD GIVEN the summer of 1920 to the restoration of the house on Pepperell Street, Annelie, Myron, and I gave the late summer and early fall of 1945 to the restoration of the Manse Calvo — as much the house as the souls dwelling within it.

A glacial civic process, which hamstrung Annelie to a limited accountability — overseeing a cleaning service and redrafting my damage assessment for the city council — was a source of annoyance to her.

"If we really have to wait for this place to be co-opted by the city, we'll be totally forgotten. It'll be like starting all over again. Flyers on the ferries and so forth. The name Manse Calvo will have no cache whatsoever."

"Have you tried telling that to Myron?"

My question was meant to be diplomatic, but Annelie, sensing a tone of condescension, pounced on me.

"No, Walek, I thought I would just let him read my mind."

I let that go. Her propensity to come out shooting in moments of frustration and insecurity was nothing new. Still, my diplomacy bore its intended fruit. The practical terms of the hotel's restoration were arranged with terrific speed once Annelie, now in full command of her body, goaded Myron, whose patience was otherwise thinning with the matter, to throw up his hands at government sponsorship and do what most business owners do, which was take out a loan.

"So, I took that advice of yours," she said one afternoon about a week after we'd last discussed it, throwing herself in a breaststroke down on my duvet. "At first, my uncle started giving me the usual line about smart business. 'You have to take the long view of things, dear' and all that. But I could tell it wearied him. It didn't take long for him to admit the overhead we'll experience in order to get up and running again is just way, *way* more than he's capable of scraping together. He didn't seem particularly comforted by the fact that we are far from alone in this kind of trouble. I mean, you've seen the state of Barrington Street. Then I flat-out told him one way or another this hotel will be back in business by year's end. Even if it means going it alone. I even stomped my foot, like a child who dropped her sweets. That didn't make him flinch, but I think the idea of me taking on such a crazy amount of debt did."

The month of September then saw the house and grounds become a veritable construction site. One outfit or another was in each day, often for a good part of the day and occasionally some of the evening-time. The Calvos were so buoyed by the flush of borrowed cash they were not content to simply fix what was damaged, but executed a few other enhancements to the property as well.

An open-air gazebo was erected adjacent to the bocce pitch. The area was tucked into a far corner of the back lawn that, owing to an absence of tree shade, went brown in summer, puddled in spring and fall, and froze over in a ribbed shell of mud in winter. A perfect spot, as the earth there was otherwise useless. The dome of the gazebo was designed with understated ornament and topped by a small weather vane whittled to look like a set of four waving flags. I recall how pungent the lacquer was after its application. For more than a week, I had to hold one of my father's handkerchiefs over my face when stepping outside, for the entire structure had been double-coated so as to quash any concern about potential weather damage. Annelie ordered that no windows in the Manse be opened — despite the acrid stuffiness within the house — until the stench fully and finally subsided, lest it somehow lay a fetid taint on the surfaces within.

The garage roof was replaced, as well. It had been a long time coming and would have been necessary within the next couple of years anyway. It was the original roof still in place. It had become a nesting ground for birds, squirrels, and, due to warped, curling tiles that created attractive little nooks, a hive of wasps. I was quite pleased with the decision. I felt Myron and Annelie were acting strategically, making the best use of the funds.

With Myron personally assuming a supervisory role over much of the work, Annelie and I found ourselves with unexpected free hours in which to restore the inimitable bond we had only just forged before her injury. Though some days required one or the other of us to stand in for Myron (or both if there were multiple crews at work in different parts of the house), the weeks of September and early October were generally a time of renewed courtship.

We went to the movies quite a lot, alternating between the theatres within walking distance of the Manse, in order to catch every offering before the reels were swapped out. We once more caught a showing of *The Island of Lost Souls*; a few early Humphrey Bogart pictures, including Howard

Hawks' *To Have and Have Not*, which Annelie said she much preferred to the Hemingway novel ("They're really nothing alike."); a few pre-war John Wayne B-reels, as well as the recent (and excellent) *In Old California*; and Alfred Hitchcock's *Sabotage*, which I found superior to the Joseph Conrad novel (*The Secret Agent*) it was based on.

When the afternoons cooled, breezes arriving in seeming sequence with the fading of the sun, we indulged in long, aimless walks, figuring out where it was we wished to go only once we realized we had lost track of where we had already been. On occasion we took the house car out to the far north part of the city to investigate the bookshops there. Our aim was to replenish the Tilde Salon's vanquished library. It was a fine thing to step out of mean morning heat or warm, stinging rain into a cool, dry shop where the very walls were lined with undiscovered treasures. On one such occasion, I filled in the gaps in my father's Oxford Press series of Henry James, of which I had kept only a few volumes. Now that it was complete, I planned to remand the run, whole-hog, to the hotel's collection.

When I told Annelie of my intention, she balked. "You can't protect them. They may get damaged. Maybe lifted. We don't have a card catalogue, you know."

"But they'll get read, which is more than they're getting from me." A true statement; try though I had, James was just not for me. "I think my father would like the idea of his books becoming happy accidents for strangers to stumble on."

With the kitchen still nonfunctioning, we dined out every night, sometimes at Myron's though mostly at restaurants in town. In this way, my savings was coming in handy. I had refused Myron's offer to continue my salary until the hotel reopened. (This was less a gesture of principle than an acknowledgement that despite the significance of the loan Myron had secured, every penny was earmarked to salvage the business.) Knowing where my money came from, Annelie picked up the bill every third night. "A fair balance, says this lady," was her line.

Though we had shared a bed since a week after her return from the hospital, at which point she felt able to control her body in sleep, thus reeling me in from the sofa, our sleep was chaste. The affection of a goodnight kiss, but no more. This was not a sign of awkwardness between us. On the contrary, it was an unspoken but mutual arrangement by which we agreed that what might regenerate between us would do so in due course, even if due course meant the same prolongation that had marked the beginning of our courtship. Neither of us were explicit about this, which testified to our confidence that it was not a matter of *if*, only of *when*.

I had given Annelie the basic facts about Fenella's situation — engagement, new job prospect, the decision to move into Nate's flat — but that was all I could tell her. So far as I knew, Fenella was keeping house and waiting to see if the promise of getting on at the brewery would come through. Fenella herself brought both of us up to date.

"I thought I would be out there in the dregs wearing overalls and testing hops," she told us. "But I guess that takes quite a lot of learning and experience. So, I'm in charge of pushing all the paper around."

Fenella's two visits during the reconstruction and restoration of the hotel showed us just how much she had changed in the weeks since relocating down to Lower Water Street. The ballooning dark slacks and simple blouse that I was accustomed to seeing partly hidden beneath her ever-present apron had been replaced by a pencil skirt with exposed, off-color seams and a cardigan sweater than cinched at the neck and shoulders, and stopped, as if in mid-hem, exactly where the skirt's waistline began. When she sat, several inches of her bare back were exposed. Her shoes were practical, non-descript, but were real leather and looked like the type of small detail a man might take note of, if only to register the dimensions of the ankles they left uncovered. She looked every inch a success.

"There are some nice girls who work in the office pool, and I get to eat lunch with Nate in the brewery pub every day. I would feel a bit like a kept woman, seeing him all the time at work and then coming home to what's basically his apartment, but it turns out I make just about what he does, so I think that squares it up all right."

"You really have changed," Annelie said. She made this remark at some point during each of Fenella's visits. To which Fenella both times replied, "I don't know about that. The clothes are new, but the head and heart are same old, same old."

Fenella offered to help Annelie with interviews to bring on a fresh kitchen staff, but since it would be catch-as-can at first (and who knew how long thereafter), we didn't really need a full staff, only a cook and maybe a couple of girls from Dalhousie or St. Mary's who wanted to earn a bit of going-out money to do the serving.

"I can at least help you find a cook," Fenella insisted. "I feel like I ran out on you."

"We've been closed," Annelie said. "What else could you do? Sit around here with Walek trying to find things to do?"

"I might have appreciated the meals," I said, which got a polite laugh out of them both.

"I've already done about a dozen interviews for your old job," Annelie went on. "Got it narrowed down to two people. You could sit in on those, if you really want, but it might not be worth your time. I've scheduled their follow-ups for mid-morning, and you have a job. I doubt they'd look too kindly on you asking for time off to help your old employer find someone to replace you."

"I suppose," Fenella said hesitantly. "Still, I feel like I owe you something. I mean, I wasn't going to be much good to you when —"

Annelie, unfazed, finished the thought. "When I wasn't able to even realize you were here."

"Oh shit." Fenella shook her head. Her eyes welled and the very tip of her nose grew pink.

But Annelie had broken out in a brilliant smile. She reached forward and took Fenella's hands in her own.

"You *have* changed. The Fenella who worked here would have said what she thought and then wondered, 'What's the big deal when all I'm doing is telling the truth?'"

The three of us laughed, a chorus that severed whatever buffer of social awkwardness there was between us. Once I felt Annelie and Fenella had eased nicely into cordial conversation, I excused myself, promising to meet them later for a drink in the new gazebo, and went off to find something to do.

The conflicting time constraints of our respective jobs would put a heavy damper on our ability to see Fenella. She and Nate were a part of the traditional workforce, home in time for supper at sundown, by which time Annelie's and my workdays were only just getting going. But we would eventually work out a perfect way to get around that.

Neither Myron nor Annelie wanted any future hire to be done as a live-in, for the simple reason that Myron wanted to convert the servants' quarters into useable guest rooms. But as I was still billeted on the second floor and, so far as Myron was concerned, despite his knowing where I spent my nights, entitled to private quarters as part of my employment, my room would go untouched. There would thus always be a room available to our friends, free of charge. They didn't abuse the privilege, but took advantage often enough that we did not lose track of one another. Annelie and I were not, as individuals, built for constant social imposition. This, therefore, suited us well enough.

Fall blew in almost too quickly, and we were suddenly bundled up anytime we ventured outside. A few days into October, it was decided, in a democratic vote among the three of us in the Aaron Salon over a glass of ice wine, that the time had come to bring back the Manse Calvo.

The vote was unanimous.

xxiii. What Lay Ahead

THE MANSE CALVO WAS SET to officially reopen
on a provisional basis (to say, weekends only) on
Friday, October 12, 1945. Check-in time 5:00
p.m., dinner service 8:00 p.m. Commencement of
full operations contingent on cash flow permitting
the hire of a full staff. Hopefully by the beginning
of 1946.

We had nine rooms booked, all thanks to
Myron's wheeling through the ranks of his beloved
Collier Club, every one sourced from personal
recommendations made by sympathetic club
members to their friends and associates, none of
which cost Myron a penny in advertising.

The penultimate evening, October 11, I stood
beside Annelie at the back of the grounds, looking
not out at the gray water of the Arm, but back at
the fully-lighted house.

"It looks from here like nothing ever
happened," I said. "You can't even really see the
gazebo from here through all the trees."

"But we know, don't we?"

"Are you nervous about tomorrow?"

"These are all friends of Myron's friends. It
almost doesn't matter if something goes wrong."

"I suppose there's some comfort in that."

"I see it as a rehearsal. Next weekend, if we
get any bookings, is the actual performance. I
expect most of these people, if not all of them,
have heard some third-hand version of what
happened."

"What happened to the house, or to you?"

"Both, I imagine. Not that I think Myron was a sieve of detail, but he must have said something about my away time." Annelie laughed lightly. "As a sales tool, you understand."

Overhead, the low rumble of an airplane traced the sunset sky.

"Now that the war is over, I suppose the airport will have new patterns," I surmised. "We'll have to get used to hearing planes overhead."

"I suppose." She stared at the house and its squares of glass from behind which soft, gauzy light shone through curtains half-drawn like half-closed eyes. "I don't know what I would have done if this place had closed up. I don't think I would want to do anything else. Work someplace else, I mean, like Fenella."

"Name me one person who can imagine going from being in charge of a place to just punching a time card someplace else."

She leaned in and brushed a kiss against my temple.

"All that money we have to repay. I get a headache just thinking about it."

"Let Myron think about it."

"That's what he does, isn't it?"

"He is a very smart businessman, in my opinion."

"What do you know about business?"

"I know I'm looking at one that could have failed but didn't."

Annelie tucked her hands into the pockets of her skirt. She turned away from the house and faced me. A band of light caught her like a mystery finally revealed.

"I love you, Walek. Those are new words between us, aren't they? We don't really say that to each other. But it doesn't follow that I don't feel it, even when you're not right here next to me."

"I love you, too. I really mean it."

"Of course, you do. I'm eminently lovable."

In the kitchen, we made a simple supper of tomato and cream cheese sandwiches and the leftovers of a lobster bisque one of the candidates for the cook's position had brought in to her second interview.

After tasting the soup, I said, "I hope you've hired this person."

"I did. But not to be in charge of the kitchen. She's far too young. Twenty only. This will be her first job. Apparently, her mother taught her how to cook, no formal training. But she will be doing the meal planning."

"Who will be in charge?"

"Me. Don't look at me like I'm crazy. Fenella spent most of her time doing the food, and I've taken care of that part of it. I can run the servers and whatnot. Monitor the sideboard. Answer questions. Anticipate problems. It might even help me cut down on desk hours at night. I know how things ought to be. It won't be so bad. When we're really back on our feet — I mean completely — I'll either find somebody, or Ms. Bisque will have hopefully proven herself capable beyond her years."

"I suppose we save from not having to pay someone."

"That's exactly what Myron said when I told him. Funny, that."

In the morning, we lay in Annelie's bed and allowed the early morning light to slowly draw us from a sleep that had come only a couple of hours before.

When you share a bed with someone you get to know the language of their body, the postures you know they won't sustain and those to which they turn to achieve actual rest. While we lay silent but awake, I felt an underlying hum vibrating from the other side of the bed, as though Annelie's entire form were poised on the tip of a question that required the barest sign of interest from me to justify asking.

I propped myself on an elbow and looked at her, silently.

"*Fine*," she said, rolling over to face me. "I'm a little terrified. I know it's only dinner, for Christ's sake, but ... What if this all doesn't work? What if our time is just up? That happens to businesses all the time. Something happens to them, and whoosh, they only *used to be*."

"Annelie."

"What would happen then? This is still a home. A private residence. It's taxed. And it would have to be maintained. I suppose I would have to finally put my incomplete college education to work for me. For what it's worth."

"I volunteer." I smiled sleepily. "Does that help at all?"

"I was born in this house, you know. I don't think that's ever come up between us. Lottie may have mentioned it, or Myron. In my mother's salon, actually. When I was a girl, I must have asked an awful lot about how I was born. After Lottie finally told me, out of exasperation I'm sure, I would sometimes go into the salon and peek around in the corners and behind curtains and under the furniture, thinking there would be some trace of that day left behind, as if by magic. I don't know what kind of trace it was I wanted. A dropped handkerchief or something else equally romantic. It was a very strange thing to stand right where you came into the world and to not be able to reach out and somehow touch that moment. Even stranger, I suppose, is to *want to* in the first place, but it seemed perfectly natural to me. I haven't thought about doing that, the searching, in a long while." She laid the soft, cool flat of her hand against my cheek, and nestled up to me. "You know, in a way you've adopted my feeling of home. You've become it. How did I let that happen, I wonder?"

When standing, Annelie was almost exactly one head shorter than me, so lying as we were I could feel every part of her, from the rogue hairs peaking off the very top of her crown, to her mouth tender against my throat, to the full weight of her midriff, to the soft tickle of her toes over mine. I let out a long breath and draped my arms over her.

We kept this careless repose and watched the sun resolve from behind the trees until it made of them little more than a blurred suggestion of shapes marking the horizon.

Lovers with no inkling of what might lay ahead, and fine with it.

GREEN FIELDS TIE THE LAND into a single net of life. Field flowers bloom at the roadside, opening to the currents rolling up off the Bay of Fundy.

We are renting a cottage near Suffolk, a hamlet tucked into the very heart of Prince Edward Island, which for the past several years has become our annual escape from running the hotel.

This vacation is not merely a respite; it is also a testing ground. Effective January 31, 1959, the Manse Calvo will cease to operate and become bequeathed to the city of Halifax as the Calvo Residence for Iterant Women and Children. We arranged this date to give ourselves one last Christmas on Lemarchant Street.

Since Myron's passing in 1954, Annelie and I have made an earnest go of it, but a stigma remains that we cannot wipe entirely clean — *that woman was in a coma, did you know that, and I heard someone got killed on the street that night, too* — and of late, it's become useless. Funny how a city can sometimes behave like a village, the sort where everyone knows everyone else's business and what cannot be known is readily invented. Added to which, glossier franchise hotels from the mainland and the United States have put down footprints in the city, and against them the Manse is simply not enough competition. Our arrangement with the city, which was Annelie's idea in much the same regard that the founding of the Manse had long ago been Myron's, ensures that the property will be put to some responsible use, and that the Calvos and Szeyks alike will contribute to a hopefully better future. Our family will move into Myron's former house on Owen Street, which was left to Annelie in his will. We intend to persist in making the cottage a seasonal retreat — unless, that is, the children give us an indelible signal that our life become more of a permanent vacation.

Aaron and Marianna, only just turned a fraternal eight, have come to see the island house as a second home, as I have been fortunate to rent the same property now six years running, years that have seen both children develop their first, and possibly strongest, lasting memories. Annelie and I are banking on this connection to soften the news we will break to them tonight.

The children are twenty meters ahead of us, hunting wildflowers along the dirt road. They entertain themselves with relative simplicity. Theirs is that tender age when expectations are not predetermined but come wholly out of experience itself.

Annelie and I walk lazily behind them, keeping an eye but also straying toward a cluster of goldilocks peeking from a patch of tall grass where they don't belong. Low clouds of dust are kicked up by our footfalls. We have all been out long enough for the peak of the cottage's roof to appear small as a sifter behind us.

When Aaron screams suddenly from somewhere in the scrub, I look just in time to catch Marianna cross from the other side of the road at a breakneck run and disappear into the tall grass behind her brother.

We set after them.

Bridging a ditch about half a meter wide, cut for rainwater irrigation, we find the children crouched side-by-side before a large tree that stands like a beacon in the middle of a wide stretch of level ground, already in the middle of a disagreement.

Marianna says, "No, don't touch it. I read about these things. They are trapped." To which Aaron replies, "You mean traps. They are *traps*. And no, they're not. Do you even know what you're talking about?"

Marianna, fuming quick, having inherited her mother's temper, snaps back, "I read about it in the library. Where *you* have never even been. Where *you* don't even know *where* it is. I read that soldiers leave these things laying around so that they blow the hands off whoever picks them up. You better not pick that up."

We come up behind them soft-footed, trying to decipher the argument, the preciseness of grammar only just beyond Marianna's grasp. The idea of bombshells in Suffolk! We cannot yet see the object of interest. Aaron's birdlike shoulders block its view.

I creep slowly until I stand right over them. The sunlight is blocked by the tree's great arms. I cast no shadow. The children do not know I am there. Annelie keeps a few paces back.

When I am sure they do not suspect, I leap into the air and yell *BOOM!*

Marianna screams. Aaron lets go a loud *uh!* and pitches the object, which he had just begun to wrap his hands around, into the grass.

As my and Annelie's laughter subsides, the children's begins in earnest, as they are slow to peel away their fright. Laughter explodes from them, a manifest combination of joy and surprise and performed comedy. It is always easy to spot the exact moment when genuine delight segues into a performance for our benefit. Marianna will begin to clap her hands almost spastically, and Aaron will clutch a hand to his belly like a stage actor. These are their tells, and we love them. We never correct them, never say it is obnoxious to playact.

I find the object where Aaron hurled it and sit down in the grass with it in my lap. With her arms gently snuggled under their chins, Annelie guides the children over.

Marianna resists. "I'm telling you. We're all going to blow up."

"No, we won't," Annelie assures her. "Whatever it is, it's too old to blow us up." Her voice is calm, but we have both heard of such things as traps laid for poaching.

"It's not even dangerous," I say, turning back to face them. "Come look."

It is a tin box of the kind that has a lid opening upward from a single hinge like a lunch pail. Deeply black, it is very heavy and scored with nicks and scratches and runs of dried grey mud. It looks like it has been in the ground twenty years.

As they gather around me, I shake the box and from inside comes a muffled rattling. Annelie hunches over me, turns her fingers through my thinning hair. This, she knows, makes me greatly aware of time, though I like to think this thinning is my only obvious betrayal of age, that decades on I will still carry a youthful countenance. She rests a knee on my back. My body accepts the pressure easily.

"Everyone ready?" I bring my eyes in turn to each of them. A fanciful expression spells out their collective curiosity.

Aaron rings his hands impatiently. Marianna kneels beside her mother, half-shielded by her shoulder.

The box opens with a sharp pop that makes us all flinch. Inside is a mess of cards and colored pencils and flowers decomposed nearly to dust. The cards, once white, are now vinegary yellow. I gently remove a pile of them. There are maybe two dozen, each depicting a different scene. Some are still lifes of the box's dead flowers in bloom, though most are drawings of specific settings, recognizably rural landscapes, an action occurring in each. Annelie, I can tell, is touched by one of a small girl with a swift circle of yellow hair on her head, dunking a pail into a water well, while close by a horse, remarkably detailed on the small card, bends low toward the grass. There is another of the same girl with her arms wrapped around the horse's neck; in it, the horse smiles with full teeth like a person.

There is also a series of five cards depicting what seems to be the story of a boy who battles a fierce blue monster and rescues a girl who, as in the other drawings, has a whirl of maizey hair, to which Marianna, having finally warmed to the fact that she is not in danger, remarks definitively, "That monster needs redder eyes." Yet another series shows a family standing in a green field, each figure bent forward plucking at flowers.

This one Annelie takes with her fingertips. The paper holds a fragrance of sweet flowers and wet earth. The drawing was done with short strikes of color, giving the impression when holding the picture at arm's length that the grass moves, as by wind. The people are likewise defined only by distance from the eye. Bring the drawing closer and their faces fall apart, their bodies dissolve into

329

small blips of random color. A brief inscrutability passes over Annelie's face, but when she looks at our children it falls away, or perhaps she tucks it back into herself, as a letter is tucked back into its envelope for safe-keeping.

As she hands the picture back, a low wind draws into the closest branches of the tree, flustering its birds.

"I wonder about the child who made these pictures and what family had been his or her model," she says. "Where they are, what has become of them."

"They might come back," Aaron says, with a child's mixture of vague hope and suspicious intelligence that wants it to be true but knows that hope is just hope, it isn't a sure thing.

I gather up the rest of the cards and set them back in the box, shut the lid and latch it. Aaron and I walk over to where he first discovered the box. With our bare hands, we dig a hole in the wonderfully cold dirt beneath the tree deeper than the one before and lay the box to rest.

We go on for another half-hour until the children's baskets are filled with flowers and dandelions and baby's breath. My jacket and trouser pockets, too. Then we turn back for the house, passing the same tree, our chatter withstanding a momentary pause.

Aaron and Marianna will make spring wreaths with what we have collected. Annelie will teach them. We will gather around the kitchen table, the children's red knees clambering on wooden stools, the dig of their wrists and elbows on waxed paper. The vision of what is to come shimmers before me. I have the pleasure of lying in wait for it like a prowler of joy.

Birdsong. Something skitters just out of sight, squirrels perhaps, playing a flirting game of chase. The road bends around a swath of tall grass — and suddenly the house is there.

The children scamper ahead.

A glance — and Annelie takes off after them.

In an interview some time ago, Howard Norman said that fact is useful until it begins to trespass upon the imagination, upon the truth sought through creation. This pretty well stands up for my working philosophy in writing this story.

Ex.: Lemarchant Street does exist, but not as depicted here. The street runs directly along the east end of Dalhousie University's main campus, and is several blocks from the water of the North-West Arm. Placing the Manse Calvo on Lemarchant Street suggested to me an intangible enchantment — and this I chased to the cost of plain geographic fact. Also: There is no Bedford Brewery; but Oland Brewery did suffer severe damage in the Explosion of 1917, and amidst the VE Day riots Keith's Brewery did voluntarily distribute its product to avoid looting. Dalhousie University's location and curriculum (not to mention its hiring practices) have been presented with all imaginary detail. The VE Day riots, Churchill's visit, and the off-harbour explosions in 1917 and 1945 all occurred, but with a reach and reverberation very much different to those who actually experienced them. To echo Walek, all errors are mine alone; I bear sole responsibility for them.

I am, however, indebted to the following books, excellent all, that limned for me this period in Halifax's history: Stephen Kimber's *Sailors, Slackers, and Blind Pigs*; David B. Flemming's *Explosion in Halifax Harbour*; and William D. Naftel's *Halifax at War*.

The Manse Calvo itself is, of course, fictional, but it was inspired in some regard by the very real Waverley Inn, where my wife and I spent several wonderful nights on our honeymoon and subsequently on an anniversary vacation. In real life, the Waverley no longer functions as a hotel, but is a supportive housing facility for women and gender-diverse people.

The first draft of this novel was written many years before this change was brought about in early 2024, and I see it as a remarkable felicity that the Waverley's real destiny and the Manse Calvo's imaginary one tow the same line of function and public service.

Finally, Maljenka and the Collier Club exist only on the map of my imagination.